An Authentic
Captain Marvel Ring
and Other Stories

Other Books by Alan Cheuse

Fiction

Candace and Other Stories

The Bohemians

The Grandmothers' Club

The Light Possessed

The Tennessee Waltz and Other Stories

Lost and Old Rivers: Stories

The Fires

To Catch the Lightning

Song of Slaves in the Desert

Paradise, Or, Eat Your Face

Nonfiction

Fall Out of Heaven

*The Sound of Writing: Stories from the Radio.
(Edited, with Caroline Marshall)*

*Listening to Ourselves: More Stories from the Sound of Writing.
(Edited, with Caroline Marshall)*

Listening to the Page: Adventures in Reading and Writing

Seeing Ourselves: Great Early American Short Stories, Edited

*Writing Workshop in a Book: The Squaw Valley Community of Writers
on the Art of Fiction (Edited, with Lisa Alvarez)*

A Trance After Breakfast

Literature: Craft & Voice (with Nicholas Delbanco)

Alan Cheuse

An Authentic

Ring

And Other Stories

www.sfwp.com

Library of Congress Cataloging-in-Publication Data

Cheuse, Alan.
  [Short stories. Selections]
  An Authentic Captain Marvel Ring And Other Stories / Alan Cheuse.
    pages cm
  ISBN 978-1-939650-09-2 (alk. paper)
  I. Title.
  PS3553.H436A6 2014
  813'.54—dc23
                        2013029691

Published by SFWP
369 Montezuma Ave. #350
Santa Fe, NM 87501
www.sfwp.com

Find the author at www.alancheuse.com

For Kris, The Years

Contents

An Authentic Captain Marvel Ring

and Other Stories

An Authentic Captain Marvel Ring:

Perth Amboy, New Jersey, c. 1947

Originally published in *Superstition Review*

Jagged reddish-orange lightning-shaped scores, a circle with compass arrow and points east west north south within, and in the center of the circle, an oval, an opening invisible unless you held it directly up to your eye, an opening—

Peep inside, that is, press it in a dark room to one eye while the other you keep closed tight, and as soon as you become accustomed to the dark you'll begin to see light swirling within the ring, halos and rings of glittering pieces of light, particles of atoms, of atoms growing smaller and smaller in the depths of the once tiny but now everexpanding space, a peek into another space, into a seemingly infinite galaxy of galaxies, dancing, spinning, sparkling, exploding now! oh, that flash of fire in the distance! but where? but how? how far away? a fingertip and an infinity!

And what if this could be real? And what if there were stars in all those flashing rings of light, stars with planets and planets with creatures living upon them? what if there were other human beings living there? what if, what if you looked long enough and hard enough, squinted at this peep-hole all night long until you might see into the lake of stars and into the small galaxy with the yellow star and the green-blue planet resembling earth and on down through the blue-white atmosphere to the continent of North America and in the east of that formation to the state of New Jersey and the town that lies at the confluence of waters, where the river meets the kill to form the bay, and a boy lies in the dark, his heart beating with excitement, with the expectation of worlds to come while he squints into the peep-hole of a ring?

O Body Swayed

Originally published in *New Letters*

The airplane touched down so lightly that Jane, moving in and out of sleep, didn't even know she was home, at least not until she heard the roar of the engines in braking mode. She had been dreaming, yes, and performing beautifully in this dream, making up in her sleeping mind for her current lack of mobility. Old bones. Her body ached, where she still had feeling in her hips and legs. Thank God she was coming home to fix things. One way or another.

"Miss Harrison?"

At the voice of the flight attendant she immediately banished the other thought with which she awoke—remembering thinking flying above the ocean and wouldn't it be nice to plunge into the sea and end it all.

The flight attendant spoke to her from the aisle, the same woman who had so graciously helped her survive a humiliating experience some hours before.

"We'll have a chair for you in just a moment."

Remembering their little dance together in the lavatory, Jane, as she always did, took the offensive.

"Thank you, Marion," she said.

The flight attendant responded with a smile. "You remember my name."

"I'm not losing my mind," Jane said. "I just can't use my legs very well."

"I hope your operation goes well, Miss Harrison," the flight attendant said.

"Thank you," Jane said, sorry that she had revealed anything to the girl. But then there she had been, needing to pee. The attendant had helped Jane into the tiny cubicle, and in exchange Jane had made small talk, something she usually despised. "It's been eighteen months since I've been like this. If the operation doesn't help I might as well just die. Or perhaps I should just die and skip the operation." Before she left London she had said the same thing over the telephone to Stephen and he had gotten quite upset. To get his sympathy—the poor boy whom she had deprived, as he often told her, of a normal childhood—she would have to be dying every day.

"The chair will be along just as soon as we open the door," the attendant said.

And so it was.

"How are you today, ma'm?" said the black man pushing the chair toward her.

Jane went completely still as the man with his rough dark hands guided her into the chair. She stared fiercely forward, studying the gray walls of the ramp as he rolled her toward the terminal.

"Sorry you're not feeling well, ma'am," the man said. "It's a tiring trip…."

"I'm not at all tired," Jane said. "It's just that my legs don't work."

"Yes, ma'am," he said.

Had she frightened him? Annoyed him? She didn't care. She didn't care about anything. Well, that's what she told herself. But here she was, surveying the crowd waiting on the balcony as the man pushed her into the terminal. Her audience! Someone waved—to her? But not Stephen, where was Stephen? She craned her neck, scanning the faces behind the glass.

He was waiting for her when she rolled through Customs.

"Mother," he said.

"You hirsute creature." She held out a hand.

"It's nice to see you, too," he said. Stephen handed some dollar bills to the man who had been pushing Jane's chair.

"Do you have much baggage, Mother?" he asked Jane.

"I am baggage," she said.

"Mother, please," Stephen said.

"So you think you know now how I feel?"

"Please," he said again.

But right there in the middle of the terminal, with throngs of people moving back and forth, she shook her head and waved her arms as though she were back on stage.

"I used to soar across the floor, I used to fly like a crane and bend like the rushes in a fierce wind." She pounded the flat of her hand against the arm rest, and her hand stung, as though from the cuts of little knives. "I was a beautiful mover, Stephen. And now I'm a prisoner in my own body."

"Mother, I'm sorry…." He looked around, as though worried that people might be staring.

"Oh, never mind…." And what if they were staring? They couldn't have recognized her. Even at the height of her career, she had been an ensemble dancer. It was Martha they knew, it had been all Martha, and it still was, long after she was gone. Jane inhaled deeply and tried to calm herself. *Do I want to be a ghost that everyone recognizes?*

"Fina is sorry that she couldn't be here," Stephen said.

"Fina? I'm still trying to remember the names of your other wives." Jane focused all of her strength on her right leg. *Move!* The leg twitched.

Still, she felt like baggage, Stephen piling her into the car along with the suitcases—leaving the airport—all this passing so quickly that Jane thought she suddenly might be regaining her patience.

But a traffic jam just before the tunnel into the city annoyed her terribly. The cars, the white smoke of their exhausts, the black film passed by the trucks and buses, too much too thick too noisy.

"What an awful mess," she said, leaning forward from the back seat. "They could do something about this if they wanted to."

"Oh, Mother," Stephen said, his eye on the lake of vehicles in which they sat in the middle.

"They could," she said. Jane sighed, sinking back into her seat, exhausted. Clean it up," she said. "Bloody choreograph it better. They do in London."

"Mother," Stephen said, "Why do you speak like that?"

"Because it's the truth. I've always striven for the truth in my art and in my life. And now that I have no way to make art anymore, I just have my life."

"My stupid immobile life," she added. "My wasted life."

"Well," Stephen said, "that's not how everyone sees it."

"Is that so?"

"There's someone named Amy Kunstler. She's called and left two messages for you about setting up an interview."

"I don't want to see her," Jane said. "She phoned me up just before I left London. In a moment of weakness, I gave her your number and I'm sorry about that. I don't want to talk to anyone."

The traffic inched forward into the tunnel. Jane shut her eyes and hummed to herself the music from "True Blue." When in doubt, always think of your own work. Something Martha once told her. She didn't know if it was right or not, but it kept her busy during the remainder of the uncomfortable ride.

The apartment building—their destination—stood tall and antique at the corner of a street in the eighties and Central Park West. A doorman with an insidious smile ushered them into a grand lobby, and toward a gold elevator that carried them up to one of the highest floors—the apartment dear old Milly Pearson had bestowed upon her for as long as she would need it. Stephen fumbled with the keys.

"Hurry," Jane said. "I've got to tinkle."

He swung the door open and they were met by a curtain of slightly stale sweetened air.

"Do you need help?" Stephen looked down at her.

Jane looked up from her chair.

"I'm the mother, you're the child. I can do quite well for myself, thank you."

"Just asking," Stephen said.

A new chair always made for problems and it was with some difficulty that she wheeled herself toward a door halfway down the hall.

(Long hall, leading to a room filled with light, she could see as she swung the bathroom door open and wheeled in—thinking that this might not be such a bad place in which to convalesce after the operation.) But what was that odor? A man had been here long ago, and he had been a dapper fellow, used rum-based aftershave and smoked cigars.

Milly Pearson had never married, though Jane had always been certain that she must have wanted to, yet what about that friend of hers, that dark-haired girl from Smith—what was her name? gone now, lost in the dust-bin of the past.

So who was the man? Milly's father, perhaps? Unless Milly was the sort of rich bohemian at the center of whose life, turned inside out, there remained a rather conventional core. Never thought that about her, though. And then sitting there in her chair, trying desperately to raise the courage to begin her ablutions, Jane remembered with a chill in her chest and arms. Milly's father had hanged himself!

"Mother?"

"Don't you dare come in. I'm still trying to figure this out."

Jane shook off the odd fear that came with the thought of the suicide. Dr. Gronski had instructed her, yes, practically scolded her. No catastrophic thinking. If the thought comes, dismiss it. Begone! she said in the otherwise quiet of her mind. I've got enough to do right now just to pass some water. (Fear death by—begone!)

In the airplane, the flight attendant had risen above and beyond the call of duty by assisting her in the small cabinet thirty-thousand feet above the ground. The two of them in that small space, it was like a strange little dance. But then she saw everything that way, didn't she? Here, by herself, twelve floors up, another dance. This one a solo, unless she asked Stephen, which she was not going to do.

But a moment later, trying, without success, to hoist herself out of the chair, she called him.

"Yes, Mother?"

"Come in here, please."

And for the next five minutes they engaged in something she never imagined would occur in her life.

As he wheeled her back out into the hall, she said, "I'm exhausted. Christ knows what I'm going to feel like after the operation. Perhaps I should just give it up and die."

"Oh, Mother, please."

Stephen always pretended that nothing upset him. When small, he never could fool her. Or his father. (His father—fear death by suppression. You're going to tour? Good—I'll sulk for a while and then have an affair and blame it on you. Jane wondered if Stephen's first two marriages were any better than that. Even now as a grown man he was still his father's boy, so she couldn't imagine that they had been. Maybe his third? To Mina. What's in a name?)

"A nice view," he said, rolling her up to the window and looking down into the park.

"Of places I'll never go anymore," Jane said.

"Mother, don't be so pessimistic. This operation is going to give you back your legs."

"What use are they to me now, anyway? I'm too damned old to dance and have been for a decade. I don't know why I should have my hips replaced. I'm sorry now that I agreed to all this. Damned sorry."

Stephen turned away from the window and looked at her.

"You used to scold the hell out of me when I was kid. Now it's my turn to scold you. I want you to stop complaining about everything. The operation is going to go well. I've been doing some checking up. This doctor is the best guy—"

"Best guy, best guy. Your father was the best guy," Jane said. "And he turned into a fool. Such a fool! He had me, what did he need of other women, he himself told me that he only did it out of revenge, because of all my touring."

"I missed you, too, when you were on the road, Mother."

"But you didn't decide to find another mother, did you?"

Before Stephen could respond, if he could respond, the telephone began to ring and he went off in search of the receiver. In a moment, he called to her from the bedroom.

Jane sighed and wheeled herself along the hall.

"Amy Kunstler," Stephen said.

"I told you I don't want—"

Stephen forced the receiver into her hand.

Jane stared at the instrument for a moment and then held it to her ear.

"*Miss Harrison?*"

The voice at the other end of the line sounded much younger than it had when Jane had taken the call in London.

Jane said, "I told you that I am not interested in—"

"Mother!"

"Stay out of this, Stephen. Young lady?"

"*Yes, Miss Harrison, but I wanted to—*"

"I don't care what you want. I don't give interviews. I never have and I never will. Goodbye."

"Mother!"

"I will not," Jane said as she pounded the heel of her hand against the armrest of the chair, "I will not demean what we had by trivial interviews in the American press."

Stephen's face squinched up in exasperation.

"She's not the 'American press', for Christ's sake. She writes for *Dance Magazine*, Mother. She is a very good writer and she is interested in your work. She knows just about every solo piece you ever choreographed and performed."

"No," Jane said, feeling suddenly as though the walls of the apartment, the building, the sky itself were caving in upon her.

And then came a call from the doorman.

"Yes," Stephen said, "we're expecting her."

"I told you—"

"Mother, it's Milagros, the woman I've hired to take care of you."

"Oh, yes, to help me pee," Jane said. "You did a fine job just now. Why don't you stay?"

"I'm glad to see you're not losing your sense of humor. But I'll leave that particular chore now to this woman. She'll help you bathe and make your meals."

"What does she cook? 'Milagros?' Is that a rice and beans sort of name?"

"For Christ's sake, Mother, will you stop this? If it's up to me right now, you can just damned well starve to death."

"No, I won't starve. I'll eat my heart out first. Thinking about all that I've done and all that I can't do now. It's not you, dear boy, that I'm fighting. It's gravity. And old age. Perhaps I should just give in to it and sink into the ground."

"Mother...."

"You sound just the way you did when you were a little boy. 'Mother....' I'd be going off to rehearsal or on a tour, and you'd speak to me in that little voice. A little squeal of a voice. Begging me to stay. But I went. And did it deform your life irreparably? Did it do you terrible psychological damage?"

"No, Mother, I really don't think so. You were consistently absent. If you had deviated from that, I might really have been damaged."

Before Jane could respond, there was a knock at the apartment door. Stephen went to answer and admitted a big dark-faced woman in a white uniform about whom swirled a cloud of spicy odors.

"Milagros!" Jane nearly hoisted herself out of her chair in mock enthusiasm. "Well, don't expect to work any of your miracles on me!"

The operation was scheduled for the following week. Her idea had been to give herself plenty of time to settle in before going to the hospital. She would visit museums, go to galleries, perhaps even see a dance performance or two. But she had lost all heart for it now, stuck in this chair, unable even to pee by herself let alone shower or make an outing of an afternoon. Better that her airplane had dived into the dark ocean.

"No, thank you," she said to Milagros when the woman asked her if she wanted to get out and get some air. "I just want to sit here and sulk." Which she did, looking out the window at the building across the street, a modern design with sloping glass at the penthouse level and even and odd casements all the way down to the floor above the street. At the corner, the park's green bled out of her sight. The touch of green reminded her of London, but the geometry of the streets called back every year she had spent here in the city ever since arriving as an eighteen-year-old dancer from Sacramento, determined to turn her body into art.

"Now look at me," she said.

"What you say, ma'am?" Milagros called from the kitchen.

"I said I'd like some tea."

"Yes, ma'm," Milagros called back.

"And I'd like to be just the way I was," Jane said, closing her eyes.

"What, ma'am?"

But Jane didn't answer, already going under, into memory, and then sleep, the way a swimmer slips beneath the surface of a heaving sea. And only when she awoke did she understand what had happened. Hours had passed. The odor of steam and spice drifted into the living room from the narrow kitchen where Milagros was working. It was already nightfall, nearly time for her dinner and bath. She enjoyed the spicy meal—anyone with any sense living in London as long as she had cultivated a taste for such spicy imported cuisine.

"I had a beau once when I was growing up in California," she said to Milagros as the woman served her a heaping dish of rice and bananas, fried fish and beans. "He was a Mexican boy, son of a farmer, and now and then I ate a meal at their little shack. I loved that food. But when he found out my father nearly went through the roof. All I had done was eat with the boy. Mother suspected me. Didn't she know how innocent I was? Father was sensible, but she rode him. They never got along. At least not that I remember. It was the most difficult thing I have ever done, leaving them behind. But I knew that if I stayed, I would never dance the way I wanted to dance. Funny. I can scarcely recall Father's face. But I do remember that boy, eating that meal with him."

"You like this cooking," Milagros said. "It's island cooking."

"Yes, yes," Jane said, feeling suddenly quite exhausted. "I am grateful for it. See, I'm not all old bitch, am I? It's just…." She felt an odd sensation in her chest and a flame sweep across her face. She was crying.

"You alright, ma'am?"

"It's nothing," Jane said. "And I have to pee again."

Oh, God, it was so pathetic! The lifting, the shifting, the hauling, the holding on, the holding off, the holding up—and then gushing all over herself.

"Now for a bath, ma'am," Milagros said.

"Why not just put me in the electric chair?" Jane felt herself blush. How can it be that someone who performed before audiences all her life could feel such shame in the presence of one woman? Not to mention with Stephen.

Oh, God, throw me out with the rubbish! she said to herself later as she lay in bed, listening to Milagros quietly humming a tune and turning magazine pages in the other room.

"What is that?" she called to her.

"What is what, ma'am?"

"That song you're whistling?"

"Sorry to bother you, ma'am."

"It's not bothering me. I would just like to know what it is."

"A song my mother used to sing to me, ma'am. I don't know the name. I always called it the 'bird song.' It tells about a bird flies to the island and then flies away."

"My mother never sang to me," Jane said.

Milagros came to the doorway of the room.

"Is there anything I can get for you?"

"Another life," Jane said.

"Coming right up," Milagros said with a little laugh.

But Jane wasn't so easily seduced. She turned her head away, thinking of her mother, her flinty eyes and low harsh whiskey whisper. Bed time for girls—that voice still in her mind after eighty-and-more years. No wonder, Jane said to herself, the earth itself still bears the marks of glaciers millions of years old. That pathetic drunken bitch marked me all right. Thank God that I could flee into dance! Oh, all this swirled around in her mind with a terribly abrupt and broken rhythm. Yet despite her agitation sleep again came as a dark surprise.

"Good morning," said Milagros, looking in on her room, dressed in the same white uniform as yesterday.

"Don't be so bloody cheerful," Jane said, making a quick catalog of her aches and twinges, most of them in her hips and lower back and legs. She pretended she wasn't present as the woman got her ready for the day. "Were you here all night?"

"On the sofa, ma'am," the woman said as she wheeled Jane into the living room. Hearing this report, Jane guessed that she hadn't removed her clothes but had fallen asleep while watching television. She gave off an odor now that was not entirely unappealing, a mixture of sweat and cooking spices.

"And how did you sleep?"

Milagros stepped back and gave Jane a wide smile, showed her rows of uneven teeth, with a black tooth at the left side of her mouth and several gold teeth on the other.

"I should be asking you that, ma'am."

"Don't bother," Jane said. "I don't remember a thing."

"That's the pill you're taking, I think."

"It's a blessing, whatever it is. In London, I used to be afraid of going to sleep. I used to worry about what I might dream about. Milagros? Have you ever been to London?"

"No, never been there, ma'am."

"Jane."

"Oh, yes. Jane. I never been there."

"Too bad. I think you would love it."

"Maybe," Milagros said. "Maybe not."

The telephone rang. If it's—but it was Stephen, inquiring about her night. I slept, she told him. Good, he said. And today?

Jane looked at Milagros. The words came out, unbidden.

"I'm going to meditate on my condition," she said. "Milagros and I have had some very interesting conversations about faith, and I want to think about how that might help me."

"*That sounds lovely, Mother,*" Stephen said.

"Yes, yes, just lovely," Jane said. "Bloody fucking lovely."

"*Mother!*"

"Yes?"

"*Fina and I are going to come over and take you to dinner.*"

"In this bloody chair?"

"*Mother, you have to eat.*"

"Milagros made me a wonderful supper last night. Spicy and delicious. Just the way I like things."

"*Fina wants to see you, Mother.*"

"Is she still on that drug?"

"*Mother!*"

"When will you come?"

"*Later this afternoon? Say, about five?*"

"If I'm here."

"*Now where do you expect to go?*"

"Oh, I thought I might just go directly to the bloody graveyard."

"*Mother!*"

"You were always such an excitable child, Stephen," Jane said, handing the instrument over to Milagros, who gave her a squinty look.

"So would you like to go now, ma'am?"

Jane gave her a look right back.

"No," she said. "That's just something I told him to keep him quiet. He wants to see me. He wants his new wife to meet me. He thinks I owe him something because I stole his childhood. A grown man, still thinking about his childhood. He hasn't learned, as I have, to fend it off. I'm all for analysis, Milagros. I put in my years at it myself. But for a bearded man his age, still holding a grudge? In any case, I don't feel like going out right now. I don't know that I'll feel like going out ever again."

With that same squint in her eye, Milagros said, "You got to go to the hospital next week, ma'am. That you got to do."

"I don't have to do bloody anything," Jane said. "Do you understand?"

Milagros seemed to study her face.

"Yes, ma'am," she said, after a long pause.

"I may just turn right around and go back to London."

"Yes, ma'am."

"Or I can bloody well die, if that's what I choose."

Milagros nodded, turned away, and went about some business in another room, whatever that business might be.

Jane wheeled herself around the room, parking herself close to the bookshelves. Freud, Marx, Tolstoy, Balzac. Baudelaire, Whitman, a cook book, some titles she did not recognize: a melange she might have expected from the likes of Milly Pearson. Or was it her husband's reading? Or Milly's father's, the man dead by his own hand? But couldn't be his. Her father had been long gone by the time Milly had married. Joyce, Steinbeck, Hemingway. No books on theatre, none on dance. What a narrow life her old friend read her way through. Toynbee, Winston Churchill. Michener. Jane had done all this reading herself. At night in various apartments while her husband drank and raged about the world. And after he left, alone, content to know these stories about love and deception and mercy and triumph and betrayal and death. But she couldn't read in green rooms, no, in green rooms it had always been cards. Bloody cards. She could almost hear the riffling of the deck as she sat there, immobile, cursing her condition.

Next thing she knew she was shaking herself out of yet another bout of slumber right there in her chair.

"What?"

Milagros had been speaking to her.

"Telephone, ma'am."

"That damned boy. Why doesn't he worry about his own life?"

"Ma'am," said Milagros. "He is your child."

"Yes," Jane said, "and he regrets it, bitterly."

"Oh, no," said the woman, "he is talking about you so beautiful."

"He was?"

"Yes, about the dancing."

"Yes, well, I don't do that anymore. I haven't moved in a long time. It's a power I had and it's gone. It used to be my salvation. Terrible things would happen around me, and I began to move. My father died and I made a dance. I lost a child—"

"I'm very sorry, ma'am," Milagros broke in.

"Yes, oh, Stephen had a sister. But it got me to make 'American Blue,' my most famous piece."

"Yes, ma'am," Milagros said.

"You don't know my work, do you? No, of course, you don't. I'm a choreographer, Milagros. I make dances. And I was quite a lovely mover myself, a dancer of some repute, as we might say. Until I fell."

"You fell, ma'am?"

"I leaped, and I fell, and I broke my back and haven't danced since. This operation, it's for my hips. Nothing to do with the accident."

"I like to dance myself," Milagros said. "Before the children came I danced many times a week. At parties. In the house. In the kitchen."

"I don't see you dancing in this kitchen."

"Oh, no, not now, no more," Milagros said. "I think the children wear me out."

"How many children do you have?"

"Seven, ma'am."

"Seven!"

Milagros showed all her teeth, bad and good, in a smile.

"Is not too many where I come from, ma'am."

"I don't know how you did it. I had two. The first, the girl, died very young. And so I have only Stephen. But he was quite a burden. Mastoid problems and asthma and such. Also, he's quite handsome, as you may have noticed. That's always a liability in a man. It makes him think he's worth something just because of how he looks, not for what he does. And it made him attractive to empty-headed women who wanted only good-looks in a man. Beauty! Oh, in dance, I can't tell you, how many beautiful young people I've seen waste such great possibilities, only because they believed they didn't have to *do* anything, they just had to *be*. It's a miracle—oh, a miracle! your name!—but it is, that Stephen's survived, especially with having his father's temperament. He's not really overbearing, he just thinks that's how a man is supposed to act."

Jane looked around, almost as if someone other than herself had been speaking. Milagros stood in front of her, motioning for her to take the telephone receiver.

"Who is it?"

"Mister Stephen," Milagros said with a smile.

"You like him, don't you?"

Jane's hand trembled as she touched the instrument to her ear. "Hello?"

"*Hello, Mother. We're running a little late. Fina had a doctor's appointment. But we should be there in an hour or so. We're going to take you out to dinner.*"

"I have a perfectly good cook in residence here," Jane said, with a nod to Milagros. "I don't want to go out."

"*Fina thinks it will do you good. I do, too.*"

"I really don't care what she thinks, darling," Jane said, shifting in her chair. Was that movement? Or just imaginary movement? For an instant, it seemed real.

"*Please, Mother. It's difficult enough for both of us here. If you—*"

"If you stop marrying difficult women, things won't turn out to be so difficult. I'm surprised that you're surprised about it."

There was a brief silence at the other end of the line. "*Why do we always have to have conversations like this over the telephone and not in person? Maybe if you stayed in New York, we wouldn't—*"

"I am not staying in New York. I am here for the bloody operation. Just get that idea out of your head."

"*We'll talk about it, Mother. We need to talk about it.*"

"We most certainly will not," Jane said.

Jane could hear a woman's voice at the other end of the line, either Stephen's wife feeding him instructions or some sort of crossed connection. Finally, he said, "*We're coming over. We'll see you in about an hour or so.*"

"If you can," Jane said, unsure herself of what she meant. But she didn't have much time to wonder about it. She was just handing the telephone to Milagros when it rang again.

"What is it now?"

"*Miss Harrison?*"

"Who is this?"

"*Amy Kunstler, and I—*"

"I told you —"

"*Please, Miss Harrison. Give me a moment. I've been planning to write about you for years. This magazine assignment is just the first piece. I have a book in mind and I—*"

Jane suddenly felt a tingling in her hips and a great pressure, as though someone had just inserted a soccer ball or a hard pillow directly beneath her rib cage.

"Amy?"

"*Yes, Miss Harrison.*"

She felt a gush of air from her lungs and her mind leaped.

"Just come the hell over. I'm hoping to take a stroll, if that's what you can call it when I do it in this bloody chair, in the park. I need to see something green. You can push me around and we can talk. If you can get here within half an hour, I'll speak with you. Otherwise, not."

"*I'll be right there,*" the young woman said.

"I need to use the loo," Jane said to Milagros.

Twenty minutes later there was a call from the doorman just as Milagros was finishing with Jane.

"You're older than I imagined," Jane said a few minutes later as her helper led a pudgy red-faced woman in her early forties into the living room. Amy Kunstler was wearing an old pair of sweatpants and sweatshirt, and a beat-up pair of white sneakers. "And you ran all the way?"

"I was about to go for a run when you asked me to come over," the woman said. "I didn't have time to change."

"No, you didn't," Jane said. "Well… I'm Jane Harrison. And this is Milagros. Her name means 'Miracle', do you know?"

"Hi," the red-faced woman said, turning to Milagros. She then offered Jane her hand.

"You've written some interesting books," Jane said.

"You know them?"

"I liked the one about Nijinsky," Jane said. "But if we're going to talk we'd better get going. Milagros?"

"Yes, ma'am?"

"Hand me my purse, please. Put a door key in it. And I'll want a sweater. You can take the rest of the day off."

"Thank you, ma'am. But Mister Stephen—"

"He's a big boy. Just like his father. I don't owe him anything. And now," Jane said to Amy Kunstler, "we're out the door." And into the elevator and down to the lobby and maneuvering through the front doors and onto the sidewalk.

"To the park," Jane said, feeling every imperfection in the pavement as Amy Kunstler pushed her along. "And hurry."

It had been a bright day earlier, but now some clouds had moved in to the spaces above buildings and the streets. A light breeze—it felt good on her face as she looked the traffic up and down.

"I'm glad I wore my running clothes," Amy Kunstler said. "Who are we running from?"

"My son and his wife," Jane said. "Bloody bores. After an hour with them—I'd scream for help."

"So you're talking to me to escape them? I know what you mean, I'm recently separated. My in-laws, they were as crazy as my ex-husband."

Jane didn't respond. They paused at the traffic light at Central Park West while cars cruised up and down the street in packs. When the light changed she nodded toward the park.

"Does it matter why we're talking? It's what you want. So, as we used to say, onward and upward with the arts."

Midweek on a late spring day—Jane was amazed there were so many young people gathered on benches at the edge of the park, girls in jeans and sweatshirts and boys in jeans and sweatshirts and mothers with children and children with nannies. Music in the air, too, ringing and clanging above the sound of the nearby traffic. A young boy on a skateboard rolled slowly past the benches, gracefully balancing as he moved. Two older boys on red bicycles raced ahead of them, turning to yap at each other in a muffled language as they moved along.

"Lively," she said over her shoulder to Amy Kunstler as the woman steered her up the curb and over the rough pavement. "I haven't seen much of London since my hips went on me. I just go from my apartment to the school and back again. But sometimes after class the school will get this lively...."

"It's been what, Miss Harrison, thirty years since your accident?"

Jane felt a little jolt in her stomach and chest. But nothing in her legs.

"Is that what you want to talk about? How a dancer in her fifties falls from a stage platform in the dark and ends her career?"

"No, no, Miss Harrison. I only brought it up because you mentioned your hips."

"Well, it's true, my hips deteriorated because after the accident I couldn't move anymore. It's the Lady or the Tiger. If you move, your hips eventually go. If you don't move, they go anyway. And now I'm going to have both bloody hips replaced. I'm going to become a mechanical woman. At my age, just imagine, wiring me up and putting me out to dance. Can you see it?"

"I love the way you move, Miss Harrison. I love your work."

"This is the part in the interview where the old bitch tears up and says, 'Well, it's been a very long time since then.'"

"I've seen videos," Amy Kunstler said. "And reconstructions. I wish I could have seen the real thing."

"No, you don't. Because then you would be nearly as old as I am."

She felt the jolt as Amy Kunstler pushed her chair forward over a rise of cracked concrete and they rolled down into the park proper. A few men, some obviously retired, others obviously drunk, sat on stone steps near a fountain. More mothers and nannies pushed and tugged along their tiny charges. A trio of hunched boys wearing black bandanas clattered past them on skateboards, rushing away into the deeper recesses of the park. More boys on red bicycles tore through the scene.

"All these things that people do when I'm in the studio."

"Are you rehearsing a new piece, Miss Harrison?"

Her temporary caretaker came around to the front of her chair, which made Jane feel like a small child looking up at a parent.

"Do I look as though I am?" Jane felt a terrible rush of bile through her gut. And then caught hold of herself. "Sorry," she said. "I don't mean to snap at you. It's just…being immobile, makes me quite cross with the world."

"Someone had mentioned to me that you might be in rehearsal. I can't remember who it was."

"Someone with a good imagination," Jane said. "I haven't had a piece in rehearsal for five years now. Only Martha could do that. She didn't even blink at eighty. Well, she might have had another drink. But she just moved right past it."

"So you're not making anything new?"

Something about the way the woman tilted her puffy body to one side, then the other, suddenly made Jane feel terribly sad.

"I am, actually," she said. "A very new piece. Quite embryonic right now, though. But definitely in the works."

"In the vein of 'True Blue,' or something different?"

"Something quite different," Jane said, amazed at her sudden burst of confidence.

"Well, do you think we'll be able to talk about it," Amy Kunstler said.

"I imagine that you're a dancer yourself?"

The woman began to smile and then caught herself. "You don't want to talk about it?"

Jane nodded.

"Well, I wanted to be a dancer," Amy Kunstler said. "I took classes for years. But…I'm a better writer than I am a mover." she said.

"And you want to write about me, do you?"

"It's my hope."

"Well, don't get your hopes up," Jane said. "I'm a bit more difficult in person than my pieces might make me out to be."

"I don't write psychological criticism of movement, Miss Harrison. Unless I'm trying to find some connection between a piece and the American psyche."

"The American psyche?"

"Yes."

"And if there's an American psyche, then we can have a national nervous breakdown?"

The Kunstler woman seemed suddenly quite agitated.

"I suppose you might say that."

Jane pulled herself up in her chair about as high as she could.

"That is just silly bullshit," she said.

But Amy wasn't really listening, her body stiffening as she stared over Jane's shoulder.

"What is it?" Jane said. She strained in her chair but couldn't really turn fully around.

"I thought I saw someone I knew."

"Pay attention to me, Miss Kunstler. That's what you're here for, isn't it?"

"Sorry, Miss Harrison," the woman said. "Do you mind if I ask you some questions?"

"Ask them, and we'll see if I mind."

"First of all," Amy said as she came around behind the chair and started pushing again, "I just want to confirm some facts."

"Confirm away," Jane said, looking down the path that sloped gently toward a large grassy field.

"You were born in Sacramento."

"Yes. I went to high school there and left for New York as soon as

I graduated. I came to dance. I'd always known that was what I wanted.

"Your parents. Did they oppose your decision?"

They were picking up speed and Jane clutched her purse to her chest, afraid that it might fall to the pavement.

"I was seventeen and decided to go east by myself and live by myself and train as a dancer. I don't think you can imagine just how difficult that was." Her stomach seemed to make a sort of kick and she had to catch her breath. "Can we slow down? I feel as though I'm going to fall out of this chair."

"Sorry," Amy Kunstler said.

Jane could feel a slight decrease in speed as they approached a path along the inner roadway, cars and taxis rushing past. A few old people sat on benches nearby. Two more boys on skateboards clattered past, and one of them, without turning, waved in their direction.

"It's usually boys who set out on their own," Jane said. "But with dancers, at least back when I started out, it was women. Young women. Girls, still. Maybe it was the Californian in me that gave me the courage to do it. Isadora was a Californian, of course."

"Of course." Amy Kunstler increased their speed—Jane could feel the vibrations in the wheels and in the armrests and her purse, looped around her neck, bounced on her chest as they rushed along.

"Don't rush," she said.

Amy seemed to ignore her. "Did you meet Martha almost immediately on arriving in New York?"

Another boy on a skateboard shot past them, disappearing up the path before Jane could even make out his face.

"I arrived at the train station and hailed a taxi and went directly to her studio. I marched in and told her that I was going to be her student. I began taking classes with her even before I ate my first meal in New York, before I knew where I was going to live."

"Wonderful," Amy said. For the moment, she was entirely enthustiastic, but something came in to her voice. "Can you tell me…."

Jane looked around to where she was looking.

"Excuse me a moment, Miss Harrison," Amy said, "but I've got to...."

Jane wheeled herself around to see a man hurrying toward them.

"I don't believe this. Are you following—" Amy stepped forward to meet him.

"Just a coincidence," the man said—thin fellow with a lot of dark hair, dark jacket and striped tie, tie askew. "Small world, all that, Amy."

"Miss Harrison," Amy Kunstler said, "this is Jack Wisher, my ex-husband."

"Small world, yes, indeed," Jane said, forcing a smile at the man before seeing the two figures in the distance.

A dance, she said to herself, staring for a moment longer at the couple coming down the path and then at Amy and the ex-husband who just happened to be walking in the park, life is a strange and beautiful dance, and a wicked dance sometimes—and then she wheeled about and began rolling away.

"Miss Harrison!" Amy called after her.

"What's going on?" Amy's ex-husband shouted.

Oh, that noise! the noise of his voice! Her ex-husband's whining voice! Stephen's indifferent voice! Her own sure voice, the mask behind which she lived in fear. Jane worked her arms and worked her arms. She'd escape all this if it killed her!

A boy on a red bike zipped past her, calling something as he ripped along through the thin air of late afternoon. Jane kept on moving, moving, until her arms turned to lead, and then she pushed herself even further. A pair of long-legged female joggers brushed past her and kept on moving, not even looking back to smile or out of curiousity cast an eye. Jane sighed to herself for the days when she had legs like that. But rolling along, she hadn't felt so free since she had been confined to this bloody chair, and understood of a sudden that she hadn't lied to Amy Kunstler because she was rushing toward something new.

A piece flashed whole into her mind. On stage, moving chairs, and women with strong arms—stronger than hers—spun themselves about, the large wheels making great circles in the eyes of the audience. It all came to her in great circles itself, as she kept moving along the path.

It would be a great piece, the greatest piece she had ever done, and it would crown this miserable old age in which she built muscles in her arms, lost her legs, and wished that she would die.

Cars flowed by, their exhaust mingling with the odor of new plants and leaves. A cloud hovered almost directly over her, and she prayed that it wouldn't rain. And now—damn it all, she felt it!—she prayed that she wouldn't pee before she found someone to help her with it. She was breathing hard, rolling as fast as she could, talking to herself, hoping for more women running along from whom she might secure some assistance, when she saw the first boys skating-boarding up the path in her direction.

"Hello!" she called out to them and waved, slowing down a little so that they might slow to meet her. Glancing over her shoulder, she saw that she had covered a good bit of ground and that no one was following her. "Can you help me?" Jane forced a smile. "I need to get to a lavatory."

The taller of the two, his black bandana stained with sweat, squinched up his face in a question.

"A lava-what?"

"You stupid or something?" the other boy said. "A laboratory. Like she's a scientist or something. Right?" He nodded at Jane.

"No, please, a lavatory," Jane said. "A bathroom."

"Aw, that's all?" The tall boy grinned at his friend. "Sure, we can get you to one. Can't we do that?"

"I know where," the other boy said.

As they maneuvered themselves around behind her chair a gray-haired man in sweatshirt and shorts came jogging up the path.

"Everything all right?" he said, moving a moment in place.

"I'm having a perfectly cheerful conversation with these boys," Jane said. "Thank you very much."

"Just asking," the man said and continued on his way.

"What kind of voice you got?" the shorter boy said.

"What kind of *voice*?" Jane stared at him. "Do you mean my accent?"

"Yeah," the boy said. "I mean your axment."

"I'm an American, just like you," she said.

"Oh, that's cool," the taller boy said as they began to propel her forward.

"Wheelchair Granny," one of them shouted as they picked up speed, the noise of the rollers grating on her ears.

"Granny Wheelie!" the other shouted with obvious glee.

"Not too fast," Jane called to them.

But they didn't slow down, not even when another boy on a red bike rolled up alongside them.

"What you doing, man?"

"Heping this old lady," the taller skateboarder said.

"Yeah, so pass away, my amigo," the shorter boy said.

"I ain't your fuckin' amigo," said the boy on the bike as he pumped hard at his pedals and rushed away.

"Where is it?" Jane said, feeling the wind roughing up her face and her heart pumping.

"What?" one boy said.

"The lavatory? the loo? The *bath*room!"

"Yeah," said the other boy, pushing along behind her as they came to a fork in the path and took a mud-streaked trail off to the right. Jane grew annoyed with the bumps and ruts that jounced and jostled her.

"We must stop now," she said, feeling a tear in her neck as she tried to turn far enough to catch the boy's eye.

Two other boys on bicycles came rolling toward them.

Her captors—for she knew that's what they were now—pushed harder from behind, steering toward a tunnel under a walkway flush with trees.

"Whoa!" one of them called.

"Fuck me!" another cried out.

The bikes came steaming upon them, throwing stones as they skidded alongside, and Jane felt her chair—herself—rolling free into the tunnel as the skate-board boys turned to meet the bike riders.

"Help!" She cried out as the left side of the chair hit the tunnel wall and tilted forward leaving her hanging on to the armrests.

Behind her came the grunts and thuds of battle, and an even louder noise—a bottle smashing against stone, she guessed, without being able to turn. Then a scream, a string of snapping noises like tiny firecrackers at Chinese New Year's, and then silence. And then Jane felt herself shaking, someone was shaking the chair, shaking her out of the chair and she fell forward like baggage onto the cold, damp, rocky bottle-strewn ground that reeked of urine and feces and decaying food. Some feeling had returned to her legs and it was agony.

"They took the fucking chair!" a boy said with a groan.

She looked up to see one of the bike riders in a black bandanna crouched above her.

"Least we got something," another rider said. This boy, lean and glowing light-skinned in the shade of the tunnel, held out a hand to her.

She reached out a hand toward him, hoping to say, You'll have to squat down and lift me, because my legs don't work very well. But nothing came out of her throat.

The boy beckoned again.

"Come on, grandma, I'm not asking you to fucking dance. The purse," he said. "Give me the purse."

Jane let her hand fall to her lap and took several hard short breaths— she was soaked with sweat but felt the cool sour air in her lungs all the same—and bowed her head forward. The boy leaned down and with two hands lifted the loop holding the purse from around her neck.

In a clatter of rocks and a humming of tires on dirt, the boys departed, leaving her to lean her head against the damp wall of the tunnel and feel her body wind and unwind and wind again. *Ah*, she thought she heard herself moaning, or was it humming? *Ah, ah, ah....* As if on signal, her bladder released, and she sank eyes closed into the warm stink of her own urine.

"They took her *chair*?"

She opened her eyes at the sound of a familiar voice echoing in the tunnel.

"My God, Mother!" A new voice, a woman speaking. Jane opened her eyes and studied the face of the young blonde girl alongside her bearded son.

"Miss Harrison! Oh, I'm so sorry!"

Amy Kunstler knelt alongside her as Stephen went to the mouth of the tunnel.

"Which way did they go?" he called.

"Mother?" The strange blonde woman hovered over her.

"She's all right, I think," Amy Kunstler said.

Jane felt herself sobbing, but still no sound came from her throat. She closed her eyes again, seeing wheels and skates, boards and bikes, boys, bandanas, wheels and wheels and wheels. And the tunnel spun in tune with these turning wheels, and lying there she herself began to turn.

The Distinction Between Twilight and Crepuscule

Originally published in *Pleiades*

Casablanca—1935. On the beach two small boys, one dark-skinned, one light, were playing out an intricate game in the sand. First, one of them would lie on his back and kick both legs in the air while the other ran around him in a circle, and then the other, the runner, would suddenly fling himself down while the other, prone only an instant before, would yank himself erect and begin to run.

"It's just like my street back home," Aaron said from the balcony. "We're just too far away to hear them yell and scream." He cleared his throat and touched a bony finger to his long slender nose, rubbing away a few droplets of sweat. The air was dry here, but still he soaked through his shirt as though he had returned in high summer to the very streets he talked about.

"We never played games like that on Long Island," said Paul, sitting in a chair opposite him. "My father wouldn't allow it." He brushed aside a lock of blonde hair that had fallen across his forehead and squinted into the piercing sunlight.

"Who said I played?" Aaron said, lifting a fluted glass full of sparkling wine and holding it toward the beach. "I wanted to play, but I always had a lesson."

"I never wanted to play," Paul said. "I invented reasons why I couldn't." He touched a match to the tip of a cigarette and inhaled deeply. "I was quite a busy boy, though. I made a little world all of my own without ever much leaving my room."

As if in a film in which the image and sound were completely un-synchronized a series of high-pitched squeals and shouts drifted up on the wind from the water.

"Those boys seem to be running themselves into the sand," Paul said.

"They live there," Aaron said. "Like crabs. They burrow into the sand at night and sleep. At sunrise, they dig themselves out."

"No?" Paul said.

"No," Aaron said. "But it amuses me to think about them that way."

"And this amuses you?"

"What do you mean?"

"You're amused by my company."

"That's why I suggested that we do this together."

"I thought that it was for the instruction."

"Yes, that."

"I need the instruction."

"First sign of a pupil who no longer needs the teacher," Aaron said.

"That sounds rather Buddhist," Paul said. "Are you reading about Buddhism? I've been reading a little about it."

"I've been raised in Jewdhism," Aaron said. "I'm a Jewdhist."

"Funny," Paul said, blowing smoke across the table only to have it ripped away by the wind. He hummed a little phrase and then wet his lips and became silent.

"Talking about Jewdhism," Aaron said.

"Were we?" Paul said.

"I was," Aaron said. "And talking about it, I'm reminded once again of that first sight I caught of Miss Stein."

"Yes," Paul said. "And?"

"I was shocked at how Jewish she looked," Aaron said. "And how old."

Paul again touched a hand to his forelock. "To tell you the truth I'm shocked at however it is I look."

"You don't look Jewish," Aaron said.

"Should I take that as a compliment?" Paul said.

"Merely as a statement of face," Aaron said. "And you don't look old."

"Thank the gods."

"And you don't look like a woman."

"It's just a stupid accident how I look. It's how I feel, how I see, that worries me."

"After lunch, we'll work again," Aaron said. "We'll see how you feel."

"That's what I'm here for," Paul said.

As if at a signal they both turned to look at the beach where the boys still frolicked and wrestled, and then they found themselves gazing beyond the white sand at the gently breaking surf, and staring past the small breakers to the stable edge of ocean horizon. Several birds flew in a line from south to north. The sunlight bounced off the water with a strange resilience, as though it were a solid, buoyant substance skipping and dancing across the tops of the waves.

"I'll confess," Paul said. "I don't know why I'm here most of the time. Though sometimes I do have an inkling."

"What's your thought on the subject at the moment?" Aaron said.

"My thought on the subject. So formal. It's less than a thought."

"Your inkling, then," Aaron corrected himself.

"It's not New York, and that's why I'm here." Paul fingered the temple piece of his sunglasses. "I'm tired of America," he said. "For a young country, it feels all worn out to me. That's why I came here. It feels like an old country that's still in infancy."

Aaron stared at the remaining liquid in his glass.

"It feels like no country to me," he said. "That's why I'm here. I feel no connection to it at all. So I can listen without distraction to the sounds in my mind." He raised the wine glass to his lips and drank. "Or with minimal distraction, I should say. There are, of course, some native sounds."

"Those young boys out there?"

"I meant native music," Aaron said. "Native noise."

"There are some noises, yes, one can't deny," Paul said.

"Yes, yes, some noises." Aaron tapped his glass against the surface of the wooden table. "Ready to go inside and work?"

"Yes, I'm ready."

"So then…"

It was the only piano in the quarter, an ancient instrument, legs scarred as if by the beaks of attacking birds, surface blistered from the ubiquitous heat. There was no stool, only an old broken-backed wooden chair that Aaron pulled close to the instrument before sitting himself gingerly down. He raised his hands and then worked the keyboard lightly.

"Appropriate, don't you think?"

Paul murmured along with the music, his body perfectly still.

Aaron abruptly broke off his playing.

"Sit."

"Uh-huh," Paul said, changing places with his teacher.

"Play."

Paul commenced to touch his fingertips to the dry bones of the keys.

"Wait," Aaron said. "Go back to the—"

"Here?" Paul remade a phrase.

"Yes, yes…"

Paul played on.

"And yes," Aaron said. "And, stop there. But wait, all right—"

The afternoon rose with the music in the heat that gathered up near the ceiling fan, gathered near the edges of the shuttered windows, leaked away slowly, unnoticed.

"That last piece," Aaron said. "Play it for me again."

"It's new," Paul said.

"Something in the sound attracts me. Cantabile, it's all cantabile."

"I had a suspicion," Paul said.

"You're being wry, yes?"

"Where I come from, we're often quite wry."

"Where I come from," Aaron said. "We're often quite rye ourselves. That's r-y—"

"I understand," Paul said. "Droll. You've missed your calling. You should have gone into vaudeville."

"Have some respect," Aaron said. "I'm your teacher."

"I couldn't have more respect if I tried," Paul said, raising his hands above the keyboard and producing the opening phrases of the last piece. Now the music drifted through the air like smoke, like mist on a Long Island early autumn morning. When he stopped playing the two men sat in silence as the noise of the street insinuated its way into the room, the noise of the clicking of tongues in odd speech, the clack of wood against wood, wood against stone. The heat. Dry and overpowering. Without the sun it seemed desperate and meaningless. With the sun it at least seemed to play some part in a larger plan, though of course no less debilitating. The heat. The dry hot shade of the room.

Aaron said, "I'll show you something now."

Paul stood up and they exchanged places once again.

"Blues, I hear blues," Paul said.

"And aquamarine?" Aaron said, his fingers never hesitating.

"Yes, that too."

The music rolled out into the room, liquid now rather than smoke, and it cooled the air between them, serving both as river flow and bank of the river, as salt tide seeping slowly back up into a freshwater estuary.

"So American," Paul said, turning his face toward the dark wood of the shuttered window.

"What else would you expect?" Aaron said, playing on.

Now the melodic line emerged, like some living figure in the air, appealing and yet so honest and full of truth that it made Paul turn back toward the piano and cock his head to one side and listen as if to catch the measure of some passing animal or bird.

The animal, Aaron created, a bird, fluttered its wings in air. But it had paws too, claws that slapped and scratched against the ground, pounding out the rhythm in this forest, in this sky—it went back and forth from ground to cloud, from earth to horizon—but why forest, why living creatures, who could say? To have heard this tune while walking along the path to where the standing water catches the sunlight, so translucent, so blue and at the same time translucent. And the green of things, the odor arising from the damp beneath our feet, this dream, this fantasy, fantasia, where all light and all color and all sound seem to move together in a pleasing motion, the water, the particles of brilliance making up the very horizon, cloud and tree and rock—but on this shore all white sand blinded brilliantly, and Aaron blinked and signed, and the vision came apart in mid-air, the pieces falling around his head and shoulders and onto his wrists and hands, his fingers the last things coming to rest.

"Pretty," Paul said.

"That's what you have to say?"

"I don't know a better compliment."

"But you don't like it."

"I do like it. It's just not—"

"Not?"

"Not—what I want to do."

"I won't make you do what I do," Aaron said, sitting motionless on the chair. "I couldn't anyway. You can't tamper with genius, you can only get out of the way."

"I don't want you to get out of the way, if it's me you're talking about."

"I don't see anyone else in the room," Aaron said. He fingered his collar. Sweat broke out in small dots all about his collar and along the lines of his nose.

"Beautiful, I should have said," Paul said.

"If that's what you thought. But it's still not good enough for you, is it?"

"I have this feeling that I can scarcely explain. I want to turn everything inside out and upside down. I want to make the beautiful ugly and the ugly beautiful."

"I'm glad you finally said so," Aaron said.

"It just came to me, the way to say it."

"It's going to take quite a bit of work. I'm not sure you're genius enough for that."

"If I'm not, then I'll give it up," Paul said.

"I didn't suggest that you come all this way so that I could discourage you," Aaron said. "Though I know people who are capable of doing that."

Something trickled against the shutters as though it were raining, an impossible occurrence in this city at this time. The sound came again, and it might have been the noise of the shifting of the light itself, the air overflowing with the fullness of heat and the hours so that afternoon itself could no longer go on—not for much longer.

"You know who," Aaron said.

"I don't," Paul said. "Can you name them?"

Aaron laughed drily, and got up from the piano.

"Outside," he said, going to the window. "I meant you know who it is outside."

As if he were addressing the piano keyboard, he raised his hands and with a flourish pulled open the shutters, flooding the room with white hot light.

"Blinding," Paul said. "I like that. Blind them so that they might see."

"Deafen them so that they might hear?"

"Who is it?"

Aaron looked down into the street. A small trail of dust rose along the way to the beach where the boys had run after tossing their stones against the shutters. The salt odor of the ocean drifted into the room, and the stink of mud stippled with dung, the smell of roasting meat, and certain odors that he would never be able to define or identify, no matter how long he stayed. The sea, the stench of the streets, the charmed heat that rose to meet the now blinking line of the horizon.

"Our little friends," he said.

The air swelled around them despite the closing of the shutters, heat all around, like warm drowsy water.

The two men yawned almost simultaneously. They looked at each other.

"Siesta time," Aaron said.

Paul went to his room, lay back against the perfumed pillows, and smoked a cigarette. He found himself nodding, put out the cigarette and closed his eyes. Bright brilliant flakes fell all around him, making a cool blanket that covered his legs, his thighs, his chest, his chin, his mouth, his nose, his eyes. The snow fell silently, and in spite of himself he began to invent a cool yet melodic music to accompany it. He touched a hand to his genitals and gently began to move.

Aaron went to his room and undressed to his undershorts, plumping up the pillows and then curling into a fetal ball and closing his eyes. A distant cry in the street. He pictured clouds over the ocean horizon. Another cry. The afternoon call to prayer, yes, it was. He released himself, his hands folded beneath him. He signed. He breathed in deeply. He let go. Allah Illah...

When he opened his eyes the room had faded to grays and darks, an inky drawing of what so soon before had been brilliant and gay.

The dinner hour had stolen up on them. Both men found that they possessed huge appetites.

The cook did not disappoint them. He and his young helpers delivered two kinds of roasted birds, one small and coated with a rare honey, the other dusted with powdered sugar and studded with raisins; they brought roasted vegetables; lemony sauces; tart chutneys; flat bread that still smelled of the sandy oven. The wine tasted as fragrant as the mountain groves, as dry as the nearest desert. Paul and Aaron ate heartily, using their fingers. Aaron allowed himself to belch with mighty force and though Paul held back he saw the smile on the face of the cook and his two young helpers who hovered just inside the doorway to the dining room, their slender bodies fattened and distorted by the candlelight.

They finished a second bottle of wine.

"I'm quite ready enough now," Paul said, standing up, "to recite my favorite poem,"

"Oh, you are? And what is that?" The wine, the intake of breath, Aaron felt such pleasure.

"Vintage Schwitters. One of his best."

"Say it then, if you can remember it."

"Oh, I can remember it."

"Then say it."

"I will," Paul said, pushing back from the table and standing up. He took a deep breath and began to recite: "Lanke trr gll./ Pe pe pe pe pe / Ooka. Ooka. Ooka. Ooka./ Lanke trr gll./ Pi pi pi pi pi/ Tzuuka. Tzuuka. Tzuuka. Tzuuka…"

"I like it," Aaron said.

"Like it?" Paul said. "It's the goddamned cat's meow."

"That too," Aaron said. "And now for a little night music?"

"Absolutely," Paul said.

Aaron cranked up the gramophone and the sounds of rhythmical chanting filled the room.

"What?" said Paul. "Where did you find that?"

"While you were practicing yesterday, I went out and met a German fellow in the market. We started talking. He had just come back from an expedition to the Sahara."

"You bought it?"

"Borrowed it. So exotic," Aaron said. "It reminds me of Brooklyn."

"You and your Brooklyn," Paul said.

"Yes, me and my Brooklyn," Aaron said, saying nothing more so that they could listen to the remainder of the recording. When it was over he wiped his lips with his napkin and said, in an exaggerated voice, "Me…and my Brook-lyn…"

"Anything else like that?" Paul said.

Aaron went to the shelf alongside the gramophone.

"I'm traveling light. I don't have much with me." He selected another cylinder. "But try this."

The sound rolled out, unraveled, high-pitched, more shrieking than singing, tin bells jangled, or knives clicked together, screams now and then punctuated by a deeper more mannered throbbing and drumming.

"Just like Brooklyn?" Paul said.

"All right. So it's a little more civilized."

The cook and his helpers cleared the table, the two young boys giggling and making eyes at them as they worked. Paul looked at Aaron and Aaron looked away. In a few moments they were alone and Paul was lighting up a stick of kif that he had bought in the market. He offered some to Aaron, who declined.

"My lungs can't take it," he said.

"Mine can't do without it," Paul said. "Not since they discovered it."

"Enjoy yourself," Aaron said.

"I'm going to try," Paul said.

The very air in the room soon tasted of the sweet burning leaf. Aaron blew out the candles on the dinner table and went to the shuttered windows. Had no one remembered to open them to the night breezes off the ocean? No one had remembered. The wind of salt, the tang of it, the sweet weed odor of the sea-grass, the news from outward bound upon the ocean. All this drifted in while lights winked far out on the horizon.

"Fishing boats," Aaron said.

"What?" Paul said.

"Fishing boast," Aaron said.

"My catch will be larger than yours," Paul said.

"Dark," Aaron said.

"Dark out?"

"Dark, dark out."

"No light anywhere?"

"Just the fishing boast."

"How many inches your fish?"

"Big fins," Aaron said. "Large dorsal."

"Technical talk about fish. Where you know this from?"

"From where?" Aaron said. "From Brooklyn, of course."

"Have you been sneaking this?" Paul said, holding up the smoking stick of kif.

"I don't know," Aaron said. "Have I?"

"I think you have," Paul said. "Definitely." Paul got up from his chair and went to the window.

"Light all disappeared."

"Gone west," Aaron said.

"To 'merica," Paul said.

"Tumerica," Aaron said. "Tumerica, merica, merica."

"Ta-ta ta-ta ta-ta ta-ta ta-ta ta-tahhhhh," Paul said.

Aaron rattled his fingers against the table top.

"I need some air," he said.

"A country air?" Paul said. He attempted to whistle but couldn't seem to hold his lips in the correct position.

"Sea air," Aaron said.

"I see air," Paul said. "I see the bloody luminescence of the very night wind we breathe. The tang of it. The salt-tinge of it. The iodine tick to it. The flow and the ebb, the rush and the crashing of the air waves."

"Waves of grain," Aaron said.

"There you go again with America," Paul said.

"Where else can I go?" Aaron said.

"Let's go into the desert," Paul said. "Let's take our damned recording machine and go find those chanters and screamers and drummers. Are you game?"

"Game? Like wrestling in the sand?"

"Want to try it?"

"When?"

"Now," Paul said.

Which is how they formed their little procession—just the two of them, though the two boys who helped the cook looked on from the top of the staircase as though they were watching a funeral parade—meandering down the stairs, holding to the smooth railings as they went, and out the door and across the dusty road and between the small palms that formed the border between dust and sand. The dark sucked all moisture from the air and they breathed heavily, as though they had been walking, or possibly trotting, for miles. The night smelled of tar and the ubiquitous salt and rotting fish and a particular tincture that Aaron imagined, with no evidence to back up his claim, came from the feathers of low-flying sea-birds. These they could hear in the distance, however dark it might be. Or were those muted screechings the noises of those still-errant boys in the sand?

"So damned dark here," Aaron said.

"But we can look back at the city," Paul said. He turned and Aaron turned with him and they both studied the vaulting blackness that held up the streets of the city—lights twinkling above and around its dark presence.

"Special dark out here, yes?" Aaron said.

"I'm enjoying it. But I missed the damned sunset."

"I missed that tonight. Because of siesta."

"Tomorrow I'm keeping watch," Paul said. "I don't want to miss it. The old North African crepuscule."

"Twilight," Aaron said.

"In Brooklyn you might have called it that, boyo," Paul said.

"And here, too."

"I want crepuscule," Paul said. "Show me the way. I'm already heading in that direction." He produced another stick of kif, sheltered it from the wind, and proceeded to light up under the rising moon. Aaron demurred from this second round.

"Helps my sense of time," Paul said. "As in…" He changed the melody they had heard on the gramophone. "Poom, poom," he said to follow it up. "Poom, poom, poom, poom, poom, poom…"

"All out here alone," Aaron said. "So busy, noisy, during the day. Those boys playing, wrestling, the donkeys tethered beneath those palms…"

"I don't see no fucking donkeys," Paul said.

"You what?"

"See no donkeys. Fear no donkeys."

"Hear no donkeys, either?"

"I heard one last night. Scrawling and wailing. Like some kind of wounded lion instead of a broken down half-breed genetic dead-end of a pack animal."

"Lions and donkeys in the night sound quite alike," Aaron said, walking in the direction of the water.

"That's a nice rhetorical flourish. But have you actually heard them both cry out?"

"I've heard the donkeys," Aaron said. "But I confess that the only time I've heard the lion roar is at the movies." Head down, as if embarrassed at his admission, he walked faster along the sand.

"Wait," Paul said, "wait for me, master. Maitre."

"Ah-loh…"

Off in the distance someone called out. To them? They couldn't tell, not at this distance.

"Ah-loh…"

A boyish, almost childish voice in the dark.

"See to find out," Paul said.

"Wait," Aaron said. "Might be dangerous. Robbers on this beach."

"Robbers?"

"I've heard stories…"

"Who steals my purse…" Paul advanced into the shadowy moonlight, seeing nothing but sand, trees, the impossibly delicate scrolling of the surf as it splashed onto the beach.

"I don't carry a purse," Aaron said, coming up on Paul from behind and taking hold of his elbow. "Why is it that you've smoked most of the kif and I'm the one that can hardly walk?"

"Overall unfairness of life makes it so," Paul said.

"Ah-loh…"

"Like damned sirens out there," Paul said. "Boys will be boys, but will boys become sirens?"

"Ah-lohhhhh…"

"Ahhhh…" Aaron let out a cry as he pitched forward onto the beach, finding himself with a mouthful of dry bitter sand. "Ftttt…" He spit out the fine grains. "Ftttt…ftttt…" He kept on spitting as he pulled himself to his knees.

"Paul?"

He was nowhere to be seen.

"Paul?"

His friend, student, protégé, pal….Where had he gone? Aaron squinted into the slurry dark, finding, as he rose unsteadily to his feet, that he was having problems with his depth perceptions. From chest to knees, it felt as though he were sinking into the sand while at the same time his head seemed to be drawn upward, as though that rising moon were a magnet and his facial bones and skull—all metal construction—were rising to join it. How else to explain this feeling of palpable luminescence in the cavities of his nose and mouth? In his head, in the echoing chamber where it always began, he could already sense the chords.

A horrible screeching went up just then across the water—no, it came from the beach where the moon shone down on dark shapes boiling in the darkness, the boys, the donkey, a taller shape.

"Paul?"

"Pa-w-l-l-l...?" his friend shouted back at him, mocking his nasal call.

"You all right?"

"Yoo-hoo!" his friend called back to him. "Yoo-hoo!"

"Wait a minute," Aaron said, stumbling forward in flat-footed fashion across the dark humps of sand. His heart beat hard like a bird's wings juddering as it hovered in a rising wind above the shoreline. He wanted to say something, he wanted to shout something, he wanted to sing something, he wanted to play something, he wanted to see something—but nothing—nothing!—that he knew.

Los Coronados

Originally published in *Rattapallax*

Alone, and perched on this examining table, Jere Silverman shivered and suffered, a searing patch of fire across her abdomen.

Suddenly the examining room door opened.

"So, what do we have here?"

Not a young doctor, but not old either. Full head of curly brown hair with the tiniest touch of gray at the temples, an interesting effect.

"I burned myself, a stupid accident," Jere said, trying to keep herself from trembling.

The doctor nodded as he bent toward her. She caught a whiff of his bitter-sweet cologne.

"Let's have a look."

At the doctor's urging, Jere lifted her tee shirt, feeling only the slightest twinge of embarrassment. Working at home, she wore no bra. She had breasts the size of softballs—thanks to her first boyfriend Bobby Penner for that metaphor—and fortunately they hadn't been burned. But this swathe of angry flesh just below her navel united fire and ice—fire and ice.

"Can you—?" The doctor's voice, so gentle, trailed off into the silence of the room.

Carefully Jere undid the fly of her jeans, viewing again what had nearly made her faint when first it happened. How she had fixed herself back up even halfway, she couldn't remember.

"Quite a burn," the doctor said, bowing his head toward the blistering flesh. A few coils of Jere's springy red pubic hair poked up from below the waistband of her underpants. The only pleasure in all of this pain was the way she noticed how the doctor seemed not to notice. But in order not to do that he looked up into her eyes.

"I am such a sucker," Jere said to her friend Tandy Wilentz later that day.

"Isn't it sort of unethical for him?" Tandy said.

This annoyed Jere. Here was Tandy in Fukuoka, nine thousand miles away, and who knew in what part of day or night right now, making a judgment about what had happened at a clinic in Jere's town. She had had to drive fifteen minutes, and in great pain, to get there, too, to meet Dr. Michael Hauser—Mike, call me Mike—her near neighbor.

"I guess I should lodge a harassment complaint against him, right?"

"Do you want to?"

"He asked me out. I want to go."

"So go."

"I already told him I would."

"Good."

"And—?"

"And what?"

"And so you don't think I'm crazy?"

"A nice man—at least for now we'll say he's nice since he hasn't done anything to prove otherwise, except maybe this little ethical transgression—"

"We looked at each other," Jere said. "It wasn't him looking at me in that way, it was also me looking back at him."

"So, a mutual transgression. Tell me the truth, when he called you to ask about how you were doing, didn't you think it was a little weird?"

"Of course I thought it was weird. A doctor calling a patient for a date. But I knew already. We both knew. He told me he was transferring my case to one of his colleagues."

"Wonder how he explained that one?"

"He said he was taking some vacation time."

"Where is he going?"

"We're going to dinner."

"His vacation is a dinner."

"He's invited me out, I told you."

"This is incredible," Tandy said. "How many years has it been?" (They had been roommates at Smith.)

"Te—"

"Doesn't matter. Nothing else matters. You, one of the most successful women in your profession. And listen to you. And listen to me. Both of us. We'd give up integrity, privacy, purity (if we have any of that left), not to mention our bodies, all for a lousy dinner date."

"You already have a husband," Jere said. "I'm the one who wants the date. And I hope it's not going to be lousy. It better not be lousy. Anyway, nothing much is going to happen for a while. I'm still in bandages. I have to wash this burn twice a day, put on the salve, dress it."

"Sounds to me like something is going to happen. Sounds to me like you're going to undress your burn."

"Tandy!"

"You said tha…." Her friend's voice began to fade, something to do with satellites and the position of the moon, who knew? Telecommunications was not Jere's field of expertise. All she could do about this was complain.

"I can't hear you."

"…the best…."

"Tandy?"

"—"

"I'm hanging up. Goodbye."

Here is how such things begin. Jere was lucky enough to work at home. And as she had done on hundreds of such mornings—a gazillion, Bobby Penner would have said, and God, with that phrase suddenly in her mind she couldn't stop thinking of him, but when she did the pain seemed to let up so why not think of Bobby, as awful as he was?—she had set the tea kettle over a high flame and returned to her desk to work on a speech for a savings and loan president, which she had to fax to him by four that afternoon.

For some reason, who can say why? The teakettle didn't whistle—and when poised in the middle of a phrase about the glories of long-term savings, Jere pushed back from her desk, charged into the kitchen, rushed to the stove, and, before she could figure anything out, splashed boiling water all over herself.

She explained it to her mother. Well, not her mother in the flesh, but her memory of her mother, a sweet but demanding woman who had died when Jere was twenty-two and just out of college, six years after her father had passed away. A few years ago Charlotte—her then-new therapist—had suggested that she talk to her mother when she had something to say, and so now and then they did speak.

Mrs. Silverman would come to her—in voice—in quiet moments late in the afternoons, almost as if she were stopping by for coffee. Jere let her talk, and found herself listening much more intently than she ever had when the woman was alive.

Today's subject? The same as her conversation with Tandy, of course. But the late Mrs. Silverman had different interests.

"You burned yourself?"

"Yes, mama."

"I'm sorry you burned yourself. You ought to be more careful. I remember when you were only three years old and you knocked a milk carton off the kitchen table. Milk spilled everywhere. And you cried. You cried and cried."

"Over spilt milk."

"Yes, I just told you that."

"I'm joking, Mama. Crying over spilt milk. An old saying? Don't cry over spilt milk."

"Of course, of course. Oh, you are so quick, Jere. But how quick, we will find out. You burned yourself and the doctor asked you on a date?"

"After he dressed the burn, Ma. And after he got another doctor to be my doctor."

"At least he saw what he was doing."

"We both saw, Ma. We both see."

"You both see? But he's the doctor, so he's supposed to see more than you."

"I know a few things, Mama. Maybe almost as much as a doctor knows, in my own way."

"My little Jere. Jerey—"

"Please, Mama."

"Jerey Paney, loves the rainy. Went on a ride on a big black trainey."

"Thank you, Ma. I think that's enough for tonight."

"You 'Ma' me, but you don't want to listen to what I have to say. I have to treat you like you're still a baby. When your father died—"

"Please, Ma. No. Don't do this."

"When he died, it was me alone left to take care of you. And I think I did a perfectly good job."

"Nothing's perfect, Mama. But you did your best."

"But not good enough."

"I didn't say that."

"I know what you're thinking."

"Most of what I'm thinking, Mama. But not all. Even I don't know it all."

"So maybe I do know what you're thinking. You're thinking—"

"I'm thinking how both of us know what we want, and how much we both miss Daddy, and how much I miss you, and how silly and stupid I feel when I can't even take credit for a simple decision on my own without bringing you into the picture."

At which point, Jere slammed her coffee mug onto the butcher block table in her kitchen and shook her head, staring off at a point just above the white clock above the sink.

Usually she didn't lose it when she conjured up her mother. Sometimes—not this time, but sometimes—it even helped.

But when, as Charlotte had also suggested, she tried to speak to her father, she hit a wall, remembering only the last few months of his life, when he returned from his futile expeditions to foreign places seeking experimental treatments, his clothes reeking of cigarette smoke, despite his condition, his eyes filled with worry and fear.

She was thinking about this—you know how such thoughts break right into the middle of things—while on her first dinner date with Doctor Mike—this was what she began to call him when talking to Tandy—just as they were finishing a bottle of delicious red wine and he was telling her some of the intimate details of his own early life.

"My father was a very successful businessman, known, I learned much later, for his calmness and integrity. But at home at night with us, he couldn't manage his temper and used to chase me around the dining room table, swinging his belt at me and threatening all sorts of miserable torture."

"A double life," Jere said.

"More like triple, or maybe quadruple," said Doctor Mike. "Years later we found out... Listen to me, sounds like everything I learned I learned years later. Maybe I did. But it was a long time later that we found out that he kept a mistress one town over from ours. A really old fashioned arrangement. He paid for her apartment, her clothes, that sort of thing."

"My father could hardly keep my mother," Jere said. "let alone a second woman."

"It takes a lot of energy," Doctor Mike said. "And you have to be pretty miserable in your main life to want to make a second one."

"I have enough trouble making a first," Jere said.

Doctor Mike shook his head and smiled.

"I believe you, because you're saying it, but I think it doesn't have to be that way."

Jere fought off a blush, feeling that heat rise up through her lap like another burn.

"I've made it that way myself," she said. "Work, work, work. Nothing, I'm sure, like medical school and a doctor's—"

"Oh, whoa," he said. "nothing mysterious about what we do. Just a lot of memorization and mechanical stuff, some chemistry. Speaking of which…." He reached across the table and she let him find her hand.

"I know," she said. "It's pretty amazing."

Fully blushing now, and loving it, soaking up the heat, and wondering why she ever enjoyed the cold, Jere leaned toward him across the cluttered table.

"He's a great guy," she said to Tandy the next day—or was it already night where she was?—telling her about Doctor Mike's wonderful smile, and the delicious taste of his breath—

"The taste of his breath?"

"Of his mouth."

"His mouth. Tell me about his mouth."

"I just told you."

"And what else did you taste?"

"Tandy, I'm waiting for my burn to heal, I don't want to heat things up too much."

"Sounds like you already have."

Jere shook her head, and suddenly noticed her posture, lying there on the sofa in her small apartment, the telephone crooked at her left ear, her right hand playing lazily on her chest. She shook herself out of this stupor, listening to her friend's voice in her ear. She had had boyfriends, beginning with Bobby Penner, but for the past five years her life had been vacant in that way. Too busy, she told herself. Too much work. Too much to do. She amazed herself in the next few weeks at just how enthusiastically she put the lie to all this.

Dinner, dinner, dinner.

Dinner and a movie.

And then home to her apartment—or sometimes his house—to bed.

"How does it look?" she asked him the first time she undressed and showed him the raw wound, shiny with antibiotic salve, beneath the bandage that she changed religiously twice a day.

"Jim's looking at it?"

"Doctor Watkins, you mean?"

"Yes. What did he say?"

"That it's coming along nicely."

"Best thing you can hear," Doctor Mike said, taking her in his arms and holding her a distance proper for someone with a still healing burn. Dinner. And late night walks along the river. Walks and talks.

The walks were about staying fit. Doctor Mike practiced what he preached, and thank God, Jere sighed to herself after one of their early morning forays along the old canal, that she herself had never smoked.

"From an early age, I swore I'd never touch a cigarette. The smoke was the only thing about my father I didn't like."

"Good idea not to smoke," Mike said. "Tobacco used to be one of the ritual materials of the old Taino—or was it Arawak?—Indians. They'd smoke it four times a year. Raise their crooked little smokes to the gods, I think is how Shakespeare puts it in 'Cymbelline.' In excess of that, it's not good for you."

"It wasn't good for my father," Jere said.

"Lung cancer?"

"Lungs, then brain."

"And he went for one of those miracle cures?"

"I was sixteen and had my first boyfriend. I don't remember much about that time. I had Bobby Penner and I didn't know anything or want to anything else." Jere shivered at the memories of Bobby and his manic lust, and dinners with his family, his shoe salesman father shouting at pathetic Mrs. Penner.

Jere shook her head and sighed, recalling with such misery and pain over the loss her own father's quiet ways that her wine glass trembled in her hand.

"Are you all right?" Doctor Mike leaned toward her across the table.

"Sure," she said. What was she supposed to tell him? That after nearly twenty years she still missed her father with the same intensity that she had felt when he died?

Mike reached for her hand and she enjoyed the medicinal firmness of his grip.

"Dollar for your thoughts," he said.

"Isn't that a penny?"

"I'm taking into account inflation since the saying was first coined."

"All right," she said, unable to suppress a grin. "You've done it now."

"Done what?"

"You're making me happy."

Late night, some months later, at a party in a town house in Philadelphia that belonged to one of Mike's old medical school friends, Jere discovered his wonderful little secret.

"Mike," one of his pals—now a balding cardiologist—called out to him. "Play it."

A slump-shouldered guy, wearing dark glasses—his speciality, endocrinology, Mike told her—handed him a guitar.

"Ladies and gentlemen," somebody said.

Mike plucked at the strings as though he had never seen such an instrument before. And then he began to play.

"'Mississippi water,'" he sang along to his pungent chords, "'taste like turpentine. Mississippi water, taste like turpentine…'"

"Yeah," one of these doctors said with a grunt. "Oh, yeah."

"'…Ohio River water, taste like sherry wine….'"

All the doctors and their wives shouted and clapped their hands. Jere just sat there, so in love with his voice—with everything about him—that she could hardly catch her breath.

"Turpentine to sherry," the balding doctor said. "There's a transformation a guy can really appreciate."

"Geographical," another man said. "Mississippi, Ohio, different places, different tastes. One kills you, the other gets you high."

"What about Philly?" Doctor Mike said, the guitar in his lap and a glass in his hand. "Any body ever sing the blues about Philly?"

"Try it," a doctor said.

Mike picked up the guitar.

"'Philly Philly, Philly Philly all the time…'"

Mike nodded at Jere, took another swallow of his drink. When he picked up the guitar and played again, she felt as though he were plucking the chords out of her body.

"'Going to Chicago….'"

"Yeah!" some doctor shouted out of the crowd.

"'Sorry but I can't take you….'"

Mike stared at her from the inside of the music looking out. And Jere stared right back. Her burn had healed—by now it had become a lovely swathe of baby-flesh pink—and that night she let go of all care, thrashed about ferociously, with the noise of the blues in her mind.

"I don't understand it," she said the next day to Tandy, who by this time had finished her work in Japan and was now living near San Diego. "It was okay with Mike when we first got together, but the companion-ship was better than the sex. Suddenly the sex has caught up."

"And you're caught up."

"Even more than before. Tandy, honey, I haven't felt so good… since…since before my father died…I feel so…fortunate. So happy."

"You're not waiting for the bubble to burst, I hope," Tandy said.

"It's not a bubble. It's real life, I know it is."

"I'm glad to hear that. So, his friends have interviewed you and you passed, right?"

Jere laughed at the way she described it, the parties, the dinners. "Yes."

"So it's time for me to meet Doctor Wonderful."

"The final test," Jere said.

"That's right. Can he pull the sword from the stone—or not?"

"You're my only family," Jere said. "It seems right."

"Worse than that, I'm your only best friend."

"So let's make a plan."

Tandy invited them to stay with her in La Jolla. Her husband had gone back to Japan for a couple of months on business so there was plen-ty of room. But Jere, having gotten to know her Mike, decided that it was better if they took a hotel room.

"He'll be more comfortable," she said. "He's a little shy."

"What about his music? That doesn't sound so shy."

"He's quiet, except for that."

"So if he's quiet, I won't hear him scream at night in bed."

"No, but you might hear me."

"I don't believe it," Tandy said. "You're making me blush. And it's always been the other way around."

"'The times they are a-changin.'"

"'The sheets they'll be a-changin.'"

"Don't be disgusting," Jere said.

"Stay in a hotel with Doctor Shy. I think it's a good idea. What if we don't get along?"

"That's not what I'm worried about. In fact, I'm not worried about anything. I just thought he might feel...a little more relaxed. More like he's on vacation. He works so hard."

"And you don't?"

"Now you sound like my mother."

"How is the old girl, by the way?"

"Good. We're still talking."

"And she approves of your doctor?"

"I haven't given her much choice."

"Funny, isn't it, how the dead can't fight back all that well."

"Funny, yes. But they still have power."

"Don't I know it? Just the other day, I was shouting at Paul over the telephone, and don't ask me about what, because I can't even remember, and I said something that sounded familiar, and I said to myself, where did that come from? And I remembered, it was some crappy thing my mother used to say to my father."

"Do you realize?" Jere said. "We're both complete orphans. No mother, no father. Is that why we're such good friends?"

"Maybe that's a part of it, I don't know," Tandy said.

"But you won't think badly of me if we stay in a hotel, right?"

"Stay at the Coronado," Tandy said. "The whole experience."

"The Coronado, why have I heard that name before?"

"It's a famous place," Tandy said. "Stay there, you'll love it. We'll come visit you. We'll walk the beach."

"No, but I've heard the name. I can hear someone saying it. Maybe my mother's voice, that's who."

"Why not call your friendly psychic? Maybe she can tell you where you've heard it before. Or maybe I said something. Or maybe you just read about it in a magazine."

"If I could carry a tune, I'd be making those spacey noises right now. Too-too-too-too, too-too, too-too. But Tandy, speaking about singing...." And she went on to talk about Doctor Mike's musical powers.

So, five months after her stupid accident with the tea kettle and her encounter with Mike at the clinic, Jere found herself several thousand feet above the Salton Sea as the airplane in which they were traveling made its final approach to the San Diego airport.

"Down there, that's where they made the 'Planet of the Apes' movies," Mike said, pointing at the yellow-brown desert.

"You know everything, don't you?" Jere nudged him with her shoulder.

"Blues and movies, that's about as far as I go."

"And medicine," Jere said. "That's a big chunk of knowledge."

"And speech-writing—what you do is pretty impressive, I have to say."

"Thank you," Jere said.

"Oh, and Mexico," Mike said. "All of that out that way—" he pointed south— "it's Mexico. Do you know Mexico? I've never been there."

"No, I don't know it," she said, leaning past him to take a good look but by that time she saw only brown hills and houses splattered across them, and a large block of water just ahead.

An hour and a half later they were seated in their rental car, traveling across the curving arc of bridge above the bay, looking out at clouds and light and the golden shape of Coronado Island—"a peninsula, actually," Mike said, pointing with one finger at the map in Jere's lap as he steered them through the blue air, the city to their right, all of Mexico to the south of them.

"Mexico," Jere said.

"That's Tijuana down that way," Mike said. "Big border town."

"That's where I heard it," Jere said. "Coronado. Tijuana."

"What?"

"Oh, just something…."

"What?"

Jere shook her head.

So beautiful here, the palm trees, the light behind the palms, wisps of ocean cloud brighter on the underside where the sun struck the water and relighted the sky. From the window of their room in the huge sprawling old ornate turretted hotel on the beach she could study the ocean and a pair of islands just to the south, low, dark, green shapes hugging the water.

"What are those?" she said to Doctor Mike.

He turned from the dresser where he was stacking his shirts.

"Don't know," he said, peering into the brightness beyond the glass. "Santa Catalina or some place like that. I have a vague recollection. The channel islands? Hey, ask me about the Isles of Langerhans, that I can tell you about."

"What are *they*?"

And as he described them she watched a military airplane of some sort make a slow approach to the landing field to the north just below the cliffs.

"War games in paradise," Doctor Mike said.

Jere laughed and turned around, and he was standing right there.

Later, they arrived by car at a large noisy restaurant on the north side of the city.

"'Kiva,'" Mike read the sign when they drove into the circular drive in front of the low building. Across the way loomed a large oddly-designed hotel.

"Tandy says it's good. She's not in a cooking phase right now, she says."

"That's all right," Mike said. "I like hot food. It's supposed to have curative powers, you know."

"Have you studied that?" Jere said.

He handed the keys to the valet and took a ticket in exchange.

"I have a vague recollection of a lecture I heard when I was in med school. Some alternative nutritionist, somebody like that."

"Well—" Jere said. And then she was jumping up and down.

"Oh, my God!" Tandy came running toward her.

"Excuse us, Mike, but we haven't—" Jere lost her voice to a mess of squeals.

By the time the women calmed down, their table was ready.

Tandy, tall, thin, pretty, except for the hair, looked a little like Jere's older sister.

Or younger? It went back and forth—sometimes when Jere looked at her she seemed not to have aged at all since the last time they saw each other, sometimes it seemed as though Tandy had become a replica of her own mother.

While Mike spoke to the waiter—fit blonde boy, wearing all white, earring through left lobe—the women walked their way in sprightly fashion through everything they needed to know just then and there— health, weight, job, spirit, love, of course, love.

"You're still as happy as ever?" Jere said.

Tandy tossed her long dark hair to one side, glancing over at Mike.

"Phil is my first husband and my last. He is so devoted. You know why we're here tonight? He does all the cooking. When he's away, I'm just hopeless. I'd starve to death."

"'Kiva,'" Mike said. "That's a prayer cave of the Pueblo Indians. What if they were the majority in the U.S. and they called a restaurant 'Church' or 'Cathedral' and ordered grilled cheese on white bread?"

"A doctor who's interesting in addition to being a doctor," Tandy said when the two women repaired to the ladies room in the old-fashioned girly way. "You...." She hugged Jere and Jere pressed against her, feeling a warm wave of affection break over her face and neck and arms. "You just might have found the right guy...."

That's what Jere was thinking as they traveled up hills and around curves, following Tandy to her house for a nightcap. Mike hummed a blues, then a Beatles song. cupping his right hand over hers and removing it only to negotiate a few bad curves. The warm sensation stayed with Jere the entire drive.

With its opposite, a kind of wonderful chill that made goose-bumps up and down her arm when she saw the view from Tandy's living room—the velvet dark night ocean sky studded with stars. They ate a second dessert—the best tofu ice-cream Jere had ever tasted, the only kind he'd ever tasted, Mike said—and they sipped Kahlúa and stared out at the sky.

And they talked. Old times, new times. Jere worried that Mike might take all this to be something resembling an interview, but he was affable, truly at ease, it seemed to her.

"I have plans for us for tomorrow, if that's okay," Tandy said when much later they were going out the door.

A trip to Ensenada, she announced—such a short distance away you couldn't even call it a real trip. A leisurely drive down across the border, then early dinner at the beach, and back across the border before midnight.

At the hotel, Mike hummed blues to himself in the bathroom while Jere stretched herself across the large bed, savoring the luxury of the room and the delicious sense of security that staying here with Mike afforded her.

She never knew better love than what they made that night. And she was glad for the burn that had brought them together, now that it had healed and the doctor who had first attended her lay at her side. But at some point in the middle of the dark she awoke, uncomfortable, feeling pressure on her bladder and then discovering that she couldn't pee.

What? she said to herself. What? Standing at the window, she felt steadied by the sight of the silver-gray sea beneath a three-quarter moon. Those islands flickered into view and then faded again, just far enough away to seem unreal, then real, unreal, then real.

"Jere?"

"You're awake, too?"

"I'm luxuriously awake," Mike said. "What are you doing?"

"Thinking."

She turned to see him roll off the bed and stand up.

"About…?"

"Something," Jere said. "I wish I could really remember. Just something. Like some song I can't quite remember the tune of."

"I know what that's like," Mike said, walking over and putting his arms around her.

"I know you do," Jere said. "But this is different. Just…something else."

They returned to the bed and Mike let her know that he wanted to make love again.

"Let's just sleep," she said. "We've got a trip. Such a lovely day coming up."

Mike gestured toward the window where the dark had lessened ever so slightly and the moon had begun to fade.

"We'll try to sleep. But day's almost here."

Looking back on all this, Jere would have thought that she might well have been visited that night by her father in an early morning dream, some visitation in which he would have made himself known to her with a little gesture, like the way his eyebrows sometimes crinkled when he laughed or the way he leaned his head to one side when he listened to her and touched a finger to his cheek. Oh, she would have loved to have seen him, to have recognized him even in dreams. But though she lay there in the modulating light of the new morning and thought of him hard and long, lapsing now and then into a logey kind of dozing and then snapping out of it again, he never appeared before her. Except in the deep and visceral part of memory—where the smell of his skin and breath still lingered in recollection and the rough timbre of his voice raised in a hello or in dispute with her mother still echoed in her mind. And his laugh, his phlegmy old laugh, sounded in her ear as though resurrected on an old cassette player from a tape made from an old thirty-three-and-a-third LP.

"Daddy?" she said, and was sorry, because Doctor Mike stirred at the sound, like some deep-lying fish in a cool pond of dark, rising slowly toward a spinning fly or a wriggling insect (though he fell back, yes, fell back, good, and she went on—silently—conjuring up the pictures and sensations that made up her memory of her father. Silently, yes, as silent as she could be while allowing her emotion to rise through her own body toward the sounding box of her chest.).

She kept her eyes closed and told herself that in a story, any old story, he might have appeared to her in a dream. But this is life—lonely truthful real life—and only real things happen. Only thoughts about him, not the real him or even the real ghost of the once-real him. Only my memories and never the actual events. Oh, Daddy, she sighed, lying like a dead woman because she was afraid now that she might wake the doctor who slept alongside her. Oh, Daddy, what is this time that was cut so short between us? What is this life that makes me feel so all alone now that you and mother are gone?

And the moon disappeared completely into the whitening sky. When Jere next glanced at the bedside clock some hours had gone by, and it was almost time for their little journey.

It began after lunch, after a walk on the beach under the direct full spreading glare of the hot Southern California—almost Mexican—sun. Mike walked between Jere and the water, and she kept glancing over his shoulder, behind his head, at the pair of islands skulking out there in the distance just to the south, where the widening curve of the southern spit of land that joined this "island" to the mainland led directly to the low hills of the city of Tijuana.

"Still no name?"

Mike looked puzzled.

She asked again.

"Oh," he said, "I asked at the desk. Two people later, I got an answer. I saw a map of Mexico. They're Mexican, they're called Los Coronados. We're on Coronado Island, *they're* the Coronados."

"Who lives there?" Jere slowed down and peered out over the water.

"That I didn't ask. It's part of Mexico, that's all they told me. I could find out more."

"I'll ask," Jere said.

"Why the interest?"

Mike took her hand as they kept on moving northward up the beach in the direction of the rising cliff that sheltered the military airport from the ocean. A navy jet looking like some large exotic house fly made a noisy approach to the landing field.

"All this wealth," Mike said. "Cheek by jowl with the army that defends it."

"I like the way it's all out front," Jere said, slowing them down and eventually stopping and turning to take another look back toward the south. She couldn't say why, but the land down there, those hills, the islands beyond the coastline, she felt pulled by it all.

When Tandy arrived, Jere, dressed in slacks and a new white blouse, couldn't wait to leave. Graciously she insisted that Mike sit in front while she climbed into the back. Naval base, bird sanctuary, working class shopping strip—she listened to Tandy's running commentary on the landmarks they passed but kept her eyes on the southern horizon where the hills thick with houses and towers and church spires loomed larger and larger. Signs told them they were approaching the border. Jere was someone who never paid attention to her heart, but now she could feel it fluttering in her chest like some wild bird beating against the thin wires of a flimsy cage.

"They don't check us," Tandy said as they slowed down and rolled toward the Mexican border control, three or four lanes with a few young soldiers standing about with their weapons lowered. "It's more of a nuisance coming back in," Tandy pointed to the long lanes of traffic snaking out of Tijuana toward the booths at the U.S. port of entry. "But we'll be coming back late enough so we'll miss a lot of the traffic."

"It's rush hour," Mike said, glancing around as they speeded up and whirled around a traffic circle that spun them out in a westerly direction.

"The air is bad around the highway," Tandy said. "And the city water's bad. But where we're going, the food is great. It's beautiful, right along the ocean."

The highway rose as they climbed a small hill that allowed them a view of the steel fences topped by cortina wire on the U.S. side and the dilapidated neighborhoods on the left side of the road. In the air was the smell of diesel and other odd smoky odors. Small trucks and old cars rushed past them. *Ensenada*—the sign came up. Old Indian women and small children waited on the side of the road at taxi stands. A sports car full of young dark-haired men roared past them, dust and loud rock-and-roll trailing behind.

"You know your way around," Jere said, from her seat in the rear.

"It's perfectly safe, unless you're in the drug business," Tandy said. "If that's what you're asking."

"I don't know what I'm asking," Jere said. The car reached the top of a hill and she caught a glimpse of silvery ocean in the distance below, and then the road curved down and to the south.

Playas, the sign came up, with an arrow pointing to the right.

"Turn here, Tandy!" She pounded her fist against the back of her friend's seat.

"What?"

"Turn! Turn!" Pound, pound!

Tandy spun the wheel, cutting off a small sawed-off truck and nearly spinning out onto the roadside.

"Jesus!" Mike spoke up for the first time in minutes.

"Woke you up, huh?" Tandy shook her head and steered them down the hill to where the road leveled out into a strip of shops and small houses and apartment buildings.

"'Playas de Tijuana,'" Mike read off the sign.

"'Playas' is sands, the beach," Tandy said, stopping at the first traffic light.

"Do you want to go swimming? Is that it? Where we're going, there's a beach."

"I don't know what I want," Jere said.

Mike turned around in his seat.

"Are you all right?"

"I'll bet Jere wants to buy some drugs," Tandy said.

"No, no, no, no, no, stupid. Keep driving."

A block ahead, Tandy slowed down. "There's the bull ring," she said.

"You want to see a bull fight?" Mike shook his head.

"Wrong season," Tandy said.

"Turn," Jere said.

"All right, already," Tandy said, steering them into a narrow street that ran alongside the bull ring. "I'm just following your orders."

Mike pointed to the right. "There's a hospital. 'Oasis Hospital,' the sign says."

"Oh, Jesus," Jere said.

"What?" Tandy said.

"This is where," Jere said.

"Where what?" Mike said.

"Where he came," Jere said.

Tandy slowed down as they drove past the hospital.

"I don't know what you're talking about, but do you want to stop?"

"No, no, keep going," Jere said, looking back at the hospital.

They paused when they got to the end of the street. "The border," Tandy said. "Home is just on the other side." Jere looked at the wire fence and the steel fence behind it. Flags fluttered on the other side. Miles away, the buildings of downtown San Diego glowed in the sun, a toy city.

Mike leaned around and reached for Jere's hand.

"Do you want to go home?"

Jere shook her head.

"I had some kind of memory flash," she said. "I don't know what else to call it. I saw the sign, 'Playas,' and I remembered my father saying that name. This is here, this is where he came for his treatment. To that hospital. There was some doctor there who was working on an experimental cure. They gave my father laetrile."

Tandy turned the car to the left and now they were driving along the waterside in a southerly direction. Low buildings—cheap restaurants, an office, a motel—shielded them from an unbroken view of the ocean.

"Jesus," Mike said.

"So bizarre," Jere said.

"I know a little about laetrile," Mike said. "A cyanide compound made from apricot pits. It was one of those miracle cures that never worked out—like all the rest."

"He needed a miracle," Jere said.

"I could use a miracle," Tandy said.

"You're not sick," Jere said. "I'm the one who's sick."

"What are you talking about?" Mike reached for her hand, but she didn't offer it. "Your burn healed beautifully."

Jere ignored him. "Tandy, stop here," she said.

"Are you serious?"

Tandy stopped the car just as the road turned from uneven cement to dirt. A man in a dark sweatshirt rolled by on a bicycle. Atop the orange umbrella of a deserted food-stand, a red and green flag fluttered in the ocean breeze. Clouds momentarily shielded the face of the sun.

"And now, I suppose," Jere's friend said, "you're going to get out and walk into the ocean and never return."

"What the hell are you saying?" Mike sounded suddenly annoyed.

"I'm joking," Tandy said. "But hey, don't speak to me that way. We've just met."

"I'm pissed," Mike said.

Jere looked at him without speaking and left the car and walked, as her friend had predicted, directly toward the ocean.

"Hey," Mike called after her. "We're going to Ensenada."

Where the sidewalk ended, a jumble of large rocks formed a buffer between street and beach. Jere climbed gingerly down and around them, shocked at the briny stink rising from below. The clouds drifted to the south and the full force of the sun struck her just as she stepped onto the sand. A dog lay sleeping in front of her and she stopped short of it, watching it warily for fear that it might wake and attack. It took her a moment to realize that the animal was dead and its body was adding to the stench. A gull cried out, swooping down and away. Two small boys came running out of nowhere and seeing the dog's body, circled around and around it, chanting something Jere could not understand.

"Go away," she said, but they ignored her.

A gull laughed and Jere looked up toward the horizon. There lay those islands, Los Coronados, one long and narrow, the other, just to its north, more bunched up and angular, both of them dark green beneath the late afternoon sun. Some miles offshore, they appeared to her, because of the illusion created by the moving clouds and wind-blown waves, to be like two strange ships, ranging low in the water, pushing southward, ever southward, without ever shifting their position between ocean and sky.

A dog barked. A living beast!

"Jere, we'll be late!" Tandy called from the roadway.

Years and years ago, Jere's father's soul had flown from his body and until now she had not known to where it had traveled. But now she was certain that it had winged its way to these islands, Los Coronados, of this she was sure. From which he could hear her, though he did not speak in return. One day she would travel herself to see him. One day. To these islands.

"Daddy," she said into the wind, "I was burned. I was terribly burned."

A Brief Washington–Mount Vernon Chronology Followed By an Aborted Picnic at the Holocaust Museum

Originally published in *Antioch Review*

Then here are very few drawbacks, as Ashford saw it, to living in Washington, D.C., until friends come to town. Not that he minded the visitors, since they were usually pals—hardly ever family except for the boys, and they appeared rarely now—amigos from college days, say, and their often quite pleasant wives. For example, here was Hollis Burton, one of his original roommates, looking only slightly overweight and still, unlike Ashford, with nearly his entire head of hair, stepping out of a taxi with a tiny brown faced woman following just behind him into the golden light of a freshly-minted D.C. Indian summer afternoon. And it wasn't as if Ashford hadn't been looking forward to this visit. He hadn't seen Hollis in years, and when last they had met—it had been on Hollis's turf, in L.A.—they both had different wives (and Ashford, sighing to himself at the thought, a lot more hair).

Merry Butterworth, Ashford's present wife, just at that moment stepped up to him where he stood at the living room window and slipped her strong arms around her husband's still-slender waist.

"Look at you, just like a little kid, standing at the window watching your friends come to play."

Ashford waved her away, showing his annoyance (though he knew not yet with what).

"The door," he said as the knock came again.

Swooom! Hollis rolled into the house and took over, raucous, ebullient—hugging, kissing, snatching hands, pushing forward for a moment into the spotlight his new girlfriend, the reed-slender, obsidian-haired Anne Nguyen, before filling the stage once again with himself.

"I am so glad to see you!" Thrust of big beefy mitt. "It's been years!" Bang of jaunty hip against hip. Shake of head. "Wow! Anne, isn't he just as ugly as I told you he'd be?"

Anne Nguyen tilted her head to one side, smiled shyly at the ceiling, looked back hesitantly at Ashford.

"No...."

"This girl is confused," Hollis said.

"So am I," Merry said. "You're not nearly as awful as Ash described you." She offered her hand. "I'm Merry."

Hollis, as Ashford had expected, had fun with her name for much longer than was appropriate. But that was Hollis, his sense of humor, such as it was, apparently unchanged since college, which meant that he had been making these awful jokes for quite a while now. Knowing what they needed next, Ashford fixed them drinks and by the time he passed them around they were relaxing in the cool of the side sun porch as though they had all been stretched out there for hours.

Talk came easily to the two men. Ashford told him about his latest venture, writing speeches for the CEO of a big tobacco company, a guy with an interest (or at least a wife with an interest) in the arts. Hollis, he learned, was now the editorial director of a new online unit of a large international publisher.

"A chance to stay in L.A.," he said by way of explanation. "After I got fired from the Fox channel, there was a while when I thought I might have to move back East."

"Jersey boy turned native Angeleno," Ashford said with a wink at Merry.

"My family's originally from Pasadena," she said to Hollis. "Well, as originally as you can get out there anyway. My mother came east to go to school—"

"Let me guess," Hollis said. "Smith?"

"Wellesley," Merry said. "And she met my father—"

"Harvard?"

"M.I.T.—and she never went back west."

"American stories," Hollis said. "I love 'em. Well, Anne here has one too, don't you, sweetie."

"Oh, it's my turn?" the girl said with a toss of her lava-dark hair. She had been distracted, it appeared, by the shadows on the porch ceiling, or perhaps she was just day-dreaming at the end of the day.

"You don't have to say anything right now." Ashford shook his head. "We've got all weekend."

The girl looked over at Hollis.

"She's a boat person," he said.

"You sail?" Merry blushed as soon as she said this. "Oh, I know what you mean. The war. Refugee."

"Washed up on the beach like my own little Aphrodite," Hollis said.

"Really," Anne Nguyen said, giving Hollis another look.

"You guys must be getting hungry," Ashford said.

Merry stood up.

"I'm going to start dinner," she said with great enthusiasm.

She cooked. They drank. Anne Nguyen went into the kitchen to help Merry. Evening settled over the house. The men spoke of old times.

"It can't be ten years, can it?"

"Oh, yeah," Hollis said. "I can believe that. It's not like we're rocks in a stream and the water flows around us. It carries us along, and it wears us down."

"We're wood? That's your metaphor? Twigs? Flotsam and jetsam."

"That would make for a good comedy team," Hollis said. "Let's do it. Do you want to be Flotsam or do you want to be Jetsam?"

Ashford was feeling the alcohol, in his chest, in his throat, behind his eyes.

"I want to be the creek. I want to flow...."

They laughed, old times surging closer the louder they got.

"How are your folks?" Hollis looked up at the paintings on the wall and back at Ashford.

"Floating, flotsaming along. Dad's got two new knees—"

"No shit?"

"And Mom, same old thing. Golfing still. The family religion."

He finished what was left in his glass.

"And you?"

Hollis took a deep breath and seemed about to speak when Merry and Anne Nguyen bobbed into the doorway.

"Dinner!" "Dinner is served!"

In the cream-walled dining room—over an astonishing veal stew, sauted baby artichokes, and an otherworldly salad—Anne Nguyen, with some teasing and also some serious encouragement from Hollis, told her story.

"I was born in the American Embassy in Saigon on the last day of the war. My father worked for the Ambassador, secret stuff that to this day he never talks about, and he managed to get my gigantically pregnant mother and my big brother into the building. Seeing the pictures, the footage, I'm not sure how. I think I'm quite serene in nature—"

"Sometimes she's so relaxed," Hollis broke in, "that I think she's in a trance."

"—maybe in reaction to all that chaos that greeted me when I arrived."

"Picture it," Hollis said, "the Americans inside, hustling to shred and burn every last bit of paper in the place, looking up to the ceiling, to the sky, waiting for those last helicopters to arrive to take them to the ships."

"I was there that last year," Ashford said. "Pushing papers at a desk in Saigon." He looked directly at Anne Nguyen.

"And good for you," Hollis said.

"This fellow here hasn't made himself out to be a hero, has he?" Ashford grinned at the girl and then at Hollis.

"I flew a desk, I'll be the first one to say." Hollis skewered an artichoke and held it up to his mouth. "In Texas."

"Oh, Holly," Anne Nguyen said. "You were lucky. You didn't want to be in Vietnam."

"I've always felt as though I've missed something by not being there."

"Holly?" Ashford smiled at his pal.

"She calls me that," Hollis said.

"We used to call him 'Hollow' or 'Hallow,' short for 'Hallowed,'" Ashford said. "I can't remember why."

"Because I was a spiritual person," Hollis said.

"Your soul floated in beer," Ashford said.

"I drank to drown my questioning soul," Hollis said.

"He's not a drunk, wasn't even a drunk back then," Ashford said to Merry, knowing that she would be asking about it later if he didn't say something now. She was sensitive about such questions, growing up in the household that she had.

Merry gave a little shrug.

"Can we let Anne finish her story without all these interruptions—"

"And interjections," Hollis put in.

"And digressions," Ashford said, getting into the spirit of things.

"Enough," Merry said, clanging her fork against the side of her plate.

"Anne," Ashford said. "Please go on."

"Anne," Hollis said, reaching over and caressing her bare shoulder.

The shiny dark-haired girl smiled slyly, as if she had just thought of something terribly amusing, and Ashford, for an instant felt a little shock in his chest, the kind of spark he suffered when pulled to a woman for the first time.

"Anne?" he said, and his voice sounded to him as though the two of them might have been alone when he spoke her name.

"I don't know," she said. "Do you all really want to hear this?"

They stumbled over each other to say of course.

Well, here they were, she described for them. Her father waiting patiently for their turn to be evacuated, her mother going into labor, and giving birth right there in the Embassy, in the small office of the Ambassador's secretary, in fact.

"I wasn't the only one born there that day," she said. "My father told me about two other births that he had heard about, one in midair, in one of the helicopters—"

"Good Lord," Ashford said.

"—and another in the crowd just outside the gate, that one was a miscarriage—"

"It was all a miscarriage," Hollis said. "Because of her birth, they missed the last lift out. It took them another year to get away." He reached for her hand but she leaned away from him, as if moving in a sort of dance—and stood up.

"Which way is the...?" Her thin body emphasized the question, her eyes a little glazed from the wine.

Merry gave her directions.

"That's a pretty amazing story," Ashford said as she left the room.

"Yes, quite something," Merry said.

Hollis smiled at her.

"You've got children, yes?"

"Our boy Rick is working for a bank in Minneapolis and Jed is still at college."

"Holly's never had children," Ashford said. "It would have been like, how do they say it when they talk about inner-city kids, 'children having children'?"

"And you're Mister Mature?" Hollis shook his head.

"Merry supplied the maturity," Ashford said. "I supplied the sperm."

"Ash," Merry said.

"It's all right, Merry," Hollis said. "This is what happens when we get together, it's called regression back to the dorm."

"I see."

"Do you?" Hollis smirked. "Look, you divide a man's age by the number of years he's been out of college and you get his true emotional age."

"So you're both just toddlers?"

"Toddlers on toddy," Hollis said.

Ashford noticed the effect of the toddy, that was for sure, but he didn't feel like a toddler. Rather, when sitting here with Hollis, he felt quite old, terribly old. Once they had been thin young men with hair sitting around a dorm room talking bullshit, and now they were middle-aged men sitting around a dining room table talking bullshit. It was very disconcerting.

"Have to toddle to the potty," he said, getting up from the table.

"Can't hold it, that's a real sign of age," Hollis said.

"Hey," Ashford said. "Watch that."

"Aw, just tell Anne when you see her to come on back. I miss her."

"I don't blame you," Ashford said. "She's quite lovely." He brushed the back of Merry's hair as he left the table. "Of course, you are the loveliest."

"Of course," Merry said, giving him a certain look.

He walked into the hall to see the darkhaired woman lying on the floor outside the bathroom, her skirt rucked up over her thin thighs all the way to her yellow-spotted underwear.

"Jesus!" Ashford let out a yell.

The woman opened her eyes.

"What?"

"Are you all right?" He went down on one knee beside her.

Hollis came running.

"Annie!" He bent over her. "She's epileptic," he said. "Anne?"

The woman looked up at them and then noticed that her skirt was awry and shifted on the floor to pull it back down.

"Let me see her," Merry said over their shoulders.

"I'm fine," Anne Nguyen said, taking a deep breath and sitting up. "I guess I forgot to take my medicine. The jet lag, or something."

Both men helped her to her feet and escorted her into the living room.

"I really am okay. This happens once a year, maybe."

"Did you hurt yourself?"

Anne Nguyen shook her head.

"You didn't bite your tongue?"

Anne Nguyen shook her head again, and sighed.

"Where's your meds?" Hollis held up his hands.

She told him where to look in her bag and he went down to the guest room to find the stuff.

"I think we should call Gary," Merry said.

"Your doctor?" Anne smiled up at her from the sofa.

"Uh-huh."

"Not necessary. It wasn't that awful this time. I just saw black and fell into it, like a bag of feathers."

"Doesn't sound so bad, the way you describe it," Ashford said.

Hollis returned with the medicine. Merry had already fetched a glass of water from the kitchen.

Not much could match that for excitement the rest of the evening. Merry helped Hollis and Anne settle in to the guest room. When she came upstairs, Ashford was already in bed. They talked a little while about the next day's activities—Anne, as it happened, wanted to see Mount Vernon as part of some personal quest to discover American history—and they turned out the light.

Merry bunched close to him in the dark.

"Do you think there's a connection between the way she was born and her epilepsy?

"I don't know," Ashford said.

"Do you think she'll be all right?"

"She says."

Silence from Merry. In a moment she was lightly snoring. The house was otherwise quiet. When the boys were still living at home, he always knew they were there. Some kind of parental radar, he supposed. Guests were different. You couldn't imagine guests sleeping in another part of the house. But some things came to mind. Ashford lay there a while in the dark picturing the epileptic girl's yellow-stained cotton panties.

Next day—the first full day of the visit—and the weather was lovely. According to the *Post*, the rest of the weekend would, in fact, remain glorious, wonderful heat, low humidity, good sun. Ashford had gotten up early enough to complete some work he had pending—a speech for the CEO that he would be giving in Nebraska this coming week at the opening of some new arts center. He didn't even want to think about it once he had finished, so after making a few telephone calls he came downstairs and found Merry fixing breakfast for Hollis and Anne Nguyen.

"We're all set for Mount Vernon," he said. "It's open until five. We don't need reservations."

"Thank you," Anne Nguyen said. She looked as fresh as she had when she first came in the front door, though Ashford couldn't help but remember the way she lay in the hallway, so vulnerable and otherworldly.

"And in case you're wondering," the girl said, "I'm feeling fine. In fact, after one of these episodes I usually feel fantastic, my skin tingles for days, even my vision seems clearer."

"I should have epilepsy," Hollis said, his eyes lowered toward the food on the table. "Maybe it's a cure for jet lag."

"You're lagged?" Ashford reached for the coffee pot and poured himself a cup of the dark, nutty-scented liquid.

"Lagged bad," Hollis said. "I couldn't get to sleep. The young lady here went out like a light bulb."

"That's how Merry goes," Ashford said.

Merry made a little huff of breath in her throat.

"Anne, while they're talking about us, perhaps we ought to take a little walk around the neighborhood."

"I'd love that," Anne Nguyen said.

"Plenty of time," Ashford said. "We're off to Mount Vernon after lunch. And after that, what? Dinner and a movie?"

"Done," Hollis said, perking up for the first time that morning.

"Good," Merry said. "We'll have fun."

"The elderly on a tear," Hollis said.

"For Christ's sake, Hollis," Ashford said. "'Elderly.'"

"Over forty," Hollis said. "This is America."

"That's why I want to see Mount Vernon," Anne Nguyen said.

Later, on the sunny drive across the sparkling river, she spoke more about it.

"It's a part of the childhood of this country. Where I was born, even if I was only there for a year or so afterward, the traditions and history are thousands of years old. Here it's so different. Not that I know the old Vietnamese ways, except what I hear from my parents and their friends. But when Holly said he wanted to take this trip, I thought maybe we should explore some of the history of the place." She waved toward the window. "Just look."

They looked at statues and in the distance the white columned buildings of the national cemetery just ahead before they gave into a half turn around a traffic circle and took the direction of the airport.

"You want to know what I thought?" Hollis laid a hand on the back of Ashford's seat.

"What?"

"I thought, hey, I can get out of the office for a couple of days."

In the front passenger seat, Merry laughed.

"Ash works at home. He never gets away."

"Except for outings like this," he said.

Merry turned to look at him.

"So you're enjoying this?"

"I am," he said.

She shook her head.

"Let me call all the newspapers," she said.

"Uh, Ash," Hollis said, "is this the part where the houseguests experience a fight between their host and hostess?"

"We're not fighting," Ashford said. "Merry's right. We don't take advantage enough of living here."

"You inspire us," Merry said. "Anne, look."

She meant the river, the capitol and other monuments on the other shore. A passenger jet roared overhead and they all turned to look. Once past the airport, the traffic thinned out and the green of the parkway enveloped them.

"So tell me," Ashford said to Anne Nguyen, "is this really a serious passion?"

The girl looked confused.

"I can speak for her," Hollis said. "It's a weird passion. A July-September thing. Well, maybe June-October...."

"I was thinking about her interest in American history," Ashford said.

Merry reached over and laid a hand on his arm.

"More of us should have this passion. I've always taken our history for granted. I've never been to Mount Vernon."

"Well, neither have I," Ashford said.

"Gee, guys," Hollis said, "I have to confess...." Hollis made a little snort in his nose. "I don't even know where it is."

"Only a few more miles down the road." Ashford glanced at his friend in the rear-view mirror.

"Kind of a long commute from the White House if you're traveling on horseback," Hollis said.

"He lived in the White House and only visited the family place now and then," Ashford said. "Only about fifteen times, in fact."

"You've been doing homework," Hollis said.

"That's what I do best," Ashford said. "Actually, I looked it up on the web this morning before breakfast."

"Well, what else about it should we know?" Hollis leaned forward against the seat.

"Hush," Anne Nguyen said, "I want to discover it for myself."

Which, after they arrived at the estate and parked and bought their tickets—a ritual scuffle ensued between Ashford and Hollis about who would pay, with Ashford triumphing—she set out to do, with all of them, at first, in the group. Tourist season had ended a few weeks before. The line at the entrance to the mansion house was just long enough for Ashford, following along behind Anne and Merry and Hollis, to read most of the pamphlet that came with the tickets:

A Brief Washington-Mount Vernon Chronology

1674—John Washington, great-grandfather of George, is granted the Mount Vernon homesite.

1726—Augustine Washington, father of George, acquires the
Mount Vernon property from his sister.

1735-39—Augustine Washington resides at Mount Vernon
with his family.

All this family declension, it was getting tedious (because it reminded Ashford of his own tableside memories of conversations when he was a child) and since he had already read most of this on the web he skipped down the timeline a bit.

1761—Washington inherits Mount Vernon following the death
of Lawrence Washington's widow [his brother's wife].

1775—Appointed commander in chief of the Continental
forces. He will not be in residence again at Mount
Vernon for eight years.

Ashford broke off his reading, following his group into the mansion itself, where they entered a dining room with fake desserts on the table and the walls painted a vile shade of blue/green.

"The original color," said a chubby middle-aged docent in plaid skirt and red sweater. She then recited something about the Washington's dinner parties.

"Take a bite of one of those plaster rolls," Hollis said.

"Holly," Anne Nguyen gently touched him with her elbow.

They passed out onto a rear porch with the placid river in the distance.

"An Eighteenth century prospect," Ashford said, remembering something from an English class long ago.

"No pollution back then," Hollis said.

"You've become a complete cynic," Ashford said.

"The way I see it, I'm just being realistic."

Then up the rear stairs to view a group of tiny bedrooms. Another docent, this one a white-haired stick of a black woman, recited facts about which family members had which room and gave a short account of Washington's brief illness and death.

"George Washington slept here," Hollis said as they descended the stairs, a pleased grin on his face.

"You heard the lady." Ashford shook his head. "He died here." Overhead, Ashford could hear the docent reciting from the beginning her speech.

"I liked the four-poster bed," Merry said. "I'd love for us to have one."

"Then we shall," Ashford said.

They passed through a corridor off which sat the kitchen, and then they were out the door.

"That's it?" Hollis yawned widely. "Big country, big ideas, small house."

"We want to see the outbuildings and gardens and the tomb," Merry said. "Right, Anne?"

"Right," the dark-haired Anne Nguyen said.

Ashford eyed the broad expanse of lawn to the south of the mansion, green all the way to the river.

"Maybe Holly and I will lie down over there on the grass while you ladies finish the tour."

"We'll have our male-to-male talk," Hollis said. "We haven't had that yet."

The two women left and the two men sat down in the shade of a large pecan tree.

Ashford read: "*Outbuildings and Gardens. Washington carefully planned the grounds, placing the work buildings and yards along a lane which runs north and south from the circle in front of the Mansion....*"

"That's terribly interesting," Hollis said, lying back with his head cradled on his arms.

"Stuff about the kitchens."

"Uh-huh."

"The gardens."

"Charming, I'm sure."

"The Tomb...."

"Yeah, tell me about the tomb."

Ashford lay on his side, the warm breeze bathing his hair and face.

"George Washington died in the master bedroom at Mount Vernon on December 14, 1799...."

"Just what the lady said. Poor bastard missed Christmas," Hollis said.

"...In his will, he directed that he be buried on his beloved Mount Vernon estate...."

"How'd they keep this whole place up, anyway?"

"Slaves," Ashford said.

"Oh, de happy slaves de be woiking for the good Massa George." Hollis took a deep breath. "Can't have any thing good in our history without it being fucked up by slaves, right?"

"That's how it was in New Jersey when we were growing up," Ashford said.

"Yeah, we had slaves, too," Hollis said. "I called them mother and father." He laughed and closed his eyes. Ashford closed his eyes, too.

"So, how have you been?" he said.

"I'm in love, can't you see?"

Ashford smiled and opened his eyes.

"I don't know about the love, but you're certainly in luck. She's a lovely thing."

"Thank you."

"And she's lucky, too. You bringing her all the way across the country just to visit this crappy old estate."

"We came to visit you," Hollis said.

"First time you've done that with a girlfriend since you left...?

"Cindy."

"Sorry, I—"

"You couldn't remember. No big deal. I wish I could forget her name myself."

"What is she doing these days?"

"Entertainment law. Big deal in the movie business. I should have stayed with her, I'd be living high on the hog right now. But it's weird, I just couldn't see much of a future in eating shit in public."

"It wasn't that bad, was it?"

"Who lived it, you or me?"

"All right," Ashford said. "I bow to experience."

Hollis took another deep breath.

"We've got a few problems."

"You and Cindy still—"

"Me and Anne," Hollis said. "She introduced me to her parents and they were not pleased."

"They wanted a nice Vietnamese boy?"

"You got it. And on top of that, a Vietnamese boy at least ten years younger than yours truly."

"That's a mess," Ashford said. "Those, her people, they put a lot of weight on tradition."

"Yeah, even more than us in New Jersey," Hollis said with a laugh. "It must be like being Jewish, and then you have to come home and meet her parents. Or she has to meet yours."

"We'll have to ask old Weingarten," Ashford said. "We'll have to give him a call."

"Wish we could," Hollis said.

"Why can't we?"

"You didn't hear? He died."

"Oh, Christ! When? How?"

"About six months ago. Some kidney thing."

"Christ," Ashford said again. "The first one of us to go."

"No," Hollis said. "There was Adams. He died in Africa a long time ago, remember?"

"Yeah," Ashford said. "Now that you mention it."

He rolled on his side and looked out over the river. The birds were singing as though it were still high summer. Here and there a weak tree had turned a light shade of yellow or red, but most of the green was still intact. By the temperature and humidity, you couldn't tell that September was well on its way to ending. He lay back and closed his eyes again, working hard to push away these questions of mortality. Fragments of the speech he had been writing floated into his mind and he pushed them away, too, as he did bits and pieces—"*Greenhouse and slave quarters, destroyed by fire in 1835 and since reconstructed*"—of the tourist pamphlet. Facts, facts, they had nothing to do with him. But he was good at it, arranging, rearranging. In spite of himself, he mouthed the words of the speech and heard the CEO's voice as he would deliver it the next day. Then he saw Weingarten's face. They had been tennis friends, not much more than that. But it was something he had always counted on, a game with Weingarten, before they each moved to different cities and lost touch with each other. A weird coincidence, he had seen him on the street in Saigon just before the end. Was there some kind of damned theme for this weekend? Vietnam, Saigon, Weingarten. Anne Nguyen, her skirt up over her thighs, drifted sideways into his mind.

Next thing he knew, the birds were singing and Hollis was saying something and the women had returned.

"Interesting, so interesting," Anne Nguyen said.

"Yes, I'm awfully glad we did this," Merry said on the drive back to the city. "And you boys had a good talk about old times?"

"Yes, oh, yes," Hollis said.

"Certainly did," Ashford said. "And had us a little rest, too."

"Good," Merry said. "You need that. You work so hard."

"I do, don't I?" Ashford said. "But I don't mind."

"He's a good man, Anne," Merry said to her new friend. "A very good man."

But the real truth didn't begin to come out until much later that day, after a dinner at his and Merry's favorite neighborhood restaurant—Italian, fresh pasta, home-made bread, the works—and several bottles of a good Chianti.

"We have a plan," Hollis said. "I was thinking about old Weingarten, and Anne and I were talking about what else she wanted to do here in D.C., and we want to propose another tour."

"This is the panel in the cartoon where in the little balloon over my head you see the word 'g-r-o-a-n,'" Ashford said.

"Let's hear what they want to do," Merry said, and he knew she was right. So they listened.

Upstairs again, in that mysterious few minutes just before sleep, the two of them talked things over. The pleasant outing to Mount Vernon—"I actually went out for a few minutes on the lawn there," Ashford said—what easy house guests Hollis and Anne Nguyen were—"She is really sweet," Merry said, and Ashford felt a terrible cold rush of guilt because of his recollection, he was thinking about it even now as he regretted thinking about it, of the stained place between her legs—and the prospect of another outing tomorrow morning.

"I'll fix us a lunch," Merry said, "and when we're ready we can eat on the mall somewhere, on one of those benches...."

"Good idea," Ashford said, without knowing what he was saying. He still had Anne Nguyen on his mind, and imagined his dear pal Hollis down with her in the guest room, his belly swelled as with a money-belt beneath the flesh, rolling on top of her, the slender girl pinned beneath him, and enjoying it, opening her legs and entwining them around him.

It was more than he could take and not act himself, so Ashford reached for his wife in the dark, and they made strenuous love, so that almost immediately—miraculously!—his thoughts of the other girl vanished, and it was just him and Merry again, the way it had always been, the way it should and must always be.

Morning was here before they knew it, Merry working at the kitchen counter, packing sandwiches and fruit into a white woven basket when Ashford came into the room.

"You're serious about this picnic stuff, aren't you?" he said.

She nodded and kept on with her work.

"Man does not live by museums alone," she said. And he laughed, and shook his head, and touched her shoulder, her arm.

Hollis and Anne Nguyen soon appeared from the guest room. Time spiraled forward. After coffee and juice the four of them walked down to Connecticut Avenue and caught a cab. It was colder this morning than yesterday, almost as if in the night a line had been drawn between the seasons. A quick ride through cool but sunny streets got them to the front of a dour gray stone building a block below the national mall. A few people, adults and some teenagers stood in line at the door.

"You were right," Hollis said to Ashford, "no problem."

Anne Nguyen, dressed in sweater and jeans, inclined toward Ashford as the door opened and the line began to move. "I really appreciate…."

"Don't be silly," Ashford said.

"We only get to these places when guests come to town," Merry said.

"Isn't that only the way?" Hollis followed them in.

There were tickets available, Ashford knew there would be, and after Merry checked her basket at the coat room they lined up to enter the exhibit, quickly passing into the elevator, a drab contraption that carried them up silently to the next floor.

From there on, for the rest of the morning, it was hell on earth.

"A hell with rules," Hollis said as they reached the large chart of racial characteristics of various skulls.

Ashford's mind was still back with the first thing they had seen after stepping out of the elevator, the oddly compelling footage, looping around and around, as he discovered after watching for more than a moment, of the Nazis' celebration at Hitler's rise to the top of the German government. There were mobs of dark-shirted celebrants, torches in hand, chanting a victory song whose words he could not make out but whose rhythms—da da da dah, dah, dah, dah, dah—pulsed in his head for the rest of the tour.

Edicts, news headlines, banners, telegrams, charts, books, flags, all these things attracted him and distracted him as the four of them drifted through the mutely lighted halls. It was more than he could take in on one viewing and Merry said the same.

"It's giving me a terrible headache."

"Imagine what it was like for them," Ashford said.

"Them?"

"The Jews."

"Of course," Merry said. "It's just too overwhelming, unbelievable."

"But here's the evidence," Ashford said as they moved along past an exhibit of what seemed like a thousand shoes and eye-glasses.

"What do you think?" he said to Hollis when they stepped into a railroad box car of the variety that transported Jews and Communists and Gypsies to the extermination camps.

"I had a Jewish grandmother, did I ever tell you that?"

"Is that why you wanted to see this?"

Hollis shook his head.

"It was strictly Anne's idea. She wants to know everything."

They looked over at the Vietnamese girl. Tears ran down her cheeks. Her eyes looked elsewhere.

Voices drifted in from speakers hidden somewhere in the ceiling. Testimony from camp inmates, they soon learned. Here were rows of beds from a barracks. A model of the gas chambers. And in the middle of this particular room a place where you could see evidence of medical torture and bestial acts of sadism.

It was Merry's turn to cry.

"I'm not sure I'm going to get through this," she said.

"We can leave," Ashford said.

"No, no, our guests…."

"Don't be so damned genteel," he said.

Now she really began to cry.

"Please," he said, looking around. But no one seemed to notice.

"Let's catch up with them," Ashford said. "The faster we move, the sooner we get out of here."

But there was no rushing things. More and more people filled the corridors, making it difficult to hurry. And Hollis and Anne Nguyen were not increasing their pace, but rather were slowing down. At each turn a new exhibit caught their attention. A hall filled floor to ceiling with photographs of people from one village sent to the gas chambers.

A map of the region, dotted with camps. A corridor filled with evidence of the American reaction.

"Incredible, huh?" Hollis said to him at one point.

"Absolutely relentless," Ashford said. "The energy and attention they put into the extermination of the Jews."

"I guess, if you're going to do a thing like that, you've got to really apply yourself."

"Sure, Hollis," Ashford said. "You might put it that way."

"Well, don't look at me like that, Ash. I'm just telling you what I think, not suggesting it was right. My grandmother, remember?"

"How come you never told me that, about her, before this?"

"It never occurred to me to bring it up."

Ashford had no Jewish grandmother. As far as he knew, the closest he came to having anything other than pure English blood in his veins was the rumor of an Irish great-great on his mother's side of the family. But the English did try to stamp out the Irish, didn't they? Or at least hold them down.

He tried this out on Merry as they were—finally!—returning to the main floor of the museum.

"Really, Ash," she said. "If you're being funny, it's not the right place for it."

Her eyes were still wet with tears. Without another word, she set off across the large space and entered a large doorway marked with a sign that said *Hall of Remembrance*.

Hollis and Anne Nguyen came up alongside him.

"Hi. Where's Merry?"

Ashford pointed toward the hall.

As if they had some urgent message to deliver, the couple hurried in that direction.

When they didn't immediately reappear, Ashford crossed the floor and went in through the same doorway. A small flame flickered in a holder in the center of the circular space. Benches lined the walls and on them sat a number of people, some weeping copiously, or shaking with silent grief, or just sitting silently. He saw Merry and Hollis and Anne Nguyen off to the right, their bodies bunched together, looking like sculpture rather than living human beings. Ashford took a step toward them and then stopped, waiting a while—it seemed a long while—for them to get up.

No one spoke until they went out back through the lobby, and then it was Ashford who broke the silence.

"The basket," he said to Merry.

She looked at him, and went to retrieve it.

"Does any one feel like eating?" she said as they left the building. It was even cooler a day now than when they had started out.

Hollis shook his head.

"Not just now, thank you," Anne Nguyen said.

"I'm pretty hungry," Ashford said. "But I'm not going to make a fuss about it."

"Good," Merry said. "Shall we find a cab?"

In the taxi on the way home, Anne Nguyen began to cry again, and Hollis held her close, as though she were his child. Merry sat primly—coldly, even, Ashford had to think—with the basket on her lap. He, in the front passenger seat, stayed swiveled around so that they all might speak. But none of them said a word. The dark-skinned driver wore an off-white turban. There was a slight odor of staleness about his body. The cab itself smelled of disinfectant. From the basket a faint odor of food drifted out. Meat, warming, and the slight sharp tinge of mustard, perhaps. And apples, the sickening-sweet scent of apples about to rot.

Horse Sacrifice and the Shaman's Ascent to the Sky

Originally published in *The Land-Grant College Review*

Sting Bradford never knew what hit him. One minute he was down there in the musty basement of that woman's Glover Park house humping dry-wall on his head just like in the old days (one of his laborers called in sick that morning), and the next, he crumpled like the paper cup under a descending heel of a hand, the slab of sheet-rock sliding off to the right, and him rolling to the left so that it didn't trap him there on the cold concrete floor.

And then he could breathe again.

Jesus, he said into the dust, getting up slowly and brushing himself off. It was his big fear, and it kept him alert, when he and Paula, his wife of ten years, went to the Keys, skin-diving just off her younger sister's little sail-boat. But holding his breath in ten feet of clear water was never like this. He'd lost control, and it frightened him.

He felt worse when he went upstairs to the kitchen to get a drink of water. The woman who owned the house—a plump dyed blonde in her thirties and worked for the government, was all he knew—stood there at the stove dressed for the day.

"Hi," she said, an odd smile on her face. (Just something about that smile made Sting wonder if she was a dyke and just trying to be polite to him.)

"Are you okay?" There was an odd quality to her voice, too, a little sort of catch that came along with her smile.

"The weirdest thing…." He started to speak and then stopped, because it just seemed all so familiar to talk about it and he didn't know her at all. He drank a glass of water and went back downstairs.

Paula, he knew. After ten years, or twelve, counting the two years they lived together before they got married, you knew somebody almost as well as you knew yourself. But that night when he started to tell her about what had happened—"The weirdest thing," he started to say again, still a little shaky from the incident while Lord Jeffrey, their rust-colored spaniel, apparently noticing that something in his manner was just a little bit off, licked and licked and licked Sting's outstretched hand, Paula remained distracted. A slightly built woman with straight brown hair who, as she stood there at the stove stirring something in a pot, looked the way she must have when she was twelve and helping her mother cook for her and her younger sister, she seemed to be lost in her own worries, which usually had to do with her job at the Smithsonian.

After a while, she said, "What weird thing?"

"Nothing," Sting said, giving Lord Jeffrey a pat and sending him on his way. "That little Salvadoran guy was out sick. So I had to spend the afternoon hauling dry-wall."

"Uh-huh."

"One point, I couldn't get my breath."

"What?"

"I couldn't get my breath."

"If it happens again, you ought to see a doctor."

He shrugged off her remark the way she seemed to have shrugged him off, and went about helping her set the table. The meal started off quietly, which didn't exactly please Sting. As he sometimes thought about himself, he was in the trades, but that didn't mean he didn't like a good intellectual conversation. Currently, he was reading a book by the renowned late University of Chicago professor Mircea Eliade. (Years and years ago, in the middle of a terrible college career in Virginia that ended a few semesters short of graduation, he had dated a girl who attended classes at Georgetown. In one of those ironic situations that happen to you when you're still fairly young, they had gotten pregnant and the girl had an abortion and left school, never to speak or even write to him again. But not before starting him off on a path of study to which he was still terribly devoted, despite his decidedly amateur status.)

"Today in the supermarket?" Paula spoke to him through the steam rising from her bowl of rice.

"Uh-huh?"

"I saw George Stephanopoulus."

"No kidding?"

Lord Jeffrey brushed against Sting's leg, begging for a morsel.

"Go away," Sting said.

"I wanted to go up to him and say, how could you betray Clinton like that?"

"You think he betrayed him?" Sting said.

"He turned against him toward the end," Paula said.

Sting nodded, taking in, as he often did, almost unconsciously, Paula's love of loyalty. Remembering his own parents' devotion to one another, he admired that quality no end.

"But you think that what Clinton did was wrong, don't you?" he said, remembering his father's escapades that would have undoubtedly led to the dissolution of the household if he hadn't died first.

"Yes," Paula said. "But everybody else was wrong, too, especially all the people who kept on saying how wrong he was."

"Complicated," Sting said. "That's why I like doing what I do. It's difficult, but not all that complicated."

Lord Jeffrey returned, and Sting gave him a loving but forceful push away.

"A nice distinction," Paula said, reminding him with the sharpness of her response of just who she was and what she did for a living.

In bed that night, he picked up his book, a glossy-covered many-paged paperback, and read for a while:

We begin with Radlov's classic description of the Altaic ritual, based not only on his own observations but also on the texts of the songs and invocations recorded at the beginning of the nineteenth century, by missionaries to the Altai and later edited by the priest V.L. Verbitsky....

He took a deep breath and then another and plunged back in to the book:

> The first evening is devoted to the preparation for the rite. The *kam*, having chosen a spot in a meadow, erects a new yurt there, setting inside it a young birch stripped of its lower branches and with nine steps (*tapty*) notched into its trunk....

"Jesus, it's hot in here," he said, setting down the book on his belly. Lord Jeffrey, curled up at the foot of the bed, was snoring loudly. Paula, working on notes on a lap-board in her usual business-like way, shook her head.

"Let in some fresh air."

"I will," he said, and got up and opened a window and returned, a bit breathless, to the bed and picked up the book.

> A small palisade of birch sticks is erected around the yurt and a birch stick with a knot of horsehair is set at the entrance....

There was a footnote to that line (there were a lot of footnotes in this scholarly book, and each seemed more interesting to him than the next):

> 38 According to Potanin (*Ocherki severo-zapadnoi Mongolii*, IV,79), two poles with wooden birds at their tops are set up near the sacrificial table, and they are connected by a cord from which hang green branches and a hare skin. Among the Dolgan poles with wooden birds at the top represent the cosmic pillars; cf.Holberg (Harva): *Der Baum des Lebens*, p.16, figs. 5-6, *Die religiosen Vorstellungen*, p.44. As for the bird, it of course symbolizes the shaman's magical powers of flight....

His heart beat fast...he decided, he read quickly...as though it were some thriller or terrific movie, the kind filled with weird old rites and violence, the kind that Paula refused to watch with him.

"Jesus," he said, "listen to this."

"What?"

"'Then he blesses the horse—'"

"Are you reading a western?"

"Just listen, I'll explain. '—and, with the help of several of the audience, kills it in a cruel way, breaking its backbone—'"

"Please, spare me," Paula said, looking at him over the tops of her reading glasses.

"No, no, you got to hear this, it's amazing, '—breaking its backbone in such a manner that not a drop of its blood falls to the ground or touches the sacrificers. The skin and bones are exposed—'"

"What are you reading?"

"It's the Eliade," he said.

"You should have gone to graduate school," Paula said.

"Shit, for Christ's sake," he said, "that's not what this is all about." He took a deep breath, surprised at the vehemence of his response.

"I didn't mean that in a bad way," Paula said. "I meant, you have such scholarly instincts. Reading all that esoteric stuff."

He ignored her, taking another couple of breaths, and dove back silently into the book, reading about the extension of the ritual into a second evening and the song the shaman sings:

> Gifts that no horse can carry,
> Alas, alas, alas!
> That no man can lift!
> Alas, alas, alas!

And the address he makes to the Markut, the Birds of Heaven:

> Birds of Heaven, five Markut,
> Ye with mighty copper talons,
> Copper is the moon's talon,
> And of ice the moon's beak....

He read a little while longer while Paula kept on writing on her pad, and then they agreed to turn out the lights, kissed chastely, and fell back onto their respective sides of the bed. Lord Jeffrey lay like a sandbag on his feet and Sting shoved him aside. His muscles ached, and he wished that instead of his usual shower he'd taken a good hot soak before coming to bed. Lying there in the dark, he thought about a zillion things, the job, the dust, the noise, traffic on the way home, Paula's remark about graduate school. He thought they had settled that long ago, that she was the brain worker and he was the brawn worker, and each could gain from the other's labor.

Zah! he could feel his heart pull and jerk at the prospect of a fight with her, so, no, he didn't want that, so he'd try to keep quiet, just stay quiet and lapse easily into sleep. His breathing settled again. But he stayed awake a while, listening to Lord Jeffrey's chest and throat sounding like an unoiled machine cranking in the dark.

The next morning on the job the Salvadoran was back, sneezing and coughing. Sting kept his distance from him, not wanting to catch anything. A couple of days went by and, as it turned out, it was Paula who developed a medical problem. Just before the weekend, she was taking the escalator down into the metro and caught her heel—she still wore low heels when she went to work, when every other woman there wore flats or sneakers—and fell, breaking her fall with her hands. She didn't even bother to mention it while she was making dinner that night. It wasn't until it was time to clean up that she told him that her right wrist was bothering her and he took a look and saw the swelling.

He had a little field experience from the service, and knew to pack it with ice. But the pain grew worse and worse, and so at two in the morning he got dressed and then helped Paula get dressed and leaving Lord Jeffrey behind to complain about being left behind they pushed through uncommonly cold autumn night air and drove to the Sibley emergency room. Anticipating a long wait he brought along his copy of the Eliade, but just a lucky turn of the ebb and flow of patients on a Friday night they only had to sit about fifteen minutes.

The doctor was a neat guy, taller than Sting by almost a head, younger by about ten years, and quick with his examination—sprain, not a fracture, but they'd do an x-ray in a minute just to confirm—and also in the way, when Sting said half-jokingly that he wanted his blood pressure taken too along with Paula, he reached for his arm and went along with it.

"Yours is way up," he said when he read it, saying some numbers that passed Sting right by.

"So what does that mean?" Sting said.

"I'd see a cardiologist, if I were you," the doctor said.

"You mean now?" Sting said.

"Make an appointment. Think of it as necessary but not necessarily an emergency."

Sting was much too busy to do that, but that's how, a week later, unable to sleep, he lay there in the dark brooding about his blood pressure and the job the next day and the owner of the house, the plump blonde, yes, and a house he had seen listed that he wanted to consider buying and renovating and reselling, if he could swing the bank loan, and Paula's breathing and his own breath, slow and steady, slow and steady, and the dog's steady breathing, and then he got up to piss and he returned to the bed listening to his own now more hurried chest, and wondering what was happening inside it, and the sounds of squirrels on the roof pulled his thoughts away from himself and he wondered why the animals should be awake in the middle of the night—

And the telephone on the night table rang and rang until Paula reached over and answered it.

"Hello?" her heard her say. Her voice sounded as if it were the middle of the afternoon. How can she do that? he wondered, pick up the telephone in the middle of the night and talk as if it were the middle of the afternoon.

She burst into tears.

"What?" he said.

She made awful noises into the telephone, then held it away from her face.

"Janice," she said in a hoarse whisper. (Her sister)

"But she's all right?"

"Robbie," she said. (Her nephew)

"What about him?"

Paula drew the mouthpiece to her lips again and cried into the telephone.

"What?"

Sting gently peeled the receiver from her hand and spoke.

"What happened?"

His sister-in-law, her voice a stew of croaks and gurgles and words, eventually found a way to explain that her little boy had drowned.

"Oh, my God," Sting said. "Oh, my God…."

Almost as if he understood what was happening, Lord Jeffrey (sensing the distress in their voices, Sting supposed) got up and dumped himself between them.

Only a few hours later, with little time to digest what had happened and dazed with fatigue and suffering from a good-sized headache, he was driving Paula to the airport.

"I'll call the office as soon as I get to Miami. I'll call you as soon as I get to Key West," she said.

"Wish I could go with you, but…."

"You can't let that job go by itself," Paula said. "I understand."

"She didn't come to my father's funeral…."

"Sting, it's not quid pro quo. You can't go. It's enough that I have to. But I have to be there her for. For her. Jesus, I can't even talk…"

Sting reached over and brushed her shoulder.

"Stupid thing, living on that boat…."

"You love that boat when we go down there…."

Sting looked off into the misty dawn of monuments, water, and parkland.

"All right," he said. "I'm a jerk."

"No, you're not."

And she leaned over and kissed him on the cheek.

But he did feel like a jerk, watching her board the airplane and thinking about nothing, as tired as he was, except how hard the day was going to be. His mind seemed to wake up, though, on the walk back to the car. And he allowed his thoughts to distract him from the feeling of guilt that splashed over him when he heard the sound of a jet taking off, wondering if it was Paula's. She'd be sitting there in her window seat—did she have a window seat?—looking down toward the ground, feeling a little nervous (at least he always felt nervous on take-off), wondering about him, where he was, just getting in to his car, already driving to the job? And then she'd be thinking about her nephew, the pathetic kid drowned in the Gulf waters.

"You look awfully shaky," the owner said when he appeared in her kitchen so much earlier than ever before.

"My nephew died," Sting said as she offered him a cup of coffee, flavored with a big whiff of her perfume. "My nephew by marriage."

"I thought something was wrong," the owner said. She was wearing a black dress and some turquoise jewelry, as though she were about to go to a party rather than an office. But she didn't seem in much of a hurry. "Want to talk about it?"

Sting shook his head.

"My wife's sister," he said after a couple of sips of the strong coffee. "She lives on a boat down in Key West? Single mother, all of that. The kid, I think he was four or five, got up in the middle of the night, wandered off along the pier and fell into the water...."

"I'm sorry," the owner said. "Do you have to go down there?"

"Naw," Sting said. "I just put my wife on the airplane. She'll stay with her sister a while...."

"Some things are more important," the owner said, but by her smile Sting could tell that she was glad that he was not leaving the job.

He nodded, feeling awkward, wondering if after all he should have gone with Paula.

"Sting?" she said. She asked about his name.

Sting: Charles Dewey Bradford was his given name. "Sting" was born in that rough time when he was doing his best to drop out of college. He drank a lot, and got into bar fights. Sting—like a bee! Muhammad Ali's imperative stuck to him after some one of his inebriated friends called it out in the middle of one of those frequent battles he waged against order and civility. At first he ignored it, and then he came to dislike it, actively asking his pals not to call him that. And then, after they kept on using it, he began to answer to it naturally.

Sting.

His parents disliked it, but his father didn't have all that much time to hate it, dying of his heart attack a couple of months after Sting came back to Maryland and began working in the trades. His mother, after all these years, still called him Charles.

"How did you and your wife meet?" the owner asked.

Sting smiled, thinking of Paula, somewhere now in the air above the Carolinas.

"At a swing dance."

"Oh!" The owner seemed pleased to hear about that.

"But we haven't danced in years."

"Too bad," the owner said. "You should get out more."

Sting nodded. He really didn't know what to say.

She glanced at her watch. "Time for me to go to work. Or else I won't be able to pay you for the job."

"See you," Sting said.

"See you," the owner said.

Throwing himself into a job always kept Sting's mind off things. And with everybody showing up that morning, he had a great deal to do. The stair guy and the plumber needed some talking to. And by the time he finished checking out the dry-wall work the Salvadoran guy had completed, it was nearly lunch time and he had to take a terific piss.

They were working on the downstairs bathroom. So he had to go upstairs, where it was deserted, except for the lingering scent of coffee and the owner's perfume.

What might it be? What if he bought some as a gift for Paula upon her return home from Florida?

Stepping quietly into the owner's bedroom, he stood for a moment, looking things over. It was neater than his and Paula's bedroom, with the double bed freshly made and several comforters and pillows arranged neatly on top. From the looks of things, the owner lived alone. Sting thought for a moment of Paula and of how solitary they each had become even though living with each other, and he was wondering if somehow this little separation might somehow do them some good, and then lost himself in an inspection of the articles on the small dressing table: creams and lotions and brushes and combs, a locket, with a photograph inside of a man in uniform, probably the woman's father, a bead necklace laid out as if for display—and several bottles of perfume and cologne. He chose the first, because of its alluring name—Take Me—and got lucky. Yes, he breathed in, this was the scent, something much too drastic for Paula ever to wear.

Returning to the basement, like a boy fresh from his first encounter with a woman, as he worked he now and then raised his finger tips to his nostrils and took a breath. But by the end of the day his hands were thick with dust and oil and had lost any trace of the perfume.

At home after dark, he took a shower and changed his clothes and made himself a little supper of sausages and eggs. No salad, though. Paula was the one who insisted on the salads. His mother raised him on basic meat and potatoes and he didn't like salads and couldn't care less if he never ate one. After rinsing the dishes, he took Lord Jeffrey for a walk. The neighborhood was a quiet place with small mostly wooden houses, with here and there a brick house interspersed, the kind of place he had grown up in.

He was just coming back in the door when the telephone began to ring.

"Hi," he said.

"Hi," she said.

"How are things?"

"Pretty grim," she said.

"Yeah, I guess I should have figured. But are you okay?"

"Sure, I'm okay. It's my sister...."

"She must feel so fucking guilty...."

"I can't talk about that now."

"She's there?"

"Of course," she said.

"Well," he said.

"How are you?"

"The usual. Working hard."

"Have you had any more...?"

"Any more what?"

"Of those...breathing spells...."

"Nope. Hell, I'd forgotten all about that."

He took a breath.

"So...how's your wrist?" he said.

"Better," she said.

"Good."

"I better go," she said.

"Give Janice a hug from me."

"I will."

"Explain to her...."

"I already did."

"Is it tomorrow?"

"What?"

"The funeral?"

"It is tomorrow."

"Oh, Christ. I should send flowers."

"I'm here," Paula said. "That's enough."

But she wasn't *here*, where Sting was, and that, even with his few moments of speculation that it might be good to be separated just a little while, made him uncomfortable, it had been so long since he had gone to sleep alone. Of course, he could stretch out across the entire bed and enjoy the space of it all, and belch and fart without worry of rebuke. But after a feeble try at the Eliade, it made for a bad night of it, with a lot of turning and tossing and sitting up with a pain in his chest until some deep breathing—memory of a single yoga class he had taken long ago with Paula, at her urging, but which came to nothing, with not even Paula staying with it for more than a couple of months—seemed to calm him down, and then came a little sleep, with odd dreams, rolling around in dust, and waving at a train with his grandmother—dead for thirty years—waving back to him, and then it was light and he was wide awake, and Lord Jeffrey was urging him to go for a walk.

Once again he felt awful when he arrived at the job.

"In the old days, before I met Paula," he was saying to the owner over coffee at around seven-thirty, while the rest of the crew had begun its work in the basement and the downstairs bath, "I didn't care about what I did the night before as long as I could get to the job and I didn't care about the job as long as I could do whatever I wanted to do the night before...."

She laughed, and he noticed that she had an odd little tic in her right cheek that made the skin pulse in a sort of digital way.

"It's hard work, isn't it?" she said.

Sting shook his head.

"Not any more, really. Just now and then, like when one of my guys took sick and I had to hump the sheet-rock myself. But, naw, mostly not, not anymore."

"It's all mental?"

"Aesthetic," Sting said. "It's all aesthetic."

"I like that," the owner said, nodding slightly. "But now I have to get to the office. Help yourself to the rest of the coffee...." She paused.

He nodded.

"Thanks," he said. And now and then over the course of the morning he thought about that moment, but then they had a problem with a beam. And then it was the end of the workday and he went home to walk Lord Jeffrey and make his supper.

Paula called him just as he was doing the dishes.

"Janice is in bed," she said.

"Oh, my God," Sting said.

"She took pills. She's all right but she's going to be in for a couple of days. I can't leave."

"I understand," he said.

"Are you okay?"

"Not too bad. We had trouble with a beam this morning…."

"And how's Lord Jeff?"

"Good as ever."

"I miss him," she said.

"And me?"

"I miss both my dogs."

"Ruff," he said. "Ah-whoogh!" he said as a bark.

And she laughed. Her wrist was much better, and he was happy to hear about that.

"And Sting?"

"Yeah?"

"In the natural foods supermarket? I saw Jimmy Buffet."

He read a little more Eliade, and did some stretching in bed, as though the mattress were water and he was making a bridge across this broad liquid divide. That's what he was doing when the telephone rang.

"Hello?"

"Charles, it's Mom."

"Mom," he said. "What are you doing up so late?"

"I can't sleep anymore, at least not in a regular way. How are you?"

"I'm fine, Mom. Working hard, the usual. I'm sorry, I should have called you."

"Well, I called you first." She cleared her throat and he could hear the residue of her last cigarette, which was still probably smoldering in the ashtray near the telephone.

"Let me say hello to Paula. Or is she asleep?"

"She's in Florida." To his mother's increasing dismay, he explained about his sister-in-law, the child's death, all that, including Paula's wrist.

"The poor dear," his mother said. "All the poor dears. You're there alone?"

"Just me and Lord Jeffrey, Mom."

"Lord who? Oh, the dog."

"Right."

"And you don't know when Paula's coming back?"

"Not for a couple more days, Mom."

"In that case, have supper with me tomorrow night."

He put the book down and settled in toward sleep, feeling much more comfortable in his solitude than the night before, and feeling kind of stupid about it. Except when his father died and he spent a couple of nights at his mother's house while Paula stayed here because of her job, they hadn't been separated in ten years. He thought of that on the ride over the next day, an hour's drive, west along the river and then a jog north, right from the owner's house where he knocked off a little bit early. What if Paula's plane crashed on the way home? Or what if he hit someone head-on on his way to his mother's? All these stupid thoughts....

But that's how he came to be sitting in his mother's crowded little kitchen, a room that smelled of stale cigarettes and buttery cooking, early the next evening, something he hadn't done without Paula by his side for a long time.

"Geena made us your special lamb chops, you just have to heat them up," she said, this wizened little woman, her white hair shrunk like a skull-cap atop her walnut-shaped skull, her blank and wandering eyes moving in counterpoint to the trail of smoke from the cigarette dangling from her fingers.

"Good, Mom," Sting said. "Thanks for thinking of me."

"I think about you all the time, Charles." She held her cigarette up in the air and reached over and touched his chest. "Ah… It is really you." She ran her hand over his skull and forehead, her nicotine-scented fingers lingering on his nose and then his cheeks.

"Sorry, Mom. I haven't shaved."

"Oh, you're always my little boy, beard or no."

Sting gave his head a little shake, feeling a bit embarrassed and glad that she couldn't see him blush.

"So, hey, time to eat?"

"Will you serve me, Charles?"

She aimed the cigarette at an ashtray in the center of the table and crushed it out.

"Sure, Mom. Here we go."

He went to the stove and heated up the meal, staring at the clock above the stove and watching the second hand. He served her, they ate. After he cleaned up, she asked him, as she always did, to read, something he didn't usually mind doing, but tonight it somehow didn't sit right with him.

"I don't know, Mom," he said. "The dog's home alone, I've got to get back."

"What about this old dog, your own mother, sitting home alone every night?"

"Okay, okay, Mom. What would you like?"

"The Book is on the counter." She gestured behind her. "Geena marked the place where she left off."

He picked up the large blue leather Bible and began to read.

"'Exodus, Chapter 32.' 'And when the people saw that Moses delayed to come down out of the mount, the people gathered themselves together unto Aaron, and said unto him, Up, make us gods, which shall go before us; for as for this Moses, the man that brought us up out of the land of Egypt, we wot not what is come of him....'"

"'Wot,'" she said. "'Wot not.'"

"I guess that's 'know,' Ma," Sting said. "'Know not.'"

"Smart boy," she said.

Sting stayed silent.

"Please," his mother said.

He cleared his throat and read a little farther: "And Aaron said unto them, break off your golden earrings which are in the ears of your wives, of your sons, and of your daughters, and bring them unto me... And all the people brake off the golden earrings which were in their ears, and brought them unto Aaron...And he received them at their hand, and fashioned it with a graving tool, after he had made it a molten calf...."

Sting looked up from the page and saw that his mother had fallen asleep. But he no sooner closed the book than she opened her eyes and stared directly at him in that uncanny way that made him think she still possessed her sight.

"'Wot,'" she said. "'Wot not.' I have to remember that." She made a funny little sound in her throat and her dead eyes twitched, almost as though she'd suffered a small electrical shock. "We read the Book every year now. Why didn't I remember this part?"

"I don't know, Mom," Sting said.

"You were always such a good boy," she said. "Helping your father, helping me."

"Yes, Mom," he said, turning to look at the clock.

"Where are you going?" she said.

"Home, Mom," he said. "I have to go home."

"'Wot,'" she said. "'Wot not.'"

The telephone rang soon after he got back to the house but the dog was desperate to go out, jumping, moaning, leaping at his chest, so he let it ring and went for their walk.

"Where were you?" Paula said when they returned. "I've been calling you."

Her voice settled a bit after he explained.

"How was she?"

"The same," Sting said. "Enjoying her Bible. How's Janice?"

"I can't leave her just yet."

"Do what you have to do," Sting said, and later, lying in bed again, thinking about his handicapped mother, his own life, he wondered at this new sensation of having lost a limb, feeling so strange without Paula on the other side of him. But, he had to admit, it was also quite liberating.

"I could feel guilty," he said to Lord Jeffrey on their walk the next evening. "I should feel guilty," he said to Paula later on that night, "you're down there doing family duty and I'm up here just doing my usual thing."

"Well, now I wish you had come. I didn't know I was going to have to stay this long. But Sting, she doesn't have anybody else."

"No friends?"

"There's this guy...."

"One of her many."

"Don't be so hard on her, she's in such terrible pain...."

"I do feel guilty," he said as he got in to bed and picked up the Eliade and then set it down. He lay there, propped against the pillow, for what seemed like a long while, amazed at how just the night before he was feeling disturbed by the very same freedom that he was thoroughly enjoying right now.

Early the next morning on the job, the owner was there, offering him coffee. He drank with her and lingered a while, talking about the job, asking her about her own work.

"This is what I like best," he said, "making my own time. What about you? What's your job like?"

"A real push," she said. "I may be standing here at seven thirty right now, but I won't be home until nine tonight, maybe later."

"I thought government work was by the clock," Sting said.

"Not what I do," she said.

"Can you tell me what it is?"

She laughed, and it caught Sting by surprise.

"I'm not a spy or anything like that. I work at Treasury, in a special department." She saw the question on his face but didn't answer it.

Two men, the short Salvadoran and one of the grizzled carpenters from Maryland, came up out of the basement. They stood there.

"Guys?"

"I should get to work," the owner said. "I've got an early meeting."

Sting nodded.

"Looks like we're going to have a meeting right now ourselves."

It was always something on the job, though this time it turned out to be relatively minor, a problem with some of the wiring that Sting figured out for them within a few minutes. That was just how he was, a practical guy, sharpshooter.

"Nice looking woman," the carpenter said.

"I think she's gay," Sting said.

"Good," the carpenter said. "Makes it easier to talk to her, don't it?"

The rest of the day went smoothly. Too bad, he was thinking to himself on the drive home, that he couldn't fix his life the way he could do renovations. Or fix his sister-in-law's life. The awfulness of her loss was just sort of sinking in. How often had he and Paula joked about how lucky they were not to have kids, just a dog.

He walked Lord Jeffrey as soon as he got home and then made himself a dinner of beans and franks—a kid's dinner, he noted to himself, while shaking his head at Lord Jeffrey who begged incessantly from beneath the table. Give him nothing from the table and he'll live to a ripe old age, that was his motto. While he was rinsing the dishes, Paula called and told him that she wasn't ready to come back just yet.

"Hey," he said, "I'm not counting, but it's going to be a week pretty soon."

"Sting, she needs me."

"I know," he said. "I know. You have to stay there as long as you need to."

"Thanks for understanding."

"Uh-huh," he said, as Lord Jeffrey bumped against his leg. "Want to say hello to your dog?"

"I thought I already was."

That got a laugh out of him.

So, another night without her wasn't the end of the world. He made the most of it, watching the cable news for a while—nothing but debris, the aftermath of a bad election—and then picking up the Eliade again, but putting it down after just skimming a page or so and sitting there thinking about their childless state, their ordinary life together, sparked only now and then with the kind of spontaneity that used to be the normal way for them.

He hated himself for wondering, as he got up from his chair, if his sister-in-law would stay in Key West, so that they might visit from time to time. And then he gave himself a mental kick in the butt—worrying about his vacations when her little boy was dead!

"Lord Jeff?" he called. "One more time around the block?"

They were going out the door when the telephone rang.

"Whoa," he said to the anxious dog and pulled back and went to answer the call, worried that it might be some more terrible news from Florida.

"Sting?"

He didn't recognize the woman's voice and so found it exceedingly strange to hear her say his name.

Of course it was the owner. Her hot water heater had sprung a leak and she wouldn't have called him about it—she would have called the furnace guy who serviced her—except that the flood was beginning to rise high enough to possibly ruin the tools and materials his crew had left in the basement.

It happens, he said to himself on the ride over. He remembered wind-storms that blew new roofs into back yards, he remembered lightning that set a half-built upper story on fire, he remembered rains that turned foundations into ponds and basements into bogs, he remembered a lawn turned to mud that sucked in an old van of his up to the fenders. Yes, it happens. And this was happening, too, everything tumbling into place without him really knowing where he was going.

She was waiting at the front door dressed in a dark blue running suit with a big yellow M on the left thigh.

"Thank God," she said, touching a hand to his arm, and gesturing toward the basement door, as if he had arrived at the house for the first time.

He brushed past her, taking in her perfume. The steps to the basement were gaily lit and as he descended he could sniff the familiar scents, the dust and oils and wood, of the job, and a certain foreign odor that he could not place.

But no water. The wood-floor they had laid at the foot of the steps was dry. Back behind the new room they were constructing, the cement floor was dry. Seeing the dry floor around the water heater, he knelt down and touched the cement, just to be sure, and it felt rough and dry to his fingertips. Starting up the stairs in a rush he had to stop himself. He stood there, feeling his blood rise, and then he could move again. The owner was waiting for him in the kitchen.

"I lied," she said, holding out a bottle of beer.

"What the hell?" he said, refusing the offer.

"I didn't know any other way. I've never done anything like this before." She contracted her face into a little smile that Sting actually found rather appealing.

"This is really crazy," Sting said.

"I know," the owner said. "I know, I know."

The odd smell drifted up from the basement, now awfully familiar but still something he could not name. And then he figured it out, that the smell was the sweet stink of his own sweat.

"I better go," he said.

"You don't even want a sip?" she said, holding out the bottle.

"Naw, thanks," he said, but stupidly—a reflex—reached toward the bottle.

She caught him by the wrist and without missing a beat led him along the hall and had them standing near the front door but just as close to the entrance to the dimly lighted living room.

It was a dance, yes? Stepping this way and that. But it was also like falling down a flight of stairs. In a moment they stumbled to the sofa. And then she dropped to her knees before him and pulled his shoes off, knocking the beer onto the carpet. It was like a dream, it was wot, it was wot not. And then a mock-wrestling match with a lot of childish giggling, and then a hasty strip show, and then just plain fucking.

Hours later, it seemed stupid to be driving home only to have to turn around and return to this job. But he drove it, feeling as though he had left his body behind at the owner's house but still needing desperately to sleep.

At his own front door, in the faint first light of dawn, he fumbled with the keys, dropped them on the steps, and retrieved them, while Lord Jeffrey barked his head off on the other side of the door.

Finally, he let himself inside.

Lord Jeffrey jumped toward his chest.

"Down, damn it!" he said, pushing the dog aside.

The telephone was ringing, his heart was pounding, the dog barked and barked and barked until Sting grabbed him by the collar and slammed him against the living room wall. It left him breathless.

Moonrise, Hernandez, New Mexico, 1941

Originally published in *New Letters*

I n the first hour north out of Ghost Ranch in the station wagon packed to the roof—and him on the verge of grief—they had stopped along the river, and he helped Michael with the view-finder of the small box camera, while Cedric, his tall, jaunty-nosed former best man, wandered off along the pebbled bank in search of his own visions.

"We'll sit awhile," AA said to his son.

As if on the mark of some invisible choreographer, together they sank onto their buttocks on the hard surface, feet pointing toward the sparkling rushing water. For a short while, they watched their breath curl up in the cool air. The morning light had given him such hope—fierce cool luminescence that seemed to emanate in perfect harmony from every cliff-face, rock formation, and stand of pines. So far nothing had come of it.

"See that cliff?" he said, breaking the silence.

"Yes, Daddy," Michael said. He was a thin child, built like AA himself, with soft touches that certainly came from his mother's side. How odd that in nature you could not make out such easily divisible mathematical properties; but in your own family, in your children, you could do the math easily. Head, mine. Eyes, hers. Nose, mine. Lips? Well, he couldn't really make a decision about the lips. But chin? Yes, his chin. For his daughter, at home with her mother—this was an excursion for men and boys—he could do the same.

Insects floated past. Buzzed, buzzed.

The river sparkled.

"Do you recognize it?" AA said, pointing to the cliff face to their north.

"I don't know."

"Miss O'Keeffe made it."

"She made the cliff, pop?"

"She made a painting of the cliff."

"Did I see it?"

"It's in a museum in…somewhere. Did you like the stew she made last night? The chicken fell away from the bone."

"The peppers made me sneeze."

"Your taste leans toward your mother's side," AA said. "Your mother doesn't like things spicy."

A light came into the boy's eye.

"Do you miss her, Daddy?" Michael said.

"I do," AA said.

"She says you're happy to get away from her," Michael said.

"She shouldn't say those things." He quieted himself down and touched his son's shoulder. "Look at that."

A hawk paused high above the river, as though pinned against an azul cloth backdrop.

"Daddy, are you and mom going to get a divorce?"

AA shook his head at the thought, at the air.

"Did she say that, too?"

"She asked me not to say what she says."

"But you just told me."

"No, I was just asking."

"She writes me another letter like the kind I got last night—"

He fritzed air across his lips, trying to stop himself from further speech. Oh, speech! What good did it do? Always getting him into trouble. And her. Writing that letter.

"What did she write, Daddy?"

Foolish naïve fellow that he was, he was about to explain, when Cedric came wandering back.

"Sun's nice," he said, removing his eye-glasses and wiping the back of his hand across his brow.

"Any luck?" AA said.

Cedric shook his head. Flecks of gray in his hair caught the early sun. "I'm not like you, Ansel. I don't know what to look for. I didn't see anything."

"Oh, no, no. Everyone has an eye. It's like fishing. Some days they just aren't biting. Let's try somewhere else."

They got up and returned to the station wagon.

"What's not biting, Daddy?" Michael spoke up from the back seat.

"Things," he said.

"What kind of things?"

"The way things look," he said.

"Pictures?"

AA glanced into the rear-view mirror, seeing just the top of his young son's head.

"*Photo*graphs, *photo*graphs."

"Votographs," the boy said, catching the rhythm of the game they had played on and off in the car all the way from Yosemite.

"Smotographs," Cedric said.

"Hopigraphs." AA said.

"Navajographs," Cedric said.

"Uh-uh," AA said.

"Ok, then, Smokographs."

"Good."

"Daddy?"

"Yes?"

"Eggographs."

"What?"

"I mean, yolkographs."

"The yoke's on you, son."

"Ansel," Cedric said. "Now I know why you take photographs."

"Why?"

"Because you're not much good at anything else."

With a nod, AA acknowledged his friend's joking remark and then kept silent awhile. Cliffs made a blur of clayey orange and soft browns. The river, which they were following, curved into a small canyon and dipped out of sight.

"Daddy?"

"Yes, Michael?"

"What is it?"

"What's what?"

"What's divorce?"

Cedric frowned at his friend.

"What have you fellows been talking about?"

AA shook his head.

"Nothing. Virginia talks to the kids, tries to turn them against me."

"She says you want a divorce?"

AA shook his head again, staring at his son in the rear-view mirror.

"Let's not talk about it now."

They rode in silence. Light danced along the tree line. Miles and miles up the Chama Valley they stopped for lunch, a lovely repast, as it turned out, that Miss O'Keeffe, herself, prepared for them early that morning before she set out on her daily work.

Slices of roasted turkey.

Freshly baked tortillas.

(He had awakened to the sound of Miss O'Keeffe's housekeeper slapping the masa between her hands before setting it in the oven to bake. Patta-pat, patta-patta-pat.)

Sweet peppers.

Almond paste sweets.

Lemonade from a tall jug, which he poured into the cups she had packed along with everything else.

Now the sun poised at full mast. Nothing but approving mouth-noises as the three of them ate.

Then Michael went down a few yards toward the river—it had reappeared again at the turn of the road where they had stopped to eat—to pee.

Which gave Cedric the opportunity to speak about what—given the look in his eyes—seemed to have been troubling him.

"This makes me sad, Ansel," he said.

"What does?"

"What does? This talk about ending it."

"Me, too," AA said.

"But you're just the husband," Cedric said. "Think of how it makes the best man feel."

They both laughed just as Michael worked his way back up the slope, arms swinging for ballast.

"What's so funny?" Michael said.

Children had it both ways. They could disengage easily from the talk of adults. Then, on occasion—right now—they fiercely demanded their rights to be included.

"Nothing."

"It's not nothing. Tell me what."

Cedric spoke up.

"Your father and I were recalling something funny that once happened to us."

"What?" Michael said in a rather ferocious manner that was unusual for him.

"I…" AA talked now. "I was taking a picture but forgot to take the lens cap off. One of the oldest and dumbest mistakes known to man."

"Whose picture?" Michael said.

"I don't remember that."

"You remember the joke," Michael said.

"Sometimes that's all we remember," AA said. "A joke is like a ghost of something funny that's happened. Hey, see those trees?" He pointed up the slope. "Who's for a little nap in the shade?"

"I thought we were going to take pictures," Michael said.

"You can't just take a picture for the sake of taking one," AA said. "You have to find the right opportunity."

"All you make is trees and rocks and sky," Michael said.

AA shook his head.

"Did you just think of that?"

"Why?"

"Nothing."

The boys eyes flashed.

"Mom said it. I agree." The boy folded his arms across his chest. AA felt an icy heaviness slant along his own sternum as he walked the few yards to the spot that a few moments before had seemed ideal for napping.

Now he couldn't rest, his mind roaring with all this turmoil, Virginia's arguments against him, poisoning the children, dissenting from his art. Once she had understood him so clearly; now it seemed—now, now, the miserable now of now—that she was turning against him and, worse, turning the children against him.

The brushing of the wind in the leaves, sounding like a river running in air—the shift back and forth between light and shadow as clouds played across the face of the sun—Cedric's labored breathing as his friend sank into slumber—all this kept him awake—and then he was out—awakened by Michael's shout.

"Look! Look!"

The boy pointed up at the blue scrim of sky where a hawk rose high above them, a wriggling vine—rope?—snake!—in its talons.

Cedric sat up.

"What is it?"

His eyes followed Michael's pointing finger.

"Oh," he said, "the flag of Mexico."

***

Why was he doing this? Driving along, wrestling with life, with time, damned drag on all, himself, the children, not to mention *HER*, time and light, f-stop of things, flash and ripple sunlit river, glint of hawk's eye, eagle-claw, driving down this road look at cactus sky mountains horizon, what? Michael asks me something what? Sorry I was daydreaming, go back to sleep.

…Ice-chill in my chest thinking of her words can't even remember specific but she makes a mood even at this remove using the children I would write you my love in a myriad shining lines shine on Republic roll on Jeffers' lines there's a poet I would be the ocean The deep dark-shining Pacific Pacific leans on the land feeling his cold strength to the outermost margins let me see do I remember? Yes, I remember The extraordinary patience of things! This beautiful place defaced with a crop of suburban houses—How beautiful when we first beheld it, Unbroken field of poppy and lupin walled with clean cliffs; No intrusion but two or three horses pasturing, Or a few milch cows rubbing their flanks on the outcrop rockheads—Now the spoiler has come: does it care? Not faintly. It has it has…all time. It knows the people are a tide That swells and in time will ebb, and all Their works dissolve. Meanwhile the image of the pristine beauty Lives in the very grain of the granite, Safe as the endless ocean that climbs our cliff.—As for us: We must uncenter our minds from ourselves; We must unhumanize our views a little, and become confident As the rock and ocean that we were made from. And if I could make something as beautiful as that what would I be?

From the back seat: "Daddy?"

"Yes, Michael?"

"I'm thirsty."

"Cedric? Oh, he's asleep. Wait, Michael."

"Daddy?"

"I know you must be tired. It was an empty day. We didn't catch any fish. We're going home," he said.

"We weren't fishing, Daddy."

"That was a metaphor, son. Comes from poetry. You have to listen to some poetry. Want me to say a poem for you?"

"I'm tired," Michael said.

"All right. Now just dig into the pack, and you'll find the water-bottles. Just behind you."

"So much stuff here, Daddy."

"I know, I know. Who knows where anything is? Can you wait a little while? We'll be back in Taos before too long. You can get a long cool drink at Mrs. Luhan's. And we'll eat a good dinner. They'll roast some-thing. They're always roasting something. Can you wait?"

"I think so."

"Good. You're a good boy, Michael."

They traveled a few more miles on this rocky road.

Then he spoke out.

"What's that, Daddy?" Michael said.

"More poetry, son. I'm remembering. 'The extraordinary patience of things! This beautiful place defaced with a crop of suburban houses— / How beautiful when we first beheld it, Unbroken field of poppy and lupin walled with clean cliffs;/ No intrusion but two or three horses pas-turing,/ Or a few milch cows rubbing their flanks on the outcrop rock-heads—/ Now the spoiler has come: does it care?/ Not faintly. It has all time. It knows the people are a tide/ That swells and in time will ebb, and all/ Their works dissolve. Meanwhile the image of the pristine beau-ty/ Lives in the very grain of the granite,/ Safe as the endless ocean that climbs our cliff.—As for us:/ We must uncenter our minds from our-selves;/We must unhumanize our views a little, and become confident/ As the rock and ocean....'"

The voice—his own—fell silent.

As they approached the village of Hernandez, a moon the size of a small coin rose in the east over distant clouds and snowpeaks; and in the west, the late afternoon sun gained the crest of a south-flowing cloud bank and splashed its final brilliance upon the crosses in the cemetery of the church rough-tough O'Keeffe had painted some years before.

He steered the station wagon into the deep shoulder at the side of the road, and stopped and jumped out, running to the rear of the vehicle and wrenching open the gate.

"Cedric. Michael. We don't have much time."

View camera, lens!

He was breathing heavily, heavily but steadily.

Assembled!

Still in control of his breath.

Image, composed and focused.

"Ansel?" Cedric called out.

"The light meter, where is it?"

He heard his voice rise, nearly as high as the rising moon.

"Daddy?"

"Help Cedric find the light meter, son. Hurry, hurry."

Behind him the sun was about to disappear again behind the clouds. He was desperate, holding his breath. Here was the dream part, the rest all real. Doing the math for a celestial body as easily as he might have for someone in his own family posed there before him—it came to him that the luminance of the moon was two hundred and fifty candles per square foot. He placed this value on Zone VII of the exposure scale— with the Wratten G (No.15) deep yellow filter, the exposure was one second at f/32. He had no accurate reading of the shadow foreground values. He released the shutter and breathed deeply at last. After the first exposure, he quickly reversed the 8-by-10 film holder to make a duplicate negative, for he knew in his nerves he had visualized one of those important images that seem prone to accident or physical defect. As he pulled out the slide, the sunlight left the crosses.

"Daddy?"

"Yes, Michael?"

He was drenched in sweat, as though he had waded into a pond up to his shoulders.

"I found the light meter."

"You did? Good lad. I'm amazed we can find anything in this car."

"Here," Michael said.

"Too late," AA said, taking the instrument from his son. "But thank you. I think we did all right."

Cedric, taking off his eyeglasses, rubbed his face with his knuckles.

"What did you get? Were they biting?"

"Maybe a big one," AA said.

"I don't see what you were looking at," Cedric said.

"Put your glasses back on."

Cedric complied. The sky had darkened in the east, and now all the horizon had melted into a dense muddy line broken here and there only by larger trails of dust and smoke.

"I still don't see."

AA took another deep breath and nodded at his dear friend, best pal, member of the wedding a long time ago. And the boy standing next to him, this child he loved so much. What would happen to him? And to his daughter? To all of them?

"You will see," he said, feeling his grieving heart turn into a bright cold moon the size of a coin. "I hope. I do hope."

In the
Kauri Forest

Originally published in *Ploughshares*

When do you begin traveling? When your airplane lifts off the ground? When you leave your house for the road? When you pack? When the plan first comes to mind? When you admit to how restless and ill-at-ease, even murderous, you feel at home? When you take your first steps? When you emerge from the womb? And what is love? Do you know what that is? Could it be the opposite of traveling? And if so, then what is hate?

You couldn't ask these questions, no matter how ferociously they burned in your mind, of a man in wool products, could you?

Wool products. Avery's seat-mate had spent his life in wool products. Not surprising, since the balding, pale-faced old fellow man had grown up in a country of forty million sheep. The man informed him before take-off in Los Angeles that he had been visiting his daughter who lived in Nevada, married to a casino manager. And went on to talk about what luck! What odds! How fortunate, his little girl, born in the faraway island nation toward which they would be flying all night, to have met a man at college who emigrated to the U.S. and went into the gaming business.

The wool-man puffed foul animal breath into the air between them as he spoke. But Avery couldn't help but listen.

"All of us Kiwis know we have to travel out, because nobody's ever coming here, we're so far away from everything else. Kids these days call it the O.E. Overseas Experience. My generation, we called it going to war. Because that's where we went."

The wool-man talked on into the first hours of the flight, leaving Avery hardly any room to tell his own story. Which was just well. He became quite interested in the red wine served by the tidily efficient flight attendants. After a while the wool-man slept, leaving Avery with no ear but his own mind's ear and the sorrowful story of what it meant to be married to a woman who left you for your younger brother.

So the night-flight passed for him in a haze of dozing and drinking. Eventually they descended through fog and rain and touched down on the tarmac in Auckland.

The wool-man sat up, suddenly awake and alert.

"You'll be driving then, mate?"

Avery nodded, and the wool-man tapped him on the shoulder.

"Don't forget, keep to the left."

And then he was traveling again, in his rental car, in a light rain—early summer it was down here—keeping to the left—STAY LEFT, STAY ALIVE, said the sticker in the lower right hand corner of the driver's-side front window—powered by his own juices of anger, regret, astonishment, yearning, regret (a lot of regret), and (more anger transformed into) fury.

Four hours to the Opua ferry, or so stated his map purchased weeks before in a small bookshop in Marin. He was grateful for what he took to be an unseasonable rainstorm—after all, it was summer in the Antipodes, and summer meant warm sun, few clouds—so that about two hours north of the city limits he could pull over onto the side of the road, heavenly jade green hills and clouds white as sheep abounding, and close his eyes. Oh, wool-man! Bah-bah, so many white sheep!

And then he was driving again, noticing signs for Wellsford, then Maungaturoto then Waipu. The exotic names conjured up a lost time, a lost place, imaginary locations in stories their father had read to them when they were children. When the sun did appear at last as he approached a town called Whangarei, he found green ocean and dark distant islands to his right, hills with giant palm ferns on his left. And he stayed to the left on the road—

Now, at last, a notice for the ferry—Opua, 2 km.—with the glint of sun on the narrow neck of the Bay of Islands, a smooth ride on the ten-car auto-ferry, twelve minutes or so, and then he was driving again. But not for long. Up a hill, round a leafy curve, a few more turns, and he was gliding, exhausted, into the water-side village of Russell where he planned—it was the only plan he had made after deciding to come all this distance to get away— to celebrate New Year's Eve by himself.

***

Which would turn out to be a quiet event under the management of Kip and Mary Perkins, owners and managers of Kauri Tops, the lodging Avery had secured at the last minute from a rather uninterested travel agent in Marin. He had asked for a trip to somewhere as far away as possible where he still might speak English and a place to stay that was comfortable and private, something low-key, none of these sports and hiking lodges he had read about in the brochures, and that was what he got, a small sparely furnished room in a light-drenched house of three stories built up onto the side of a hill overlooking the Bay of Islands.

The view made it feel like a dream-accommodation. After a solo meal of roast game-fish—employing the conventional wisdom, he had predicted lamb, and flunked—in the pleasant dining room on the second floor of the lodge Avery retired to his room, and wrapped himself in his jet-lag, which was considerable after the fourteen hour flight from Los Angeles and his several hours in the car driving north.

Of course he lay awake, imagining his wife in his brother's arms, her mouth on his genitals, his brother staring wall-eyed—he was ugly from birth and would remain ugly in memory, as long as Avery lived—at whatever ceiling beneath which they performed these pernicious acts. In a break from his pornographic self-torture Avery recalled an incident in which he and Nicholas had been burning garbage in a field near their old house in Jersey when they were both quite young, deciding that he should have set the slightly younger sibling on fire and left him to die. Oh, my God, he writhed and moaned in his bed. This was worse than he ever could have imagined, to have come all this distance to get away and find that the worst remained at home in his own mind! Time was all screwed up. Light splashed across the windows and he fell finally into a deep sleep until late afternoon.

At first he tried to lose himself in the plans for the evening. His hosts were going to make a New Year's Eve meal that would be entirely organic. Didn't that sound swell?

"My brother's always teased me about my eating habits," he said to his hosts on his way out the door for a walk. (Stop talking about him! he chided himself.) But he could hear the bastard's voice in his ear, so close it burned the hairs—heat surged up along his arms, converging in his chest in a great unsounded roar of anger and despite. He'd like to cut Nicholas into bloody chunks of meat and serve them up to Carrie in a beautiful adulterer's stew.

He excused himself so that he might take his walk.

"Oh, yes, of course, do walk," Kip Perkins said. "Head down along the Strand. The water's lovely." And to Avery's back as he went out the door, said "If you'd like to take a longer hike tomorrow I'll be happy to take you on a tour of the Kauri trees in the forest near Mangamuka to celebrate the New Year."

Celebrate? Avery didn't turn around. Rude, he knew, but he didn't want Perkins to see his face, growing darker and darker with anger, hate, humiliation, and some emotions he hadn't yet found a name for playing across his mouth and lips and making his eyes burn.

By the time he reached the bottom of the hill and walked some distance along the paved path that curved around at the water's edge, some of his anger had dissipated. The curtain of the sky, bleached white near the horizon line, rose above the village of Paihia just across the stretch of water, and higher up reached the merge of peaches and mauves, neargreens. Evening was drawing near, and he felt something more than jetlag. Soul-lag, he wanted to call it.

Nothing helped with it. *Opua*…He said the word aloud, enjoying the foreign deliciousness of the vowels. *Pahia. Kerekeri.* He was a wimp that way, he admitted it, a former Marine who loved language.

A light breeze blew in off the waters. The top of the hill behind the town lay in early darkness, a few large thunderheads vaulted across the Bay. Voices echoed along the Strand, families closing ranks together in the warm dark. A few men laughed sharply, pulling their beers closer to their lips. Down the way a small dock shimmered in its legacy of bulbs and breeze. A restaurant with a few tables glowing white in the fading light—and a sign above it—*Kamakura*. In the west a last faint remainder of the day slid behind clouds like a wholeness that in its essence was loose and liquid, an egg-yoke sliding off a plate onto a table. To the east a hill blocked even the thought that an ocean lay a short distance in that direction. To the north clouds tamped down thoughts of light. To the south, the path leading him back to his lodging.

Avery—a man going in every direction at once, and nowhere, at the same time.

***

The back patio of the lodge was strewn with lights, and a small group (of guests, he presumed, though they had not been at his solitary dinner of the evening before) hovered around the goldfish pond.

"A Kiwi tradition," said his host upon seeing him approach.

"Is it really Kiwi?" his wife spoke up. "I thought it was Chinese."

"Bloody Chinese," said one of the other guests. "It's all them right now, isn't it?"

"They're a bit bigger than us, aren't they, then?" said Kip, not just playing host but being a true host. All were welcome, Kiwis, Chinese (though there were none among them), Americans (of whom Avery was the only representative), German (a couple who had sat quietly cooing at each other at dinner, so obviously in love they were either on their honeymoon or very good actors). Kip made Avery feel welcome, though there was something about his manner that was a bit too effeminate for his taste.

A cry went up around the pond as Kip Perkins released a pail full of goldfish into the water.

"One for each of you!" he announced. "Now you each have a fish, and one New Year's wish to make on it."

Avery shivered slightly as a cool breeze blew up the hill from the bay. The shape of the shoreline across the water glittered with trembling lights, so many you would think this remote location, Russell, Bay of Islands, North Island, New Zealand, surrounded by the South Pacific and the Tasman Sea, might be somewhat near the center of the universe.

"And yours?" Kip had come around to him while he had been standing there, thinking.

"Classified," Avery said.

"Of course, of course," Kip said, "just making sure you made one."

"I did," Avery said. But he was lying. And so he now went through a skein of wishes in his mind right then and there, from Carrie's sorrow to his brother's murder to more calming thoughts of finding some kind of peace and resolution over the next few weeks while he traveled. His goldfish would certainly die from the terrible burden he placed on it.

***

Kiwi dreams. Afterwards, that's how he would think of them. But while he spent his second night here in flux, he put no name to it, only ran and swam and flew—uh-huh!—in classic Freudian fashion, which he had never experienced before, only read about in his one aborted term of graduate school when he was waiting to be shipped out during Desert Storm.

Flying, flew, flown!

A few fleeting faces of people he didn't recognize, but no her, no him, a rush of air, over seas, waterfalls, great caverns, Fingel's Cave, waves lapping, sea-birds wings outstretched.

Big man, he woke in the night crying.

But in the morning he sat up feeling rested. Perhaps his jet-lag had flown? Good, good.

Still, while he took a shower and shaved and dressed, he mourned, he mourned the marriage, mourned for himself.

You don't just—

No, you don't!

***

But you can try, God damn it! You can try!

***

Twisting, twisting about under the shower-head, hoping to wash all, everything, away.

He stared down at the drain, which ran clock-wise—everything turned around down here in the Antipodes.

***

He had missed breakfast, but so what? The thought of all that food turning to shit inside him turned his stomach. He grunted through a dozen pushups and then bent himself in two for some sun salutations—Carrie's influence—in front of the window. Where was he going? Where had he been? Sunlight on the water sharpened his glance when he started to long for some sense, some hope, made him blink with over-excitation of the eye. He couldn't move. He mustn't think.

A sharp rap at the door.

***

"Onward to the Kauri forest," Kip Perkins said as they climbed into the Kiwi's little Ford.

For the first half hour after the ferry, they drove along a smooth paved two-lane highway, and then took a gravel side road that after a while became rutted dirt. Kip talked more than Avery had bargained for. Turned out he had served in Kuwait, and beyond—Arabs, sand, oil fires, bodies on fire. Avery kept quiet, observing the countryside thick with sheep [he thought of the wool-man], a few cows, a farmhouse here and there.

"I grew up in the city—" Auckland, that turned out, Kip meant. "All of this is still new to me. We've only been here a few years. Military's behind me. I'm into conservation now."

"Sounds like a good idea," Avery said, wishing he held as much of the conviction as his host.

Suddenly they stopped, and for an instant Avery was sure they had run something over. But Kip pulled the car onto the shoulder alongside a couple of other vehicles and climbed out.

Avery followed.

"We're here?"

"Just a tramp across that field," Kip said, pointing beyond the road.

Across the road and up and over a stile and into an uneven field mined with sheep-flop. Avery might have thought to have been in Vermont or Kansas somewhere until he spied a flock of large birds with sooty wings, bright blue underparts, large bright red bills strutting past with jerky heads.

"What?" he said.

"Pukekos," Kip said. "Plenty of those around here."

"Pukeko," Avery repeated.

"Now you're talking Kiwi, mate," Kip said.

To his new vocabulary, built with Kip's instruction as they climbed over another stile and walked toward a spreading forest wall about a half-mile away, Avery added Kokako, the name of a variety of native crow, a grayish bird with blue wattles at its throat that made bell-like calls of descending pitch as it skirted midway through the distance between them and the trees, and some other names of grasses and low shrubs.

There were a few other new birds. But the Kauris awaited him after one more stile.

"See them?" Kip spoke with almost parental pride. "The leafy branches that make up the upper roof of the forest?"

Yes, Kip saw them, the tallest trees riding above an already substantial canopy, and then had to lower his head and watch his step as they descended into a small draw and moved forward and up a few feet into the shade of the outer wall of the forest. From spiking sunlight to the rippling shade as if walking underwater—in a couple of steps he and Kip had transformed their surroundings. His breathing, slightly elevated from the tramp across the fields, now seemed tied to the stippled shadowing by the big trees on the other smaller trees, made by the leafy ferns on his arms and trouser-legs.

"You see these?"

Avery followed his glance.

"These ferns are the signature of our little country. This is called Ponga. And here's Rahurahu…."

"Rahurahu," Avery said after him.

"Yis, yis, and this? Para." Kip fondled a small fern growing in profusion at the base of a large tree. It was like watching a parent with a very young child. "And here is Piupiu…."

"Sure," Avery said, "I knew that," and found himself laughing for the first time in a long while. "Piupiu. Kids must have a field day with that one. Literally."

"You have kids?" Kip said, leading him past the immediate curtain of trees.

"No, never did," Avery said. "And that looks like a good thing, now."

"Really?"

"Now that I'm…we're getting a divorce."

"Well, yis, I did that once. When I came back from the service, it all seemed to have gone wrong."

"Something like that," Avery said.

"And you can't salvage it? You're down here now, with plenty of time to think. Perhaps there's a way. Time may work it out. It did for me."

Avery shook his head, meaning, I can't talk about it.

"Sorry, mate," Kip said as he led Avery along a muddy trail that wound among the trunks of what turned out to be the very Kauri trees they had come to see. "This'll give you something else to think about. Here they are. Look how big around."

Nothing a man or even two or three men could hug, the trees were that huge.

"Like sequoias," Avery said, tilting his chin up to get a glimpse of the upper story of trunk and underside of leaf.

"Older, I think," Kip said. "Two thousand to four thousand years old these are. When even the Maori were just glints in the eyes of their forebears, and white men were still black—just a joke, of course, mate— these trunks were shooting up out of the ground."

Kip pointed to a large gash at the base of one of the Kauris. "See here? Used to be my great-grandfather's generation would tap them for the resin gum. Use it in various ways, mostly for varnishes. But digging it this way kills the tree."

Avery leaned forward and studied the crude slash into the trunk that was underlined by a frozen skin of petrified sap yellowed by weather and chemical decomposition. Suddenly he pulled himself upright and turned away.

"Nasty, yis," Kip said. "We're trying to save them, these lovely old Kauris. All of this is preserved now. Even working with the local Maori village, though some of the younger people there don't like that."

"Why not?" Avery tried to become interested in the problem.

"Oh, they're pissed off at the world. Call the older folks sell-outs. It's not Paradise here, you know, mate. Or perhaps I should say, even in Paradise we have factions."

In this forest there should have been bird cries to mask the silence that Avery fell into as he thought about what his host and guide had just said, but oddly enough not many birds sang here.

He asked about that.

"Well, well," Kip said. "It's a major question. And a large part of what I just said." He went on to explain about the importation of rabbits, and then ferrets to kill the rabbits and then possums to kill the ferrets. And now the poisoning of the forest to kill the possums.

Avery shook his head, meaning, I can't take all this in right now.

"You're poisoning the forest, deliberately?"

"Yis, yis we are. Listen."

Avery stood stock-still and settled in his body, trying to listen with as much seriousness as his guide. He heard his own heart beat, he heard leaves twirling in a light breeze overhead.

Aside from that, silence. Settled. Beneath the giant Kauris, half a world away from all his troubles. All the poison laid here, it had destroyed the undersounds of animal life—rat and rabbit and weasel and possum. And then sound returned in the form of a red-muscled dog—tongue lolling, red penis slung underneath red back like a fleshy missile ready to be launched, a feathery spray of fur at its rude tip—bounding out of the underbrush, long snaky red tail extended like the antenna of some odd machine.

Avery flinched.

"It's all right," Kip said. "It's Jimmy's Bone."

Avery turned to see nothing but the trail along which the fast-moving dog had already disappeared.

After a moment, Kip said, "Here's Jimmy, now," and out of the forest burst a burly, moon-faced fellow, with bullet-shaped shaven head, in dun-colored shorts, his thick legs bearing long deep scratches as though the dog had tried to tell him something of terrible urgency and had only one way to make himself known.

"G'day," the fellow said, locking eyes with Avery.

"Hey," Avery said.

"Jimmy's on the job," Kip said. "Laying the poison. Any luck today, Jim?"

"Good bunch of rats," the man said. "Trapped maybe six of 'em." He hunkered down at the base of a big Kauri, his knee-caps bulging out like tree-knots, his shorts riding up over his bole-thick thighs.

"The rats eat the birds' eggs," Kip said. "You noticed the silence."

"I did," Avery said.

"All these vermin, they eat the eggs," the trapper said.

Avery found himself staring at the gashes in the red-man's beefy legs. "Tough work?"

"Oh, yis," the man said, "I'm out here every day, rain or sun, summer winter. It's like the record, 'Rust Never Sleeps'? These vermin, they're copulating all the time, and if we don't stop 'em they'll take over the island." He gave Avery something approximating a smile and pulled himself upright. He seemed taller than before he had hunkered down. "And now I got to be moving."

With a nod to Kip and a wink at Avery—odd, the assumed intimacy of these mates down under—the trapper charged off along the trail in the direction of his dog.

Avery was still staring at the space he had occupied when Kip beckoned.

"Got more trees to see, mate," he said.

Avery didn't pay much attention to the forest after that, drifting along the path behind Kip for another hour or so, retracing their steps through the green wood and then stumbling back up the hill to the pasture, recrossing the stiles, strutting pukekos all around, returning to the car, returning to the lodge.

He excused himself immediately, climbing the stairs to his room. Up there he lay on his back and studied the off-white ceiling and now and then turned to gaze out across the neck of the bay. His jet-lag had waned, but he felt a heaviness in muscle and bone unlike anything he had ever suffered before.

Out he went, to dream of nothing.

After dinner, feeling more like himself, he adjourned to a small closet turned office on the ground floor and in the tiny room piled high with ledgers and rolls of toilet paper used the management's lap-top to send an email back to the States.

Carrie, [he wrote from where he sat before the screen] *what is it that you want from me? You fucking whore!*

And then he deleted the message.

He felt an attack of chills, rapid trembling that went on for several minutes as though he were wired to an electrical outlet. Sitting there at the keyboard, he hunched forward and shook, and shook. His teeth chattered. When the shaking subsided he sat a moment and then wrote his brother's address and the following:

What you did…unforgivable…you god-sucking wretch of a human being!

And again, he deleted.

What hunkered in the corner of his thoughts after he returned to his room and lay there staring out at the lights beyond the balcony, the flickering stars, the appointed street-lamps of Paihia across the water at this narrow neck of the bay? Memories of childhood—rough bangs on the arm from their ignorant father, their mother's outcries at passion and in surprise at the violence from the man she had believed to have been at first so kind—the thing about thought, Avery surmised with such coolness and rationality as he swung his feet back onto the floor and took a good stance at the window, is that it allows you to range so far and wide. One instant, he was a child, the next he could see himself alone and with muscles withered in old age—alone.

He slid open the glass door to his balcony and stepped outside. Without the partition between him and the night the lights, oddly, glinted and glimmered all the more.

Here he was, nowhere, and everywhere, and he decided he wanted a drink.

Easy to leave the lodge, the stairs, the halls silent. Within two minutes he hit the Strand, where he had first wandered upon his arrival, and it immediately became apparent, amid all the shuttered dark shop fronts, that the only place that offered any haven gave off a blue glow through the plate-glass store-front.

Kamakura [in blue neon].

He opened the door and went inside the brightly lit restaurant.

A mahogany-skinned man behind the bar looked up in surprise. "We're closed, sorry. I thought I'd locked the door."

He reached for something under the bar. Out went the ceiling lights, leaving the place in the same blue-glow as the sign outside.

"I don't want to eat," Avery said. "Just a quick drink."

The man hesitated, and then said, "Well, since you're inside already, I suppose we can do it. Long as you don't kip to the authorities." In the odd shadow and light, his mouth moved like a dark wound.

"Do I look like a guy who would do that?"

Avery blinked, trying to accustom his eyes to the blue glow.

"American, are you?"

"Through and through," Avery said, though he couldn't have said why he put it that way.

He stepped up to the bar, the blue giving his hands and shirt an odd appearance. The man beneath the light, which glowed from the eye of a large mounted fish—deep-sea variety, long sword, spiny dorsal fin—appeared to be half Avery's age, and his white apron glowed blue-white as though under black-light.

"Rick Manning," he said. "I'm the proprietor."

"Avery."

He offered a hand, but the proprietor demurred.

"Sorry, mate, I'm just still washing off the fish."

A call from behind the swinging doors that led to the kitchen.

"Rick?"

"Hold on, love," the proprietor called back. "So," he said, turning back to Avery, "where you from?"

Avery told him.

"That's a long way."

"Yeah, feels like it."

The proprietor held up a glass.

"Scotch?" Avery said.

"True to our tradition, nothing but the best from home," the proprietor said. He moved his hands beneath the bar and Avery could hear the liquid pouring.

"Rick, darling?"

A girl poked her head out from the kitchen doors. In the blue-light her mouth appeared black, also.

"Got a customer, love," the proprietor said.

"I thought we were closed."

Dark oval of a mouth made words in the blue.

"A tardy American," the proprietor said.

"One last drop of the coin in the register, eh?" the girl said. "I thought you were Maori, not a Jew."

In the kitchen behind her a dog barked and Avery nearly jumped out of his skin.

"Oh," said the proprietor with a laugh, "tomorrow's dinner. No, no, just joking. Friend of mine has a dog. Against all the health regs, I know. He'll be out of there in a second. You won't say anything, will you?" He tapped his finger against the glass.

"I'm just passing through," Avery said.

"Good, well, then have your drink." He slid the glass toward Avery the way a barker might in a shell game.

Avery picked up the glass, his eye on the kitchen door.

"We're having dog fish tomorrow," the proprietor said.

Avery remained quiet, sipping the fiery liquid.

"Or tree dog. Something to do with its bark."

Avery shook his head.

The kitchen door swung open again and the girl popped out.

"Not ready yet?"

"I'm ready," Avery said.

"Oh, you are?" said the girl.

"For another," Avery said.

"One more," the proprietor said. "Then we're closed."

He took the glass from Avery, poured, gave it back.

This time Avery drank rather than sipped.

"Closed now," said the proprietor.

The girl played with the top button of her blouse.

"Got to get him out of there."

The proprietor leaned toward Avery and said, "Don't mean you, mate." He turned to the girl. "Just tell him."

"I told him."

"Tell him again."

"Jimmy?" the girl called over her shoulder, holding open the kitchen door.

"Here I come," said a voice from within.

Out of the kitchen stepped Jimmy the trapper, his shaven skull glowing blue in the blue light.

"Allo," he said.

Avery shook his head.

"We just met over in the Kauri forest this afternoon."

The proprietor shrugged.

"It's a small town. Very small. And a small sliver of a country, too, mate. Anything can happen. Like meeting the same four people over and over again." He laughed, his mouth dark in the blue light.

"A beer?" Jimmy said.

"I didn't know we were having a party," the proprietor said. "But I guess we are." He reached down under the bar and came up with a large bottle, sliding it along the surface to the trapper who in that moment came striding up to retrieve it.

"Got a cigarette?"

He had been watching the trapper, so that when the girl appeared at Avery's shoulder it seemed as if by magic. Up close, he discovered her slender arms, slightly bowed back, a regular face. She had an appealing scent, something like sandalwood. He had about two seconds to consider what it might be like to pull her close to him and kiss her on that black hole of a mouth before Jimmy clapped his hands, the dog barked in joy, and the girl moved to where the trapper stood, folding his arms across his muscled chest.

"We're off now," he said. "Tomorrow's another day for vermin."

"Always knew you were off," the proprietor said.

Jimmy the trapper guffawed as he grabbed the girl's hand and led her to the door.

"Guess I'd better go, too," Avery said, setting his glass back on the bar.

The proprietor gave him a poignant look—or was it a sense of an invitation delayed or decided against?—and then a nod of affirmation.

"Best thing," he said, as if he knew something about Avery's fate— or at least something about his present life—that Avery hadn't yet figured.

Which could have been anything.

A few moments later back out on the dark empty Strand Avery felt quite untangled and undone. No sound but a flag flapping lightly in the night breeze off the water. He walked a few steps back toward the lodge, and then stopped, and walked in the other direction, toward a small pier identified only by a single light-bulb against the dark blotter of the bay. Vermin. Kauris. Black hole of a mouth. The horror of his old home-life. It was summer here, but he shivered nonetheless, thinking of the trapper's scarred calves and thighs, his shaven head, and what he would like to do to his brother if—and when—he saw him again.

Yes, to be reminded of this was awful, though more awful was to remember that he had nearly forgotten.

Perhaps that was the nature of this place—Russell, Bay of Islands, North Island, New Zealand, 35° north, 174° west—so far from everything that it was almost back around again and near.

Against the dark all-velvet water where it merged, just above the pin-pricks of lights and lamps across the bay, his thoughts rose, the globe shrunk to the size of a human head, and he was nowhere, and everywhere, beginning and ending, up and down, front and back. 35° north, 174° west. Big man that he was, he felt as though he might swoon. Oh, for a beginning again, for a time when the Kauris were mere seedlings and all men were mahogany.

A dog barked.

The trapper's beast.

The dark mouth in the blue light of the girl in the white blouse.

The trapper's gashed thighs.

Gribnis

Originally published in *Prairie Schooner*

Ascent, a taste, a texture, a vision of thickly sliced yellow onions crackling in chicken fat in a frying pan over a blue ring on a gas stove—one thick whiff of something cooking though there was not a restaurant in sight on the street of beautiful Victorians and Marty Younis could taste the delicious memory in his mouth. The younger of two children of first generation Jews, both of them long buried in the ground, Younis had a taste-bud recollection as he wriggled out of his rental car on the hill on Washington Street on his way to his only daughter's thirtieth birthday, and he began salivating like a good old Pavlovian dog. That taste, aiee! it called up part of the ritual lunch his great-grandmother—she was long gone, too—cooked for him every mid-day when he passed by her house on the way home, which he never reached.

Where you going?

Home, gramma.

I told your mother I'll make you lunch. Come up on the porch.

He could hear her crackly deeply accented voice as if for the first time, words he heard every day of grade-school. In memory, she blinked at him, but she had blinked all the time, as if every moment of her life she was just waking up from a deep sleep.

But who was he besides the taste in his mouth and the echo of a voice in his ear? Let's be frank. He was his mother's lazy child, his father's ass-wipe. A middle-aged screw-up. A former clothing salesman, a former car salesman, among other work in sales, and currently, with the help of his charitable older brother Sherman, the CPA mogul, the proprietor of a financially shaky electronics outlet in Albany, New York. And the father of the cat-faced girl whose photograph lay creased and worn in his thin wallet. And, not necessarily in order of importance, ex-husband of the woman who gave birth to this brain-smashed daughter—and a college graduate, if you counted that crappy little proto-vocational school in southeastern Vermont as a college. (And after all these years, he had lately put it in the "No" column.)

Sherman, who still lived in Jersey, staked him to this trip to San Francisco (a birthday present, because, of all things, Marty and Sarah had birthdays only a week apart, but also a bit of charity), something Younis couldn't help but think about as he walked up to the entrance of his ex-wife's house. He patted his pocket and pressed the buzzer. The place was huge, broad columns framing the entrance, two floors with wide picture-windows above him. Fog slid in and out among the tallest trees nearby and it gave him the chills, more so than most winter days in up-state New York. He never felt so much a Jew, which to Younis meant small and insignificant and an outsider, as when he stood here before the doors of this little mansion.

Daughter Sarah—his late mother's name—opened the door with a big smile on her face, almost as if she were doing this all on her own.

"I'm wery happy to see you, Daddy," she said, in a gravelly voice in which she slurred the words ever so slightly. Her hair looked positively beautiful, the result of another two-hundred dollar trip to the beauty parlor, and Younis hated to think of all of his tiny support payments going for such fripperies.

But—if it made her happy. What else did she have in her life, this slightly cross-eyed stubby-limbed child of his?

Now thirty.

This little numerical stunner left him pondering time and age during the few seconds that he stood there alone with Sarah, giving him too much time to think about how she had grown as fat as a heifer.

"Hello, Hal," said Marilyn, his ex-wife, as she descended the wide stairway from the second floor.

"M," he said, trying to match coolness with coolness. (M, as he was wont to call her back in those days when they were still married (and probably still in love), and she was just a pretty bank-teller from a small town in Vermont.) She was never hugely hospitable and today, even though Younis had flown all the way from the East—in a great swoop across the America he loved but had not seen all that much of with his own eyes—she gave him her usual cool-eyed look, a way it was easy to look if you only had to work at charity and live in this great house and collect support payments from two ex-husbands for your upkeep. Even though the other ex, the banker, paid ninety-nine percent of that, it was killing Marty, *killing* him—but then he had felt that way ever since their divorce, nearly twenty-five years ago and he wasn't dead yet.

She surprised him by asking him to come in, leading father and daughter up the first flight of stairs, and then up a second. Going past the entrance to the vast living room he caught a glimpse of the lovely view through the large front window, a southern exposure, the palette of houses spreading up the hills below it—and then passing the kitchen—recently remodeled, he couldn't help but notice—and walking onto the roof garden, a place he had liked ever since a green-thumbed gay pal of hers had turned it into a demitropical paradise of small palms and large flowering plants.

"Still pretty," he said, scanning the bridge in the distance, the ridges of freshly stirring fog sliding in off the ocean.

"Are you talking about me or the garden?"

"The view."

M made a face at him, and—just like that sense-memory he felt when he stepped out of the car—for a flickering instant it seemed as though they had never split up and she had never remarried—and divorced again (with a settlement larger than all the cash he had ever earned piled up together).

What was happening to him today?

He opened his mouth to speak. Who knew what he was going to say? But then their daughter burst the moment by turning to M with a pathetic question on her already pathetic face.

"Did he bring me something?"

"He brought you himself, didn't you, Marty?" That voice—like a diamond, it could cut glass, except that under pressure over the years, in some kind of weird reversal of a natural process, it had turned to coal.

"Oh, I've got a few other tricks up my sleeve," Younis said, which brought a laugh to his daughter's thick lips.

"Daddy!" she said. "I see your sleeves, you can't hide nothing there."

"Something," her mother said. "He can't hide something."

"Dat's what I said." Sarah flashed him a big smile.

"You're a smarty, ain't you?" Younis said, seeing the correction rise to the level of M's twitching lips and then fall back into her mouth.

His own mouth, watery earlier, was turning dry from the strain of this encounter.

"So, hey, Sarah-girl, you ready to go?"

"I am!" Sarah said. Then turned to her mother.

"You're ready," M said.

"Den let's go!"

"Then," M said.

Younis shook his head.

"Stop correcting her. She can't help it."

M rolled her eyes.

"Can you define the word 'expert'?"

"What?"

"Can you?"

"Yes, I can. It's someone from out of town."

Marty pursed his lips.

"That's me, I suppose. Except I'm not much of an expert at anything."

"There you go again, Mr. President."

"Huh?"

"Feeling sorry for yourself. You've got a job, Marty. You've got a child who loves you."

All time collapsed again in an instant. They were still married, they were on the verge of an argument. Marty tilted his head toward his right ear. It felt so heavy, as though he might just ask if he could lie down and rest before they went out.

"My rup cunneth over," he said.

"Oh, you've been making that joke for what—thirty years?"

"It's my birf-day," Sarah said.

"Yes, darling," M said. "You heard the number correctly. That's right. And your darling father has come all the way from Albany to celebrate it with you."

"Are you ready to go?" he asked his daughter.

She was ready. She had been ready all morning, fidgety and smiling and filled with anticipation—her usual mood, ever since she had been a small child.

Her big expectant smile got him moving even faster than he had hoped for. Well, fast was a relative term when you had a daughter like Sarah who shuffled slowly along rather than walked. But the good news was he didn't even have to ask for M's keys, as he usually did—Sherman had spotted him to the rental.

"Just remember, the hills," M said.

"I've done them before," he said.

"He has, Mama," Sarah said.

"Mother," she said.

"Mov-er," Sarah said.

"Give her a break," Younis said.

"I do, every waking minute of the day and night," M said. Coal had turned to diamond again. Her voice cut with an edge. And what about his waking minutes day and night? He had remarried and divorced, just as she had, but he had no house on a San Francisco hill to show for it. All he had were a lot of cancelled checks made out to a woman whose name—given a spot quiz—he sometimes couldn't even remember. Fortunately, he had no other children. Or unfortunately.

"You ready, Teddy?" he said once they had shuffled their way to the car and he had helped the fumbling Sarah into the passenger side, buckled her seat belt, and was himself strapped in to the driver's seat.

Sarah grunted out a laugh.

"Hah! My name's not Teddy! You know dat."

"What's my name?" Younis said, starting the engine.

"Daddy," Sarah said.

"Uh-uh," he said.

"It is," Sarah said.

"Nope. My name...."

He steered them onto the street, made a right turn, sighted water.

"Daddy!" Sarah snorted out a laugh. "Was my name?"

"Puddintane."

Oldest joke he could remember—played it with his mother. Long gone, long ago. Sorrow crept over him, the way the fog slipped over these buildings.

He loved this city, though he visited it so infrequently. All he had to do was catch sight of the bay and he became suddenly cheerful again. What was it about the world that a view of water and hills and sky could take somebody like him, a failure, as he understood himself, in almost every way, and change time into gold coins for the spending?

"Tell me, honey," he said, paying most of his attention to the traffic and the hills, "How have you been?"

"I been good, Daddy. I been real good."

"That's swell," Younis said. "Your mother has been good to you?"

"Always," his daughter said. "She's always good."

"You have to be her child for that to happen." You have to be her retarded child. And I almost qualified, there toward the end.

"What, Daddy? I don' unnerstan."

"Nothing, darling. Your Dad talks to himself. Don't you remember how I am? I should come here more often. Then you wouldn't forget me."

"Oh," Sarah said in a determined voice, "I don' forget you. I think of you evry day." She reached over and touched his face. It was as if her fingers melted into his cheek.

"Are you buckled in just right? Not too loose, not too tight?" Younis said.

"Oh, yes!" his daughter said.

Younis drove them up and down hills, worrying about everything and nothing.

***

They parked at the Embarcadero and bought their tickets. They had a few minutes until the next boat and Sarah told him she had to use the ladies room. Younis, standing guard outside the door, took the opportunity to take out his cell phone.

"Hello, Sherman? It's Marty."

"Where are you?" his brother said at the other end of the line, "You got to California?"

"I'm standing here looking at San Francisco Bay," Marty said. A white lie—he was staring at the door to the ladies room.

"And it's cold? I hear it's cold out there in the summer."

"There's a breeze."

"Remember how Mama always used to bug us? Going out? Wear a hat."

"I remember. So Sherm—"

"Yeah, I'm here."

"I had the strangest thing happen."

"Uh-oh, so what is it?"

"Nothing bad, almost nothing at all. I had a kind of vision."

"What are you talking about?"

"I was walking along, I just got out of the cab from the airport, and I smelled something."

"You smelled something?"

"Remember how great-grandma used to fry those onions in chicken fat?"

"Chicken gribnis. It's been a long time."

"I smelled them."

"You smelled them?"

"Just walking along from the cab, just in front of Mary's house."

"I doubt it was that shiksa princess of yours got herself a Jewish chef."

"No, no. But I don't know where it came from. It just came to me."

"Interesting, interesting. So how is the ex?"

"Sherm—"

"I never liked her, you know."

"Sherm, I know. You tell me every time we talk. But your Eleanor, I love. How is she?"

"Good, good. She's out with her horse. A bit of a princess herself these days. So—?"

"And the kids?"

"The kids are good. Miriam just made the Law Review at Michigan. So—?"

"Congratulations to her."

"So, you got there alright. So?"

"Why am I calling?"

Static crackled along the line. Younis watched the door of the ladies room, but didn't see his daughter.

"I'm losing you," his brother said.

"You're back to tell me that," Younis said.

"Good. So what else can I tell you?"

"I wanted to thank you again for helping with my plane ticket."

"You're welcome. What's a brother for, if he can't help?"

"It's beautiful here."

"Marty, I can read the travel section. What is on your mind?"

"I told you, I just wanted to thank you."

Still no Sarah.

"And what else do you want?"

"Nothing, Sherman. Nothing. I'm here, it's beautiful. I love the hills, I love the water."

"Maybe you ought to move out there?" his brother said.

"You think so?"

"Marty, what kind of bullshit are you giving me?"

Younis shook his head, standing as close to the door of the bathroom as he could, without it appearing as though he were trying to catch a glimpse inside.

"I'm not giving you bullshit. I'm just talking."

"You like it there, you get a job and move there. It would be nice for...? God forgive me, for your Sarah, I almost forgot her name, Jesus, we're getting old, we're starting to suffer from Old-Timers, but it would be nice for her, for Sarah, if you lived there. I love my kids so much, no matter how much I can't stand their mother sometimes I couldn't even think about living apart from them. And now they're grown up and out of the house, I'm too worn out to leave."

"You really think about leaving her?"

"Oh, Christ, none of your business. I'm sorry I brought it up."

"I brought it up."

"......"

"Sherman? I'm losing you again."

Now he couldn't help himself but shuffled closer to the entrance.

His brother's voice returned. "...get a job out there. I hear it's hard, with the end of the dot-com boom, but you have talents, you can find one."

Everything all at once. Sarah suddenly appeared in front of him, a frown coating her face.

"Sherm, got to go, talk to you later."

"Bye—"

Younis clicked off the telephone.

"What's wrong, honey? What took you so long?"

"I wost it."

"You lost what?"

"Something."

"But what?"

Sarah shook her head.

"I don't wemember..."

Younis gave her his closest attention.

"Something you took in there? I didn't see you take anything in there."

"Now...."

"Now you remember?"

"Yes."

"What was it?"

"A wuby."

"One of your rings?"

"Yes."

"You took off one of your rings in there and left it?"

"I wost it."

"No, no, it's probably still in there. Let me ask someone."

Women had been coming and going and he hadn't paid much attention to it. Now he fixed his eyes on a short blonde girl with a bare midriff just about to enter the bathroom.

"Miss?"

"Yeah?"

He explained his need and she smiled and nodded and ducked inside the room.

"You shouldn't take off your rings, honey," he said to Sarah.

"I dint," she said.

"Then how could you lose it?"

"It wost me," she said.

Younis shook his head.

"Let's wait and see...."

The blonde girl came out.

"You find it?" Younis leaned toward her, admiring her tanned belly.

"Nothing," the girl said.

"Thanks," Younis said, looking her in the eye.

Sarah tugged at his sleeve.

"Daddy?"

She held up her right hand.

He couldn't help but notice the large red ring. "Is that the 'ruby'?"

"Dat's the wuby, Daddy."

"You didn't lose it?"

"Heh, heh, it was a joke on you, Daddy!"

Sarah shook with laughter, so that Younis had to turn away. The blonde girl was still there, looking at him. He shrugged, shook his head, and she walked away.

"Let's get the boat," he said to Sarah.

"You mad at me?" Sarah shuffled along, oblivious to the usual stares she drew.

"No," he said.

"Oh, I can tell, Daddy. You are mad. Well…it was just a joke."

"Some joke," Younis said. "Don't play anymore jokes."

He was annoyed, but the wind off the water soon distracted him. They boarded, and the ferry churned in reverse, spinning halfway around and heading for the shore of Marin just visible through a thin curtain of fog. To the west of their destination the great bridge towered over everything. It reminded him of the lesser bridge, the one that arched over the Arthur Kill, connecting his part of New Jersey to Staten Island, though often as children he and Sherman had taken the ferry over the Arthur Kill instead. And here he was on another ferry, and he hadn't been a boy for fifty years! Fog played in and out of the cables. The movement of the boat, the skyline of bridge and fog, white tufts of waves, the city behind them, it was all a great distraction.

Sarah got distracted easily. Just now when a gull swooped overhead she turned and waddled in the direction of the starboard railing.

"Hey," Younis called to her.

He noticed some passengers smiling at Sarah in that condescending way the normal have of regarding the retarded. Or maybe they were just looking at her beautiful hair made even more attractive by the wind mussing with it just now. It was weird, how she had his features—and he knew he wasn't a bad-looking guy—more than her pretty mother's—but in a sort of cracked fashion, not so much jumbled up as shifted ever so slightly off the mark.

"Wook!"

Sarah pointed to the passing birds.

What was that bullshit thing people were always saying? Wake up and smell the coffee? Or the roses? That was his daughter, taking every minute a second at a time.

"I see, honey!" he called out, keeping his eye on her, not the birds. It always made him anxious, caring for her, watching her. It did when she was a child and it did now.

But his immediate worries drowned in the rumbling of the engines and the cries of the gulls, and a few shouts from the passengers, as they approached the ferry slip in Sausalito. Just then, just before docking, he smelled it again, the odor of gribnis, as his great-grandmother called the dish, something, he decided, wafting in their direction from one of the many restaurants in this fancy bayside village where the pastel houses climbed nearly straight up the hills. Italian? Chinese? Who could have re-produced that same wonderfully familiar smell of cooking onions? What was going on here? Look! The houses. He craned his neck at the sight of them, trying to shake the memory that seemed now to be haunting him.

"You see that?" he said to his daughter.

***

He had meant to talk to her sooner but it wasn't until they were walking—slowly, because of her native shuffle—along the main street that he forced himself to do it. He wasn't a great talker himself, outside of his work. Wasn't that what M was always complaining about (among other things she grew to dislike about him, or maybe hadn't ever even liked from the start)? But compared to Sarah he was a debate team champion. To be honest, he had put it off, because he hated to hear her struggle to talk about things that lay, as most things did, so far out of her reach.

"Are you feeling okay?"

"Oh, Dad, I feeling jes fine...."

"Has your mother—" But he cut himself off, figuring he had better not ask a question like that, not yet. "Have you been to school?"

"Oh, yes!"

"You still like it there?"

"Oh, yes!"

"Are you drawing pictures?"

"I am. I show you when we go home."

"Good, good."

Sarah touched him on the arm.

"I draw you," she said. "Is at home."

"Wonderful, Sarah," he said. "I look forward to seeing it."

Sarah cackled, "Me too."

Younis couldn't help but laugh himself.

"You got a sense of humor, kid," he said.

They walked another block, and now and then he'd sniff the air, the cool salt breeze coming off the bay. But he didn't smell the gribnis anymore and he certainly couldn't figure out which restaurant the odor had come from. Here was a sea-food place, parked on a barge at the waterside. Across the street, an Italian restaurant, and a sandwich place. None of these would have done. The closest he could figure might be the Mexican.

"Are you hungry?" he said to Sarah.

"Oh, yes!"

"How about Mexican?"

"Oh, Daddy, I dunno."

"You don't like Mexican?"

"I jus' dunno."

"You've had it before."

"Yes."

"So you can try it again."

"Ok, Daddy, I'll try."

But having convinced her of doing it, Younis led her to the entrance of the place, took a deep whiff, and shook his head.

"We'll go somewhere else, someplace you'll like better."

They ended up sitting on the veranda of a sandwich shop a few blocks from the ferry slip. As usual, Sarah ordered the fattiest, most expensive item on the menu and then set it aside after a few bites, preferring instead to watch the pedestrians stroll by. How could she have grown so plump if she never seemed to eat? Younis gazed up the hill, chewing the food he found rather tasteless. The town was beautiful. They should come here more often. But Sarah couldn't walk up the steep steps he saw beckoning on the other side of the street. Some other time. Right now:

"So tell me about what you've been doing."

Sarah talked, in her own crabbed way, mispronouncing (but then Younis was from New Jersey so what did he know about pronouncing? All his life he had talked in a Jersey way, no matter what the correct version of English might have been), laughing at jokes he didn't get (or mostly didn't even know were jokes), slurring words, reaching, reaching in the particular dark of her own unawareness for some word that didn't exist to describe an emotion or situation he couldn't even approach or understand. For all these years, he had lived with this daughter—well, not really lived with all this time, because of the separation and divorce, but he saw her at least once a month when she was small and in the past couple of decades at least once or twice a year)—and never knew for sure what was going on in her head. But who ever knew these things, he figured, even when it was someone who wasn't brain-damaged?

He felt his appetite swell and began to eat heartily, though the food tasted nothing like what he desired. Sarah still toyed with her plate, the waiter came and went. More than half an hour passed by. What did he learn? Nothing that he didn't already know. M made Sarah's life as pleasant as she could, shopping, dressing, movies, plays, hair salon—look at that hair of hers, just as beautiful as any normal woman's!—and Sarah seemed happy enough (for someone with her problem, who was also on medication, as he knew she had been for years).

Sarah stared at him.

He stared at her.

"Having fun?"

"Oh, yes, Daddy, I yam!"

She kept on staring.

He stared back.

She crossed her eyes at him and they both laughed.

"Okay, kiddo," he said. "Now what? It's still your birthday. What would you like to do now? Just say the word."

"What's the word?"

"You tell me the word."

He hadn't planned anything, he hadn't even really thought about it, after the idea about the ferry ride here.

"Do you know what I say?" Sarah squinted out a smile.

Younis shook his head. The words came out of her mouth so clearly— sometimes they did—she might just then have been a normal person.

"What would you like?"

"I would like…." And she paused, for an instant Younis allowed himself the fantasy, as he sometimes had done over the years, that she was in fact a normal person, and that she was going to ask for money for college or a car or a trip to Mexico or a new coat—or that she would like him to meet a new boyfriend, someone she was really quite serious about this time, after all the others.

"Da zoo," she said.

"The zoo," he repeated.

"Yes, Daddy, dats what I want. I can't wait!"

So—back to the ferry slip, back across the bay. The wind had shifted, fog drifted in under the bridge. Behind them Sausalito glowed under the direct rays of the sun, but the city ahead now lay enshrouded in white gauze. Deep salt stank up his nostrils. He held Sarah's hand as the deck shifted and they swayed back and forth, surging toward the oncoming mist. For a moment, when he turned away from her and closed his eyes and kept his nostrils open, fifty and more years disappeared and he might have been back on board that ferry boat with his brother, shifting across the Arthur Kill toward Staten Island, maybe eight, maybe ten years old, ready for adventure in the world. His mouth filled with the familiar taste.

***

Once they found a parking place, the rest of it was easy. Mobs of children, scattered patches of sun poking through the thin slipping fog, balloon salesmen and food vendors, cadres of parents with strollers and kids stuffed into baby packs. Within minutes Sarah was demonstating to him (though she didn't know it) how she gained such weight, gorging on pretzels and slurping a huge sweet drink in a transparent plastic cup. But what did Younis care? Let her mother crack the diet whip. He wanted her to be happy.

But monkeys didn't make her happy. Neither did the four-footed land animals.

It wasn't until the snakes that she came to life.

"Wook," she said, giggling as a thick and beautifully orange and green python lay on the bottom of its cage doing nothing.

"Pretty," Younis said, looking around at anything but the snake. He couldn't stand them, and he bowed then toward his daughter, saying to himself, *You're better than I am, kid.*

The big cats, though, he liked the cats despite the high nose-cutting odor of their urine that made Sarah turn aside and tug at his sleeve.

"Stinks in here, Papa, wet's go."

A few more varieties of beast and bird, and then Sarah had to take another turn in the ladies room.

Younis took up his usual post outside, surveying with sneaky glances the traffic going in and out. A heavy mother, with two kids in tow. He started to picture her squatting inside while holding each kid in turn—but he cut himself off. A lanky blonde appeared, her even lankier daughter following. Legs, legs. Dark-haired foreign woman, Italian, maybe or Mexican? Younis didn't know. Or he did. For all he knew the woman could have been Armenian or Arabian. He dated an Armenian woman once, between the end of his marriage to M and the beginning of his courtship of the woman so horrible he didn't even want to say her name. Thank God the two of them didn't have children, or they would have had to have visited them here at the zoo.

Christ! He hated himself when he allowed things like that to drift into his mind.

"Sarah?" He leaned toward the open door of the ladies room.

The two small children made their exit, followed by the heavy mother. She looked right through him, herding the kids.

"Sarah?"

Two teenage girls glided past him, bellies bared, giggling. They must have been in there a while, he hadn't seen them enter.

A black woman with a behind stuffed into tight jeans brushed past him, going inside. A black woman with stick-like limbs followed her in, saying, "Mama? You see what I'm saying?" The mother didn't look around.

The blonde mother and daughter emerged from the interior. Younis took a breath, was about to speak, but they moved quickly away.

Same for the Armenian (?) woman, too quick for him.

Out came the younger black woman. Already?

"Ex-"

"I hear you," her mother said, bringing up the rear.

Younis was determined now.

"Excuse me," he said as she approached the entrance to a tiny woman in tank top and shorts, despite the usual San Francisco chill.

"Yes?"

"My daughter's in there?"

"Oh, sure," the woman said. "What's her name?"

"Sarah," Younis said, wanting to say more but not saying it.

"Sarah," the woman said. "I'll get her for you." She ducked inside the bathroom.

Sarah, Younis could hear the tiny woman calling from within. *Sarah?*

Moments passed, clouds parted and the sun sliced down onto the little microclimate of the chilly zoo.

The woman came out of the bathroom.

"Sorry," she said. "Not in there."

Younis nodded his thanks, but he wasn't feeling all that nonchalant. A young bearded fellow in uniform approached a trash bin and opened it. Younis approached him and asked for help.

"You mean, like, security?"

"Yeah," Younis said. "My daughter, she's retarded, she's missing. Can you—?"

"Right on it," the young man said, reaching into his pocket for a telephone.

Within a minute or two security guards converged on the entrance to the bathroom.

"You sent somebody in there, right?" one of the guards said.

"Of course," Younis said. "A woman."

One of the guards was a woman, and she went inside. Then stepped out again.

"What's her name?"

"Sarah."

Younis spent the next fifteen or twenty seconds rolling living through what he had thought was only supposed to happen when you're drowning— annoyed with his parents yet longing to see them again, missing Sherman, sorry he was mean to all of them sometimes, his stupid early twenties, wasted early thirties, meeting M, the good part of a marriage, then Sarah, then the difficult times, divorce, all his terrible work life, his inattention to Sarah, then catching up with her, and then her disappearance, finding her body washed up from the bay, the funeral, M shrieking at him, murderer!murderer! followed by the lonely dark years into further decline and death—

Radio static crackled around him, people raised their voices in alarm. The female security guard emerged from the ladies room her face a blank—

"Daddy!"

Sarah shuffling along with her.

"Jesus!" Younis discovered he hadn't been breathing but breathing deeply again.

"Twice in one day! What the hell's the matter with you?"

The guard shook her head.

"She were standing on a toilet."

"Hiding?"

The guard looked at Sarah. Sarah smiled. The guard nodded, unamused.

"Yep."

"What gave you that bright idea?" Younis asked his daughter.

"I sawr it in a movie," Sarah said and she laughed, folding her arms across her chest, in that satisfied way Younis had noticed in her ever since she had been a child. It was so appealing, it made him love her ferociously, yet at the same time, here among a crowd of gawking witnesses, he wanted to kill her. Worse, he wished—fleetingly, and then hated himself—that she had in fact disappeared.

***

"I died," he told M after they returned to the house and Sarah had gone upstairs to take a bath. Himself, he wanted to bathe, to shower, to shed the slightly scummy sensations of the last few hours.

"Too bad," M said, "because I would have killed you."

"But it was worse than that."

"What could have been worse?" M said.

Younis shook his head, wallowing in the empathy of this moment, more rapport with M than he had ever felt in years.

"I hate myself for it, too."

"Why is that?"

"I—didn't want her to come back."

"Marty, you're such a schmuck. Why don't you just leave?"

Schmuck. He heard that word a lot, used it a lot, when he was growing up. But on the lips of his ex it sounded different, less raucous, more exact, not so much a general attack on his character but a specific description of who and what he was.

"I'll be back tomorrow," he said.

M stayed silent a moment, as if she were considering an ultimatum: don't come back, never come back. Then she said, "She'll like that. Where are you staying?"

"Why?"

"In case she wants to call you."

He gave her the name of his hotel.

"That's quite an expensive place."

"I suppose," he said. He wasn't going to tell her that Sherman had staked him to all of this, he'd never tell her.

There was one other thing he would never tell her, something much more deeply serious, which he had kept covered over in his mind for years and years—decades!—until just now: how one night after infant Sarah had just been diagnosed he had felt sorry enough for himself to enter her room, stand over her crib, and contemplate smothering her.

M clearly could not read his mind, because she gave him a look, neither diamond-cutting nor coal and said, "Maybe next time you can stay here."

"Sure, thanks," he said, not knowing what to make of this. "I like the hotel."

"Sarah would enjoy having you here, under her roof. There's plenty of room."

"Sure," he said again, knowing nothing, still knowing nothing! about what he was feeling.

In that hotel room to which he soon retreated he sat up in bed a good—or bad—part of the night, waiting, waiting. And still nothing. But what was he waiting for? Could he tell it to himself in his own words? Nothing. Nothing. Waiting. Waiting.

It wasn't until another day had gone by, and he had made his farewell to Sarah—and M—and he was buckling himself into his seat in the airplane that he had the sudden sensation that he had left something behind. He looked around. Other passengers glanced right through him, aging guy, slightly balding, with a small pot belly. And while he was thinking about this it came to him again—the odor of gribnis. And once more he began salivating and slumped back in his seat like a hungry penned-up dog. He knew it, he knew it, he knew it, he knew it—in his heart, in his glands—he knew it: his death, Sarah's death or some other dire event would keep him from ever traveling this way again. Quite involuntarily he licked his lips. Hours later, thousands of feet above the ground, blinking into the sunlight, with the rumble of the engines and muffled chatter all around him, the taste lingered in his mouth.

A Little Death

Originally published in *The Southern Review*

...when they draw near forty men seem to undergo a sort of spiritual change of life, with really painful depression and loss of energy. Even men whose physical health is quite good. So don't fret....Often an entire change of scene helps a lot. But it's a condition which often drags over several years. Then in the end you come out with a new sort of rhythm, a new psychic rhythm, a sort of re-birth. Meanwhile it is what the mystics call a little death and you have to put up with it....

—D. H. Lawrence to Mark Gertler, December 23, 1929

June 23, 1939—I heard the voice of the Brute on the wireless last night pouring poison into the hearts of his countrymen. It was awful, like wild beasts....I much prefer the. As though it were yesterday. In front of the house on Gun Street, Spitalfields, a pavement artist turns his wrist and wields the chalk to make a rooster so real to me I can almost hear it crow....

Cock-a-doodle-doo! Cock-a-doodle-doo!

Only forty-five some years ago. And now.

Bleeding—once last night—five times yesterday. And all the air in all the sanatoriums.

I breathed. Coughing up clots the size of hummingbirds I saw once in France. In summer. In.

Stripping the bed and breathing in the familiar odours of oils and the haunting residue of Maria's last visit. Poor gifted dear. Running from the beasts.

Going to the desk. Glad that I saved. Reading David's letter again... thinking, I tried change of scene. The photograph? Marjorie and me at the beach just after we married....The waves lapping. Please do put on your bathing costume, please do come in with me. Reading while she splashes about. Longtemps, je me suis couché de bonne heure....I loved gazing at the sea. An intense blue with hot green trees silhouetted against it. The crude greens of the earth, the ultramarine of the sea, and the sun-lit whites of the cliff, clear cut and solid, like coloured sculpture…

Ah, a mattress, like a life, as if it has absorbed all the nights entrusted to it, so heavy to haul this into the middle of the room, to begin…I've hauled canvas, hauled stretchers, wood for frames. But this…The body is the hulk that follows the paintings around.

Oh, for the life of a labourer!

A chalk artist, working his wrist…

Coughing lightly. Fearing more to come. Coughing stops.

Stop coughing, Mama saying. Asking, *What kind of work is that, painting, for a Jewish boy?*

Faintest recollection, old Spitalfields rabbi—forgot his name—saying, *What kind of a Jew makes painting? Painting is idol worship.*

Painting rooms…would he have said that?

But instead, at an early age, the Slade.

Changed everything. Boy genius, a charity case, discovering the masters. Cézanne…When later that critic called me "the Yiddish Cézanne," it stung me, made me angry, yet somehow half-pleased…. Angry again now. Anti-Semitic bastard! Thinking of it now, stomach heaves. Clots forming in my lungs…

Picture the Slade instead, the hallways redolent of oil and paint, seeing…for the first time…

Her head…

Carrington! Carrington!

How beautiful, the first…

Wasted years on her, but painting, painting. With the charity of the Jews and the help of.

Oh, and then she. With Strachey, of all. A queer, instead of a Jew.

Brings back a few days before Christmas in their rooms at the Triangle—was it '14, '15? David and Frieda and Katherine and her old Murray…and Koteliansky—

Koh-TEE-lee-AHN-skee—saying it aloud…

Frieda put up some mistletoe.

Wonderful pagan rite, David said, with a sneer of a smile.

Me saying to Katherine, Come with me, come. Taking her hand, leading her into the hall and kissing her.

A little tipsy.

Where is New Zealand? I said. Is it here? I touched her breast. Where is it? Is it here? I slipped my hand beneath her shirt-waist.

Mark? She said. I could feel the heat rushing...

And her face, too, hot, hot!

The mistletoe, I said. Under the spell...

I touched her there again, and she did not flinch but did not cleave to me either.

Hauling the...Stopping to breathe.

When we came back into the room, Frieda saying, Gertler, look at your face! Murray, drunk, saying, Look at mine!

David looking at Frieda, smiling at me, suddenly crowing, Cock-a-doodledoo!

Me, in all merriment, crowing, Cock-a-doodle-Jew!

Cock-a-doodle-Jew!

All of them taking it up.

Cock-a-doodle-Jew! Cock-a-doodle-Jew!

That husband of Katherine's, oblivious to everything except his own deviousness, put something on the gramophone and we danced about, crowing all the while.

Still a bit out of breath. Sitting here a moment, the mattress at my feet...

Oh, oh, Gertler...David so out of breath he could scarcely speak. Do you know? he said. Do you know?

Do I know what, David? I asked.

Do you know—leaning way over to one side, as if this, in his inebriated state, might allow him to commune better with me in mine—Christ himself is the cock?

The early Christians, they made the cock the sign for Christ. The cock crowing at dawn announcing the new day, the advent of Christ, the new Jew replacing the old, announcing a new life. Cock-a-doodle-Jew! Cock-a-doodle-Jew!

Oh, and we laughed and laughed, and the others laughed, because in that small room of his and Frieda's there was no room for confidential speech, and there was, after all, all the crowing...!

The Jew comes to announce, David said.

All right, then, I said. Enough of this Jew business.

You've heard enough of it?

It's funny, comical, but then.

Oh, he likes you, Katherine said. She looked at me directly for the first time since we had kissed.

And Eliot? And Forster? I heard what they said about me. Don't people know?

Nothing is secret.

But that all came later, I'm...confusing, conflating...Ottoline, oh, Ottoline.

She was good too. Never a mention of Jew. Just gossip about this, gossip about that.

And always encouraging. Finding me buyers. But came the rise of the monster on the other side of the Channel. We may all be blown to bits any moment, so why fear gossip? Gossip is life. They talk about the living more than the dead. Be glad.

Celebrate...Mother's voice...Painting? You want painting?

Sighing...Breathing easier now. And so back to work.

Work? Oh, work no more the heat of the...Mattress onto the window seat.

I've read about. Look out there. Reminds me of, green. Early summer at Lyme Regis...But the awful mists, the air so heavy and liverish. Dorset, really. So much better. Hardy receiving me in the study.

Sir, I love the books. The once green time. Old man he was. A stale odour of sweat and tobacco circled about him, like a wreath. But the books, still alive.

And paintings? Oh yes, they live on, like my Merry-Go-Round, rolled up in the corner there. Studio closed. Because I'm not there. Wherever I. I am my own studio.

Breathing comes hard, lifting this mattress.

Coughing suddenly. Set it down. Taking some breaths.

Hefting it again, easing it upright against the window. Steady.

The trouble is—my work. What is my value as an artist? What have I in me, after all, besides the bloody clots?

Gertler, his blood period. Like Picasso, his blue. Whom I never. Though always wanted to. When we crossed to France that time, the master sent me a note: Come see me. But I thought, No, he'll merely be tossing me a crust from his table.

Unrolling the canvas. A great painting, they all said. But did I sell it?

The Merry-go-hellish-round under an orange helmet of a roof top, sixteen riders, soldiers and sailors and camp followers riding white horses as they scream…

Taking me back to that time. Carrington and me going around and around. And the world going around and around, the tyrants, the dictators, the soldiers, the—

A bell! Who is ringing?

Maria!

Oh, God of my ancestors, no!

I told her not.

Hurry now.

Holding the mattress in place. Maria's face. Body pressed against. Breath pushed out of me. If only it had been. If we had met earlier.

All right. Steady it. Steady. Good. Step away. It still holds. Good.

Breathing, breathing.

To the burners. Opening up the gas.

At last!

Lying here now. Thinking of dinner last month.

Woolf said, after I had described to her the first time I tried—oh, what?—six years ago. Woolf said, Oh, how very interesting.

The hiss of private opinion.

I suppose she has never.

What is it, darling? her husband said.

Get up now, stuff towels under the doorway.

Will it be a surprise to her?

Listen to me. So calm. And the hiss.

Bell again.

Maria can't get in the downstairs door.

So now I just wait.

Shame about the mattress, blocking the view.

I'd have liked to look at my last green.

Carrington's head on the grass. In Strachey's lap. I saw her. How could she have? So devastated, she.

Once more the bell.

Stay calm. She can't. She'll walk away.

And Luke? Where is little Luke?

With his mother. Will grow up better without.

Ay! Thoughts driving me.

Gas seeping.

Just a matter of.

Must distract myself. Look at. On the shelf, here it is.

One evening of late summer, before the nineteenth century had reached one-third of its span, a young man and woman, the latter carrying a child, were approaching the large village of Weydon-Priors, in Upper Wessex, on foot. They were plainly but not ill clad, though the thick hoar of dust which had accumulated on their shoes and garments from an obviously long journey lent a disadvantageous shabbiness to their appearance just now.

Ah, yes, the first old green time.

The man was of fine figure, swarthy, and stern in aspect; and he showed in profile a facial angle so slightly inclined as to be almost perpendicular.

***

Coughing a bit. Coughing, then settling down.

He wore a short jacket of brown corduroy, newer than the remainder of his suit, which was a fustian waistcoat with white horn buttons, breeches of the same, tanned leggings, and a straw hat overlaid with black glazed canvas. At his back he carried by a looped strap a rush basket, from which protruded at one end the crutch of a hayknife, a wimble for hay-bonds being also visible in the aperture.

His measured, springless walk was the walk of the skilled countryman as distinct from the desultory shamble of the general labourer; while in the turn and plant of each foot there was, further, a dogged and cynical indifference personal to himself, showing its presence even in the regularly interchanging fustian folds, now in the left leg, now in the right, as he paced along.

I could draw that…. I could draw the labourer…beginning in Spitalfields, Gun Street, the pavement artist.

Bell again!

"Won't you go away? It's not a damned piano key!"

Sorry about shouting. Poor Maria. She gave me her gift. All the youth she left behind, running from the beasts.

Coughing, coughing. Taking deep breaths. Coughing subsides. Lovely. Picking up the book again. Heavy.

Holding it up to my closed eyes.

If I could do nothing but read. Wouldn't it? Or paint. And paint. Nothing but that. Seascape, oceanside beach.

Longtemps, je me suis couché de bonne heure…

Jew remembering French prose, drawings in Spitalfields, the turn of the artist's wrist, my clowns on the merry-go-round.

Longtemps, je me suis couché de bonne…

And if Maria. Could we make a new? But, no. These lungs of blood. Maria, run, don't run in circles. The brute is shouting. The guns are massing. Commentators agree, in the autumn, some terrible beauty may be born again.

But here, now.

My wasted life.

My merry-go-round of hellish love.

Longtemps, je me suis couché de…

Longtemps, je me suis couché…

Longtemps, je me suis…

Longtemps, je…

In Spitalfields, the pavement artist turns his wrist….

Longtemps…longtemps…

A Merry Little

Originally published in *Another Chicago Magazine*

Being a Jew at Christmas can sometimes lead to more than a little wintry discontent. At least in America, decided Ron Bronstein, a bluff, dark-haired, six-foot success story of an editor from New York with, when it came to women writers, a kind of blind spot.

Cell-phone pressed to his ear, he stood in the middle of the main Delta concourse at Hartsfield, waiting for a signal. Scores of fellow-travelers flowed past, in both directions. Aside from a few in heavy coats, they gave no sign of the holiday season. (Despite his hopes for a warm, somewhat Southern holiday, the weather report told of possible snow and freezing temperatures down this way. So much for the conventional wisdom about the South.)

Look—a mean-eyed woman the size of a large land-mammal waddled toward him, her breasts dangling like water-bags. Two men in cowboy outfits strode alongside her. A gaggle of young children cackled by. Passing him on the right came a perfectly modeled young thing, about half the size of a normal person, her miniature heart-shaped behind in blue jeans receding in the distance as he half-observed it, wondering who she was and where she was going.

So that when the voice sounded in his head he was not quite yet prepared.

"Ron here," he said.

"It's me," said the woman, replicating the sound of absolute resignation.

"I'm in Atlanta," Ron said. "We had an equipment problem in New York. So they booked me through here."

"Wish I was there with you."

"Just stay where you are and we'll be together soon enough."

"You know what I mean," she said. "He's.............." In the way that it often happened on a cell phone, the voice cracked and split and trailed away. "...on the bright side..."

"Sorry, I couldn't hear you."

".............."

"I can't hear you."

Hopeless! Not the two of them, of course, but the signal. He turned off the cell phone and made his way to the gate, wondering if, with his late luck, his seat mate might turn out be the fat woman with the elongated jugs. Or the little bitty cowgirl. That would be interesting.

But as it happened the two-hour flight to Memphis gave him a dour, white-haired old fellow in carefully pressed trousers and coat and tie, a missionary just returned from dangerous Afghanistan to celebrate Christmas with his grandchildren.

"Greatest gift of God, grandchildren," the man said. "Got any yourself?"

"Three wives," Bronstein said. "But not all at once. And no children."

"That's heathen," the man said.

"No children? I don't get it."

"Three wives. Kabul, where I just been, met a number of men with more than one wife. I just can't figure that. Beside the fact it's a sin, it's a lot of trouble."

"Tell me about it," Bronstein said.

The man took him literally and talked intermittently for the remainder of the flight about sin and redemption, something Bronstein, being a Jew, and a nonobservant one at that, never gave much consideration. When he could, Bronstein stole glimpses of the manuscript—"A Life," she called it on the title page—he had packed in his briefcase, the pages that contained the story of the woman whom he was going to see:

the scenes of her troubled childhood in the Delta, of her marriage to the son of one of the great fortunes of Memphis, of his son's (her step-son's) suicide by gunshot, of the disruption of the marriage and her flight into the relatively unknown world of Memphian bohemia (which included, like most bohemias, alcohol, drugs, strong coffee, and sexual profligacy).

Only an hour after the airplane descended through shreds of snow-cloud and light rain, he was driving his rental car up the wet gravel road to the large ranch-style house on the edge of a golf course north of the city where she now lived with her husband, with whom she had reconciled. In the manuscript, soon to be, if Bronstein could do anything (and he could do quite a bit), a book a lot of lonely, miserable women would want to read, the husband drank hard and ran around, slapped her now and then, and cursed his fate. Here was the real person, waiting in the open doorway, a handsome, sandy-haired man in his fifties confined to a wheel-chair after a near-fatal automobile accident.

"Rick Paris," he said, holding out his left hand as Bronstein came up the steps. His other hand lay still in his lap. "Merry Christmas."

"Merry Christmas yourself," Bronstein said. "I guess you know who I am."

"I do, sir," Paris said.

"Nice little house," Bronstein said.

"Big old place, isn' it? You notice the pool? Built by Toots Moman, Nashville record producer? Ever hear of him?"

"No, I haven't."

"Shaped like a guitar," Paris said. "Frozen now, though. Bet you didn't think it ever froze down this way, did you?"

Bronstein shook his head.

"No, never thought about it."

"Hello?"

Bronstein looked past his seated host into a well-lighted room with exposed timbers and a large Christmas tree nearly covered with tinsel and dangling artifacts of the season. The woman, taller than he had remembered her, came striding out to greet him.

"My God," she said. "You're here."

Bronstein gave her one of his best disdainful smiles as he walked around the man in the chair and went to take her in his arms. "I was there and now I'm here."

"I'd say I can't believe it," the woman said, "but you know that I'm the kind of person believes everything."

Bronstein embraced her, feeling her large breasts flatten against his chest.

"If you weren't, we wouldn't have our work to do," he said.

"I'm still so excited about it," the woman said.

Bronstein, passing up the opportunity, one he so often grasped, for a schoolboyish wisecrack, stepped back from her and smiled again, this time showing what he hoped was his sincerity.

"You already know I think we've got a winner. We just have to do a bit of hard work between now and the finish line."

"It is Christmas," the husband in the wheel-chair spoke up at Bronstein's back, "so we're going to have a party."

"That's the way we've always lived," the woman said. "Rick, Ron's come all this way to work with me. The party's extra."

"Right now, party's all I have," her husband said. "I'm going to have me a holiday drink by myself, I suppose. Til the company arrives."

He turned his chair around with the ease of a man born to be crippled and left them alone, casting another "Merry Christmas" greeting over his shoulder as he rolled away.

"See you in a while," the woman said, leading Bronstein down a hall and into a small extra bedroom lately turned into a study bare of furniture except for a desk, a lap-top computer, and a few book shelves.

"Merry Christmas," Bronstein said, wondering where his words were coming from. He didn't feel merry, at least not yet, though Merry was certainly the motto of the season. Merry Merry. He opened his briefcase and took out the manuscript, showed her some places in the first couple of pages that he wanted to talk about. He pushed, she pushed back. He tugged, she yielded. He pushed further. A few lines went out.

An entirely new scene blossomed in their mutually agreed upon plan. Yet it seemed as though he and the woman had hardly started when people began coming through the doorway to say hello.

"We're working," she said to each and every one. "This is my editor Ron Bronstein down from New York City and we're working." Cheerful men, some bearded, and women with bright eyes gave him spectacular holiday smiles. Bronstein and the woman went back to the manuscript each time, making slow progress through a chapter. She looked up at one point and said, "I didn't expect people to come this early. They're all from the church? I am so grateful to them. I don't want to shout at them. They saved my life while I was in rehab."

"I know," Bronstein said. "I read that chapter. In fact, I want to talk to you about that when we get there."

"Too much of a happy ending? I know you don't like happy endings up there in New York." She uncrossed her legs and her foot bumped his knee. "Excuse me." She sighed, and he watched her eyes dim and then light up again, as if she were remembering something quite distant yet important enough to add to the pages they were editing. "I'm grateful to you, too, you know. I never in a million years thought—" She stood up and went to the door, pulling it shut.

"We love happy endings," Bronstein said, a little uncomfortable with the praise she was about to bestow on him. "I mean, I don't particularly. But our readers will. They'll be ninety percent women, and women love them."

Without missing a beat, the woman took her seat again and said, "Because we're more developed than men."

"I always thought that," Bronstein said, cocking his head and smiling. In some circumstances it would have been a stupid thing to say. But it was Christmas—hey!—and everybody was cheerful.

"You're flirting again," she said.

"Am I?" Old rhetorical response, giving him some time to think. Or not to think.

"Yes," she said, cutting off his time. "Not that I don't like it. It's been a real interesting experiment, staying sober and seeing if behaving badly without being under the influence is something I like to do."

"And the verdict?"

She looked him deep in the eye with the gaze of a woman who hadn't stared at a man directly for most of the years of her life and now took great pleasure in it.

"What happened in New York happened in New York. This is Memphis. I don't know what you expected when you came down here."

"Just this," Bronstein said. "Work. And more work." He reached up and touched her on the neck. She ever so slightly flinched, and then settled herself against his hand. He could feel her carotid artery as a steady pulse against his palm. With a gentle motion, he guided her head toward his lap. She reached around and touched him, worked his fly open, eased him out, and without a word tilted her chin up and took him, flaccid though he might be, in her mouth. A tiny rippling shock shot from his groin up into his gut and down along his thighs.

A rousing noise from somewhere else in the house.

She opened her lips and spit him out, like a fish rejecting an imperfect bit of feed.

She sat up. "I can't."

Bronstein looked out the window. It was snowing.

"Hah," he said, adjusting his trousers.

The woman, seeing what he saw, made a nervous little laugh.

"Don't you think we have snow down here sometimes? Sometimes even at Christmas?"

He was breathing hard but paid no attention to it. They adjusted themselves where they sat and, as though nothing consequential had happened, went a little farther along in their work. Just as they were getting to one of the good places—one of the stickier, juicier sequences where she revealed herself in a way that readers loved and writers usually felt remorseful about years later—even more noise went up in the other part of the house.

"Born Agains have wild parties, huh?" he said.

"Wait'll you see."

She stood up and grasped his hand. A second shock, this time along his wrist to his lower arm.

"You're shaking," she said.

"I'd like a drink," he said.

"Me, too," she said. "But I'll just watch you drink instead."

Walking into the living room gave him yet another surprise. A crowded space, dozens of people. He might have been back in Manhattan, except for the demeanor of the guests. A number of bearded rough-necks ("ex-hippie Born Agains," she said, leaning toward him as he paused at the edge of the room); women in cheap pant-suits, women in velvet dresses; boy children wearing ties and jackets; little girls in red and green sweaters and skirts. In the middle sat Rick in his wheel-chair, waving his good hand.

"Listen up," he said. "Dan Dollar's going to sing for us."

Applause as a young man in his mid-twenties dressed as though out of a cheap department store window stepped forward into the middle, pushing Rick and his chair slightly to the side.

"I…am…going…to…sing 'God Bless Ye, Merry Gentleman,'" he said in a stiff direct voice.

Pattering of small applause.

The fellow took a deep breath.

"It's the MOST wonderful time of the year…." He stopped, looked around, and said, without smiling or blinking, "Wrong song." He took another breath and started again:

"God bless ye merry gentlemen let nothing you dismay remember Christ our Savior was born on Christmas Day…."

He stopped and took a small bow.

A man, his father, it must have been, stepped up behind him and touched his elbow, saying quiet words that got the fellow to bow again and then to open his mouth and announce, "—And now, a duet!"

From the far side of the room, a stork-like girl with bulging eyes and long hands slipped forward through the crowd, stopping only when she stood next to the young man.

She blinked long and hard. "Rudolf the Red-Nosed Reindeer," she began to sing in a lilting off key voice. "Had a very shiny nose."

"Nose," sang the young man.

"And if you ever saw it,"

"Saw it!"

"You would even say it glows."

"Like a light bulb!"

"All of the other reindeer used to call him misery…and if they ever saw it, they played all the reindeer games…."

"Like football!"

"Then one foggy Chrisless eve Sandra came to say…Rudolf whiff your nose so bright, won' you glide my sleigh to night…."

"I need a drink," Bronstein said, looking around for the bar.

"There's Rick's supply." She pointed toward the kitchen.

When Bronstein came back, wine in glass in hand, the young man was still singing and the girl was leaning against the wall, swaying to the rhythm of the toneless song with two bearded Born Agains in coveralls.

"Have yourself a merry little Christmas…."

"Isn't he won-derful?" she mouthed at him.

"Is he…?" Bronstein mouthed back.

"Autistic," the woman said.

"An artistic autistic?"

"Many of them are."

Bronstein swallowed his wine.

"In a way, that might be nice. Follow your own rules. Pay no attention to the critics."

"That's not what you let me do." The woman leaned against him, pressing her hip to his.

"Do you want your book to be nice, or do you want to make money?"

"Making spirits bright," the young fellow sang.

"He's mixing up the songs," Ron said.

"That's only our point of view," the woman said. She gave him an unexpected burlesque bump and stood aside.

"…making spirits bright…."

"And repeating himself."

"I do that. You've told me I do that."

"Have yourself a merry little Christmas…now…."

The performer made a smart bow and stepped back into the crowd while people howled and applauded.

Rick rolled himself into the middle of the room.

"Thank you, Larry," he said. "And Tilda."

The stork-like girl stepped forward and waved a long hand over her head.

"Fank you, fank you," she said.

"And now…" Rick waved his good hand back at her.

"Have your surf…." The girl began to sing.

"Tilda!" a woman called to her. "That's enough."

"Her mother," Bronstein's companion said.

"Must be a tough life," he said. "Raising a kid like that."

"I've lived worse," the woman said.

"But soon, like a man once said, you're going to turn your worst moments into cash."

"Time to eat," Rick announced. "In the dining room, everybody, help yourself…."

"Talking about worst moments," Bronstein said. "Does Rick know that you put in that scene with him?"

"Not yet."

"Hope he likes surprises."

"He'll have to roll with the punch," the woman said. "I did."

Bronstein reached over and touched her face.

"So you did."

"Not here," the woman said.

"I was just being tender and appreciative," Bronstein said. He leaned in to her and sighed a theatrical sigh.

"That's more than enough," the woman said.

"You know," Bronstein said, "you're depraved on account of you're deprived."

"I've been," the woman said.

"Deprived?"

"Depraved. Was lost but now I'm found."

"They didn't sing that one," Bronstein said. "Where's that autistic guy? I'm going to ask him to sing that."

"That's so mean," the woman said. "Where's your Christmas spirit?"

"Jews don't have any," Bronstein said. "Or maybe we ate it at birth."

"Cruel," the woman said.

"Tell me again. Every editor loves to hear that."

"Not every editor," the woman said. "Mainly, you."

"How do you know that? You've only had one editor."

"I'm not stupid," the woman said. "I asked around."

"You asked—?"

"I asked my agent."

"She doesn't know me that well."

"Ron, everybody knows about you."

"So you walked into the lion's den?"

"Eyes wide open."

"Can I have another drink now?"

"Oh, I'm sorry," the woman said. She led him back to the kitchen where he poured wine for himself into a tall crystal goblet which he then held up for inspection.

"Family heirlooms. You've written about them. This is from Grandma Folsom."

"Yes, yes. Ghosts of Christmas past," the woman said. "You remembered."

Bronstein took a swallow. "You made it memorable. When it comes out, everyone's going to remember." In a moment he needed a refill. "I'm glad we got some work in before all this," he said.

"Before all what? Don't you like talking with me?"

Bronstein gestured toward the kitchen door as the autistic couple came striding in.

"Dan, what can I get for you?" the woman said.

"A drink of water, please," the fellow said.

"And you, Tilda?"

The tall girl said something that might have been "water."

The woman poured two glasses of water from the tap.

"Cheers," Bronstein said, raising his goblet to them and drinking.

"Cheers," the autistic fellow said, as though reading the line from a script.

The tall girl said something that might have been "cheers," staring at him as though she knew something about him she couldn't possibly know.

Bronstein had to look away. "Tell you," he said, "I'm feeling a little woozy, I'm going to go outside and get some air."

"Whyn't you do that?" the woman said. "I'll tend to a few of my guests and then we'll have us some supper."

With a nod, Bronstein stepped out through the kitchen door into the chilly dark, wishing, even before he pulled the door closed behind him, that he was wearing more than a suit and tie.

The door creaked open and he turned around.

"Careful out there," the woman said.

"I have other plans," Bronstein said as the woman closed the door again.

"Have yourself…." He leaned against the side of the house and began to sing to himself. After a moment or two he walked slowly along to the front of the building, stopping just outside the living room picture window. As though in some larger-than-life Christmas card the party guests talked soundlessly and gesticulated as the two Born Agains in coveralls stood up and displayed their guitars before bowing into an animated but soundless performance. His hostess smiled and clapped her hands in silent time. The autistic singers moved their lips, but nothing reached his ears except the faintest twangings and cracklings. In the wheel chair, off to the side of the room, crippled Rick waved one hand and nodded and smiled.

Bronstein turned his back on the scene and, raising the chilly goblet to his lips, stared out into a darkness that seemed to extend into infinity. The air was cold and growing colder. Light snow fluttered down around him.

If he had read about a man such as he was in a manuscript he would have asked the author the question that he himself right now couldn't answer.

Why didn't he just turn around and go back inside?

What motivated him, what moved him? Fiction or nonfiction (and he much preferred nonfiction because the answers always came more easily) you had to ask the author these questions.

But in real life what could he say? He was thirsty but he didn't want to drink? He was drinking but he didn't want to thirst? How to phrase it all? To hell with it! To hell with it on a holiday!

"God damn it!" he shouted, hurling the goblet into the nothing just ahead and listening in the instant that it shattered.

He moved farther along the front of the house. Branches snapped under foot. Then slippery gravel. What? As his eyes became more accustomed to the dark he could make out the faint outline of the swimming pool just to his right.

In the mediocre stories he read by writers better than he would ever become there was always some fucking traditional turning point toward the end—some warmth that descended on a cold night like this, some twist in the mind or even, God help him, in the misguided heart of the main character. But what did he have? The editor? He could make the stories better but he couldn't revise his own life.

Christ! He stamped his foot, as if he himself were some tiny plant or animal creature underfoot that he could squash with one flat blow. And as his foot came down it slid out from under him and he tripped and sailed sideways, coming down hard onto cement—no, ice!—and sliding on his shoulder and elbows along the burning surface of what must be the swimming pool.

Except it was frozen.

When feeling returned to his face and limbs he felt as though he was beginning to freeze himself. Since he couldn't get up—he tried but couldn't—he lay there a while projecting his fears and worries onto the screen of the deep snowy Tennessee night. His legs felt suddenly colder than cold, as if the feeling were coming back into them only to make for a worse than freezing sensation.

There while shivering and listening to the emptiness of the property around him he recalled an incident from his first marriage forty years before. Why, he couldn't say, but nonetheless it came to him while he lay there on the frozen surface of the guitar-shaped pool.

She was a chubby girl—he liked her like that—who had blonde hair but had dyed it green for a costume party, some maul of a party with their friends, Halloween, perhaps, not Christmas. Her nipples, dark as raisins, showed through a see-through blouse. He had gone outside to smoke a cigarette and when he came back into the house—whose, he couldn't remember—he couldn't find her. As if in a dream—maybe it was a dream, after all these years he remembered it so hazily, so it might as well have been—he wandered through the house asking if anyone had seen her. People laughed in their cups, blew smoke into the air. Shanking up two flights of stairs—where was this house? A city triplex? An old country house with two stories and an attic?—he found a door. His heart gave a jump as he reached for the knob. Opening the door he stepped into a store room and found her sitting on the lap of a large man dressed as a sultan. Clearly, they were having a good time.

Oh, he shivered and sighed a sigh of loss for that wife, for the years gone. Miserable, miserable youth, for all of the success he won early on.

And he sighed in remorse for things he had done to the other two women he had married and divorced. And all the women in between and during and since.

A door opened somewhere in the dark. Faintly, faintly Christmas music drifted to him from the far part of the house, distracting him from his pathetic recollections. His hostess and the two Born Agains in coveralls arrived at the edge of the pool and with a lot of clucking and cawing led an unresisting Bronstein, trembling inconsolably from the chill, back into the house, remanding him to a place before the fire.

"You're mumbling," the woman said, touching a cool hand to his forehead.

"Put me in your next book and I'll kill you," he said.

"Hush, you," she said, sitting next to him.

"Just leave me out of things."

"But you're in them now, Ronnie. (Ronnie? No one had ever called him that since he was a child!) Just by knowing me. You should have thought better of it."

"I don't know you, really," he said.

"Oh, but you do."

"I don't. I fucking don't."

"You've read my pages."

"That's not you. They're only pages."

"But one day they will be me. The only me that's left. Thanks to you."

"Thanks for nothing."

"Oh, hush now."

"I don't want to fucking hush."

He looked across the room. One of the Born Agains was plucking at his guitar. A song went up. Soon everyone in the room was singing, with the voices of the autistics loud and clear and off-key above the crowd.

Everyone.

Nailed!

Originally published in
The Literarian, Magazine of The Center for Fiction

After a restless night—one of many in a restless year—when he awoke several times feeling that he was on the verge of something, a cold, or an allergy attack or who knew what? a perplexed Bill Wicker called in sick—and after a lazy morning of looking at the newspaper and the weather channel and drinking one cup of French Roast after another, he allowed Marcie, his wife of two years, to talk him into driving her down to the nail salon.

"If you were really sick, I wouldn't have asked you," Marcie said when they were already in the car. She then made what turned out to be a quite fateful remark. "You should come in with me. That big toe-nail of yours, you turned over in bed last night and scratched me."

"I don't remember that," Wicker said, keeping his eye on the road. He felt a little bit of whirling in his head, and he recalled that his therapist, when he went to her, referred to this state as a "complex." Perplexed—complex—it was just difficult, when you never counted on feelings things this way, ever.

"Trust me, you did it," she said.

"Well, that's what happens when you live together. Where?"

"Where what?"

"Where did I scratch you?"

"I said, in bed."

"No, where on your body?

"On my leg."

"Show me." Though he felt rather listless after his night of waking and turning, he managed to leer at her, his old college-boy way of feigning desire.

Marcie gracefully pulled up her skirt enough to show him her tan calf, and twisted around in her seat to reveal a long fresh white tear in the fleshiest part of it.

"Sorry," he said, "I don't remember doing that."

"It was the middle of the night. Just keep driving. It's almost noon."

He conducted their small, fuel-efficient car down Macomb Street and into the traffic on Connecticut. It always amazed him, a man usually in his office at this hour, that trucks and buses, ambulances and automobiles and fire-trucks made such a mess of things just before noon.

Though what the hell, he didn't know anything these days. The big boss, Jewish and knowledgeable, came down on his ass, his immediate manager, a black guy with a Harvard MBA, nagging him the way his mother used to nag his father, not with any straight-forward challenge but just sniping here and there. No wonder—Wicker felt this thought rising as a hot sensation in his chest—I lied and took the day off just now, in the middle of the big deal and all that. Malingering at home, he had forgotten about it for a while, as he did with a lot of things, and now all of a sudden remembered, thus producing more heat.

"Here you are," he said as he pulled into a space just around the corner from the address she had given him, which happened to be just around the corner from their neighborhood liquor store, a route he knew quite well.

Marcie got out of the car, but leaned back in the open passenger window, showing cleavage.

"Bill?"

"What?" He pulled his iPhone out of his pocket, ready to spend time in space with music on the drive home while she had them do, whomever they were, whatever they did for her toes. Toes—it remained for him one of those mysteries in the world of women from which he was, as he saw it then, forever barred—and gladly.

"Come in with me."

"What?"

He kept his eyes on her chest.

"Come on, come in and get that nasty toe-nail fixed," she said, showing him even more of what he always took a good look at at night.

"Nails are for girls," he said. He turned his head aside, not wanting to prove to her that all he really cared about these days was her body, though both of them had sort of gotten the idea that this was, in spite of every tenderness he had showed her in the early days of their marriage, just about the truth.

"Men are girls too sometimes," Marcie said.

Now she was playing to one of his perverse little habits.

"If I were a girl," Wicker said, "I'd never get out of the house. I'd take my clothes off and stand in front of the mirror all day long."

Marcie nodded at his familiar joke.

"You and your tits," she said.

"'Balls!' said the Queen. 'If I had 'em, I'd be King!'"

Marcie kept a straight face.

"You sure you won't come in with me?"

"I don't have an appointment," he said, feeling rather definitive. He was ready to return home, drink a beer and do he didn't know what else, except it wouldn't have anything to do with work.

"Yes, you do."

"No, I don't."

"You do. I made an appointment for both of us."

"How—?"

"Tricked you," she said.

"You did," he said.

"So come on," she said.

"Are there—?"

"—going to be any other men up there?" She gave him a big smile. "Now how did I know you were going to ask that question? Sometimes there are. Men do this, too. It's healthy for your feet, whatever you have between your legs."

Her remark sparked him around.

"I'm your slave," he said.

"I wish…"

"Yeah?" he said, motioning her away from the window while he pushed the button to raise it. "You wish what?" he said when he got out of the car. "Do you have any quarters?"

"I do," she said, reaching into her purse and fishing out some coins. "But I wish you listened to me more often. That's not being a slave. That's just what you and your friends think is being a slave."

"But look at this," Wicker said as they walked to the entrance of the building.

Toe Tally Nails by Nan
Luxury for Less

"At what?"

"I'm doing what you tell me. I'm coming along with you. I *am* your slave."

"It's called being a good companion," she said. "I could have made it easier for myself, you know. I could have come alone."

"Puh, puh," he said, alluding with his mouth noise to one of the things that sometimes passed between them in the night. It seemed to make her wince, and then laugh.

"Men are beasts," he said as she led him up the stairs.

"Why do you say that?" She turned around and gave him a guarded look, realizing—he could sometimes read her thoughts, at least simple thoughts like this—that he was staring at her buttocks as she moved. "Oh, I get it. Well, behave yourself when we get up there."

"What could I do wrong in a nail salon?" he said.

"Really—?" She took another breath but cut herself off. But not soon enough.

"Sorry," she said. "I was just kidding you."

"I was not guilty," he said. "And you weren't kidding as much as you think."

"You brought it up."

"Not exactly. It's just that it always seems to be on your mind."

Marcie paused on one of the upper steps.

"I wonder why."

Wicker stopped just below her.

"So now what am I supposed to do? More penance?"

"No," she said.

He could see the veil fall between her face and his.

"No," she went on, "we are going to have our pedicures and have a good time."

"Christ, that's what I want as much as you, having a good time! That's why I took the day—"

"You took the day off because—"

"Because—"

"Oh, Miss Marcie!"

He was interrupted by a raven-haired Asian woman, surprisingly bosomy compared to his stereotypical notion, poking her head out the doorway of the nail parlor.

"Hi, Nan," Marcie said. "Look who I brought."

The woman smiled appreciatively at Wicker.

"Just as you say, a handsome fellow. Come in, come in…"

She ducked back inside.

Wicker found himself blushing.

"You talked to her about me?"

"Bill, women talk."

"I've learned that the hard way," Wicker said.

Marcie put a finger to her lips.

"Not another word," she said.

"It was *your* friend who blabbed," he said.

"My *ex*-friend. And she might not have blabbed if you hadn't fucked her."

Her use of that word hit him like a hammer to the chest.

"I was drunk, men do that, I've told you every time you bring this up." He turned and spoke as if to the wall only a few inches from his face. "Christ, when is this going to end? You make me breakfast, we fight about it. I buy you flowers, we fight about it. We take a trip, we fight about it." He took a deep breath. "Look, if I come in here with you can that be the end?"

He turned around and Marcie gently touched a finger to his lips as the woman returned to the doorway, her head bowed, as though she were ashamed of listening.

"Please, Miss Marcie, Mister...?"

"Bill," he said. "Bill Wicker."

The woman inclined her head toward him and went inside. Marcie followed her, and Wicker followed Marcie into a large room glowing with light from the large windows overlooking the street. Wicker nearly went temporarily blind, and then he blinked his vision into submission. Green-tinted water swirled in basins set in front of large adjustable imitation leather chairs. Before he knew it, he had his shoes and socks off. Standing there, in that bright light, he stared at his ill-shaped toes with their odd-angled nails, beneath some of which a whitish-yellow fungus grew as if in a home garden. Ugly feet, but they were his feet, and he had decided to give in to Marcie's plan and allow these women to care for them. Within moments he was sitting back in one of those large chairs, his toes buffeted about in a basin of warm churning greenish water.

Marcie sat next to him but had the decency to ignore him, chattering instead with the woman in charge of her feet.

"Ah," was all Wicker said for a good 20 minutes, while his bosomy woman bid him raise his feet and lower, raise his feet and lower, so that she could clip—ay! now and then a little nip from her clipper pierced the solitude of his condition—his toe-nails and lave his soles and heels and shins and calves with various oils and lotions, hot and cold. She and the other women who worked here spoke to each other in a tonal tongue, voices rising and falling in songlike fashion. Now and then he glanced at the woman bent before him, but she gave nothing back to his eye, continuing to work on his feet, treating him like a patient, or a king, with warped toes and fungus-laden nails.

How many hundreds if not thousands of years had this kind of manicuring endured in Asia? His father had served there in that war. Of all the mysteries in his life this one leaped foremost to mind. What kind of grooming had the women he met there given him? This tenacious clipping? This rough filing? Now that the woman had finished with her clipping, things down there felt wonderful, soothing, exhilarating, ah... Look at the way she splashed about with the water and the oils! Stain herself in his service? She didn't care. She was devoted, she was his, or, at least, his foot's. The way she worked his calf muscles, the smoothness of her fingers on his sole. Ah... This is the kind of care women gave you, if you paid for it. He might even have blanked out during the paradise of it all, because when he looked over at Marcie she had a restful smile on her face as she looked back at him.

"Like it?"

"Um," he said. "I could stay here, I could...live here. Just bring me food, and so forth."

"And so forth?"

"Christ, you know. Fill in the blanks."

Marcie's chest rose as she took in a breath to speak.

"Shhh..." he said, reaching over to touch her hand. "Don't ruin this."

"And you're not?"

He might have said something just then but someone tapped at his foot, and he glanced down as his toe-woman motioned for him to raise his leg so that she could work on his other calf. This went on for a while, and then back to the other foot, and he honestly wished that he had more feet and legs for her to work on, all this was restful and stimulating at the same time. Ah—again, again, the ahs—if life were only this! He closed his eyes and imagined himself one of those kings—or a prince at least—of Thailand, with all of these luxuries and services at his beck and call. He would be a kind and good ruler, he would be benevolent, he would try not to harm anyone in his entourage, especially any of the women. Ah, a chance to start over, to become a better man. He opened his eyes.

The light coming through the windows seemed to have softened ever so slightly as the noon hour had worn on. Ah…

And then, as in all good and wonderful sensual matters, eating, massage, hoops, kissing, boozing, swimming, fucking, it was over.

He sat there, in the bliss of it all, slumped back in his chair, staring wistfully at his feet. Physically, his toes had changed, trim now, where before they were ragged and jagged, odd and almost alien to him. So had *he* changed? Take a look!

"You like?" the woman said.

He nodded.

"Yes, yes," he said, finding himself speaking pidgin. "I like, I like."

She bowed her head toward him, and he imagined how his father must have felt when he was his age, still young enough not to have been defeated, and yet old enough to anticipate the end of such physical pleasures. It was a pathetic thing, perhaps even verging on the tragic, that he had not paid much attention to his father's war stories when he had had a chance to ask questions about them. It was something, he figured, like what he might have felt if he had grown up listening to this tonal talking—near-singing it was to him—and had not chosen to learn it.

As he pulled on his socks and tied his sneakers, he felt a completely unwarranted surge of pride. From now on I will be different, he told himself. I may stumble, but I will pick myself up and surge forward, maybe even on my fucking toes! Gallant figure that he was, he paid for both of their pedicures while the women called out in their bird-language to new customers entering the salon.

"So that's it?" he said as he and Marcie walked down the stairs to the street.

"I think you liked it, didn't you?"

"I did," he said. "And now I know a little more about your secret life."

"It's not at all secret," Marcie said. "You can know as much about my life as you like. I'd like you to know it. I want you to know it."

"Well," he said, quiet until they reached the ground level, "a man can only know so much."

"Is that right?"

There was something in her voice he couldn't identify, except that he knew he didn't like it.

He might have said more, but just then a tall young almond-skinned woman in a short skirt and sandals came in through the street door. She might have been the daughter of the woman who had cared for Wicker's feet, she could have been another customer. Wicker stared at her beautiful calves and ankles and toes as he made way for her to climb past them.

"Damn!" he said as he and Marcie stepped out onto the sidewalk.

"What?" Marcie stopped and folded her arms across her chest, quite a sight herself, a storm in the making.

"My toes feel so good!"

He gave her a big big smile, which turned out to be exactly the wrong thing—who knew why?—to do.

"Ah, fuck you, Wicker," she said. "You know, I saw you looking at that girl just now, and I saw you looking at Nan when we first came in. You like your toes? Fuck your toes, fuck every one of your ten fucking toes, fuck them! I hope they turn black and drop off. I hope you never walk again!"

"Wow," Wicker said, "what did I do to piss you off? I did everything you wanted."

"You don't know what I want," she said, quietly, as though they were standing in the middle of a crowd of strangers, except that no one else was anywhere near them.

"Do you know?" he said. He clenched his fists, really, suddenly, angry.

She turned and began walking away from the shop. A car came around the corner but she kept on going.

"Hey, you'll get killed," he called after her.

"Not unless *you* kill me," she called back.

"*Bye-bye, Miss Marcie, Mister Bill! Hope you like toes!*"

Nan, the nail woman called to them from the upper windows of the building.

Marcie paid no attention. Wicker looked up.

"What did I do to deserve this?" he said. But the Asian woman couldn't hear him.

So he walked away, delicately, as it happened, because he suddenly felt a pain in his toes, in the big toe of his right foot, to be specific. Had the woman cut him with her clipper? He stopped a moment, hoping to ease the pain. Marcie walked on. She didn't even look back. Was this how things would end? Ridiculous! With him standing there alone, his toe aching, possibly bleeding, people moving along the avenue oblivious to his pain? And then the face of his father came up between him and the people on the street, the cars, the traffic light. Is that what this is all about? His toes, his life, lying to Marcie, his father—unspeakable Vietnam? Now he found it difficult to breathe, and he nearly forgot about his toes. His father opened his mouth as if to tell him something—how long since he had heard that voice? Could it speak from beyond the grave? Well, what the hell did he think was happening now, anyway? Did his father congratulate him on having become so well-groomed? Did his father say how proud he was of the man he had become? You tell us, Bill. Take a deep breath and tell us what happens next. What in this whole wide world happens next?

Ben in Amboy

Originally published in *Witness*

But the Wind abating the next Day, we made a Shift to reach Amboy before Night, having been 30 Hours on the Water without Victuals, or any Drink but a Bottle of filthy Rum: The Water we Sail'd on being salt….
—The Autobiography of Benjamin Franklin

The swimmer's hairy head broke through the surface of the river and he barked a salty-tongued and joyous gasp for the Jersey air, the yowl that followed coming right up from his empty belly.

A sunny early autumn day, with clouds sliding eastward, from the far frontier, dark places boiling within them, like his temper, oftimes flaming when he'd quarrel, fruitlessly, with his older brothers. His feet got tangled in sea-weed as he moved and here; low shore on the south bank about a mile off, and dusted with ocean sand on this side, the beach smelled of some recently dead animal, probably someone's dog. Or the glove-shaped horseshoe-crabs, ancient, ancient creatures that slid sidewise past his toes?

With a leap or two he yanked himself from the water and stood dripping with arms outstretched, as he had once seen a traveling juggler pose in a small square in his own town, and announced—

"Behold! Ladies and Pilgrims, one of the wonders of the world…."

He had the muscular body of a swimmer and his franklin, as he sometimes called it, dangled long between his legs despite the teste-shrivelling cold of the river.

Alas—or fortunately—no town in sight, and no ladies present, only two small dark-complected boys, one in deer-skin, the other in tattered cloths.

"Why are you staring?" he said as he bent to pull on his own raggedy clothes. He patted his trouser pocket, pleased to feel his old stocking still lumpy with coins.

The young one in deer-skin shook his head.

"Water's not good for you."

Ben licked the top of his own hand.

"It's a mix of fresh and salt here, lads, where your river runs into the bay. Depends on the tides, I suppose. But salt is good for you. Where would your meal be without salt? Where would you?"

"He's a mad one," the shorter boy said, the one in deer-skin. "Ain't he?" he asked his ragged companion, who shook his head in agreement.

Ben felt a twist in his belly.

"Say, we're out of vittles. Nothing but filthy rum to drink all night."

He jerked his thumb toward the boat anchored out in the shallows where the skipper worked on repairing his sails for his return trip to Manhattan. "I love the sea but I'm not much of a seaman yet. Last night out on the water I felt a bit queasy, seeing nothing but the dark. And we had no sleep. And now this swim has given me an appetite. So, do you fellows know where I can find some?"

The boys stared, as if he spoke in another language.

"Vittles?" Ben said. "Something to eat?"

The boy shrugged.

"Might you ask your mother?"

The boy winced, as though Ben had cursed him in a language he understood all too well.

"You were born out of nothing?"

The boy shook his head.

Ben tilted his head toward the east, as if out of deference to his own past.

"Everyone's born of somebody. And lives with somebody, at least until you get to be my young age. Then you can run away. As I did."

"You run away?" the boy said.

"I did," Ben said. "I'm out to make my fortune. I have a position with a printer waiting for me in Philadelphia. But for now I happen to be without food. Will you ask your mother if she will feed me something?"

"Got a sister," the boy said.

"Yup," the other boy spoke up, pointing toward the rocks where the beach ended and the fields began.

"Fetch her then," Ben said.

He lay himself gingerly down on the pebbly beach, squinting into the sun.

Those clouds, boiling away, took shapes like bull-dogs, horses, and far to the west a darker mass, like a plump woman without a head. He took a breath, as was his way of giving up the struggle of life's temporary obstacles, in this case, his decision to leave his brother's print shop in Boston, travel to New York, sail south to Jersey and then some. The smell rose from the sand, and when he looked around, a pair of those humpty glove-shaped horseshoe crabs skittered by.

The stink reminded him of his first employment, at his Father's tallow vats, to be specific: the thought came to him as he craned his neck to watch the boys walk away toward the field: home, wrestling with his father about learning a trade, his mother's demurral, brother James' physical overbearingness. Another sort of stink in his nostrils. From all this he was running. Or sailing away from, to be exact.

And then the squall had come up.

Stranded on the Long Island shore.

Then tacking for Amboy.

He sighed, delighted now with his exhaustion, because he had come so far.

Did it matter that he had so much more to go?

He closed his eyes and opened them again to see a tall creature appear as if out nowhere at the north end of the beach, where the sand met the woods.

An urge in his franklin: he reached down and scratched, adjusted himself beneath his thin cotton coverings. When he looked up he saw the girl approaching and exhaled breath through imperfect teeth.

She had straight dark hair, and a narrow face with high cheekbones. Her eyes spoke an odd green-blue, the light playing off the water changing them as he looked. And the color utterly compelling against the clay-shade of her skin.

"Good afternoon," she said.

"Good afternoon. My name is Ben," he said. "And I'm hungry."

"Felicity," she said, making a mock-curtsey. She made some sounds in her throat. "My sur-name. You can't say it right in your tongue."

He scrambled to his feet, finding that his chin came to her throat. How odd—he wasn't a small fellow, but here she was, taller than he. And with an ample chest.

"So pale," she said.

"Am I?"

"For a fish comes out of the water."

"Some fish are pale," Ben said. "White sharks. White whales. Others are dark."

"Most whales are dark."

"Never seen those," she said.

"Oh, coming over from Long Island we saw a big fish. A whale."

"A whale?"

"You seen a whale? My ancestors fished here for many years and no one ever tells of seeing a whale."

She folded her arms across her chest.

"Your ancestors?"

"Ompoge," she said. "The town is named after us. Ompoge. Amboy. A pale copy." She made that growling noise again, the other tongue.

"My ancestors came from over there," Ben said, jerking his thumb eastward toward the lighted space of sky above where the bay met the ocean. "Old Angleland. Home of us all."

A frown wrinkled across her lovely smooth dark face.

"Not all of us. We come from there." Mocking him, she motioned with her hand toward the west, where those storm clouds boiled more furiously than before.

Ben knew his geography.

"From the west?"

"From the ground under the west," she said with a laugh.

"Oh, and so you are a devil?"

She whirled around in a delight of rags and angled body.

"Am I?"

Her eyes lighted up more brightly than the approaching western storm. His franklin tingled, as though held too close to a fire.

"Feed me and I'll treat you like an angel."

She led him up the beach, in that westerly direction, and he couldn't help but eye the clamorous clouds. When he wasn't glancing at her handsome hams.

The girl smiled at him over her shoulder, as if she could read his mind. Clouds, hams. Yes, he was a busy thinker.

A small hut made of wood and stone waited for them at the end of the beach.

"This is home," she said.

"You haven't always lived here?"

"My brothers and I built it ourselves after our father died."

"And your mother?"

"She's under the ground."

"Sorry to hear it," Ben said. "My parents are both alive. And both quite adamant about anything I do that pleases me."

He ducked his head and peeked inside. His family's humble house in Boston was a hundred times grander than this, but it lacked the warm scent of the woodfire and the reassuring rough odor of drying vegetables.

She gestured for him to enter, following him inside.

"Rest yourself here," she said, motioning toward a pallet made of straw and old rags.

Ben gratefully lay his long self along the length of the pallet, gazed up a moment at the brown-faced girl and then allowed his heavy eyelids to close.

Pressing his hands to his thighs he brought back a memory of a cross-eyed girl who wore a stained white apron and smelled of fish. His first! He could picture clouds scurrying overhead near the Boston harbor. Ah, water! Where would he be without living near water! And girls!

Wind reflected on waves.

Sound of a bell.

And horses, he rode a horse, he held his arms out at either side, as though trying to catch the wind.

Feathered wing, feathered head.

Excuse me, sir, but do you know the way to—

Had he been dreaming? He sat up, sniffed the scent of the fire, recalled himself to where he lay.

The girl squatted in front of the fire, holding a skewer with something delicious—by its odor—over the smouldering wood.

"Is that meat?"

"Clams," she said.

Ben rubbed his stomach, one of his favorite parts of his body.

"Delightful."

He ate with his fingers, braving the toasted clam-flesh without fear of burning his lips or tongue, so delicious!

"I was dreaming," he said. He described to her, as best he remembered, what he had seen. "A wonderful thing. But confusing. Was it real what I saw? Or something my fancy threw to me in my sleep?"

The girl listened quietly, watching something beyond his head but when he glanced around he saw nothing but the hut.

"Do you dream?" he asked her.

"I don't know," she said, giving a shrug. Such an English gesture!

"I knew an old Indian man back home," he said. "We often sat and talked. He told me he dreamed."

"I knew an old Indian man, too," she said. "He was my father."

"Oh," he said with a lusty surge of breath, "you have a subtle wit!"

"'Wit'? What's 'wit'?"

Young Ben shook his head.

"Nothing nothing."

He sighed.

"Listen, my girl. I can give you only a coin or two for this lovely repast." He reached into his pocket, came up with the stocking, and fished out a coin. "A token."

She took it, looked at it, put it away somewhere on her person.

"I can repay you further in another way," he said.

She snorted out a laugh through her nose.

"Oh, you do have a witty charm about you," Ben said. "I'm just thinking that I could say a story to you. It's one of my favorites."

The girl looked blank. "Tell me."

"I was remembering it while we tacked across the bay. The skipper had a translation in the Dutch. From Amsterdam. A place I'll see one day, I hope. And Paris. I'd always thought I wanted to go to sea, you know. But once we got out on the waves all I wanted to do was read. And all I had was the Dutch. But here is the beginning..."

He settled back on the pallet and took a deep breath.

"'As I walked through the wilderness of this world, I lighted on a certain place where was a Den, and I laid me down in that place to sleep: and, as I slept, I dreamed a dream.

"'I dreamed, and behold, I saw a man clothed with rags, standing in a certain place, with his face from his own house, a book in his hand, and a great burden upon his back. I looked, and saw him open the book, and read therein; and, as he read, he wept, and trembled; and, not being able longer to contain, he brake out with a lamentable cry, saying, What shall I do?...'"

She held up her empty palms. "What does he do?"

"Well, then, that's the rest of the story."

"You said he dreams. Is this a dream or a story?"

"It's a story. But a story's the same as a dream, it's a waking dream." He reached for her hand. "You and I, we could both be dreaming now, together, in a dream."

She shook her head but did not take her hand back.

"I like stories better if they are real," she said. "Can you tell me a story about my Father? Can you bring him back to me?" He couldn't be sure whether the smile she put on was a sly sign that she knew what he was doing or purely pleasure.

"I don't know him," Ben said. "P'raps you can tell me a story about him?"

"He was a kind man. All this once belonged to him."

"This?"

"The river, the woods."

"He was a rich man."

"As rich as any of us," she said.

"Tell me more about him."

"He came from the west, following the deer. He fished for clams, and hunted the deer."

"I haven't seen any deer," Ben said.

"They are still here. Though my Father is gone."

She fell silent, and he tried to discern what it was he saw in her eyes.

"Tell me more about him."

"I'm not a story-teller. I'm a story-listener."

"Tell me then of a dream you had."

"I don't dream. Yankees dream. My people…we live." She drew her hand back from his.

"How do you live?"

"I fish and cook and work in the garden. That is what I do." Her voice dropped into nothing.

Their good cheer was rapidly disappearing—Ben did not enjoy it. His way was lightness, a good time, despite hard work.

"P'raps you would like to hear some poetry?" Ben said. "Would you like to listen to a poem?"

She gave him a look that made him think she had never heard the word before.

"It's different from stories," he said. "It's closer to music and song."

"I like music," she said. "I like song."

"You may like this." He cleared his throat and began to recite:

"'Of Man's First Disobedience, and the Fruit / Of that Forbidden Tree, whose mortal taste / Brought Death into the World, and all our woe, / With loss of Eden, till one greater Man / Restore us, and regain the blissful Seat, / Sing Heav'nly Muse, that on the secret top / Of Oreb, or of Sinai, didst inspire / That Shepherd, who first taught the chosen Seed....'"

"It's a very odd song," she said. "It makes me thirsty."

She pointed to his pocket and he took out the stocking. When he gave her another coin she shook her head until he gave her a second one. These she took and left the hut.

"'Say first, for Heav'n hides nothing from thy view / Nor the deep Tract of Hell, say first what cause / Mov'd our Grand Parents in that happy State, / Favour'd of Heav'n so highly, to fall off / From their Creator, and transgress his Will / For one restraint, Lords of the World besides? / Who first seduc'd them to that fowl revolt? / Th' infernal Serpent; he it was, whose guile / Stirred up with Envy and Revenge, deceiv'd / The Mother of Mankinde, what time his Pride / Had cast him out from Heav'n, with all his Host / Of Rebel Angels, by whose aid aspiring / To set himself in Glory above his Peers....'"

He went on a while longer and was still entertaining himself when the girl returned with a large bucket of what tasted something like horse urine. He swallowed and managed to keep down his gorge.

"Amboy beer? Tasty," he said, forcing a smile. "Distinct from filthy rum, yes?"

The girl smiled back.

"You?" Ben said, proffering the half-empty bucket.

She took it from him and retreated from the hut.

"Oh, my oh my," Ben said, "which do I like better, beer or rum?"

She returned a while later with more beer.

The fire began to smoke. Ben struggled to his feet so that he might poke his head outside the shack and breathe in some of the good salt air. The sun had set and sea-birds sat on the stones just outside the hut. A breeze blew freshly off the bay. Thunder boomed overhead, but no rain fell.

"Sing to me again," the girl said.

She tugged at his hand and drew him back into the hut.

He took a deep breath, lowering himself next to her on the pallet. His franklin tingled.

"My uncle wrote a poem for me. Would you like me to say it?"

She gave a nod and he cleared his throat.

"'Be to thy parents an Obedient son;/ Each Day let Duty constantly be Done;/ Never give Way to sloth or lust or pride/ If free you'd be from Thousand Ills beside....'"

She touched him at the groin.

"Will you give Way?" she said.

Her chest—johnny-cake breasts, with nipples like raisins, flesh the color of a young fawn's flank.

They spoke with their tongues. Her mouth tasted of that awful beer and tar and salt. He touched the light furze at her groin—noting the squint between her legs—and played his fingers there a while before raising to his nose a perfume as pungent as the fishy shoreline, but also mingling smoking wood, and island spices....

She lay with her eyes closed, giving him the opportunity to lick his fingers and compare the flavor to the scent.

Like the local beer, an acquired taste.

He climbed atop and almost instantly bucked like a young ram as he pulled away, spurting his seed in retreat in snaky strings of viscosity across her sand-colored belly.

He was breathing hard; the girl did not appear to be breathing at all.

Thunder boomed outside the hut. After a few moments she said, "I will tell you a story now."

"It's about time," he said, rearranging himself for comfort. A deep breath, sighed.

"A young girl," she told him, "went to sleep one night with her mother and father in the house and about the time the moon rose heard a knocking at her door. She leaped out of bed and asked, 'Who is there?' 'Tis I,' came a voice [the girl put on a scratchy voice as she said this], 'And who is I?' [going back to her natural voice] 'No one but the

River Spirit, that's who,' [in the scratchy voice] and the girl began to cry...."

Ben was already drifting, thinking about the crossing on the ferry to south of the river that he must make tomorrow, thinking that he would rather be going out to sea instead of merely crossing a river, but water was water and one day he would travel across the ocean, he was as sure of it as he knew he was going to Philadelphia to work as an apprentice for Andrew Bradford, or so he hoped. He was hungry, but he would not ask for more of the girl, she having given him what she had, the ease of coming in to her, the spice of her cunt, Amboy Indian girl, Ompoge, River Spirit knocking at the door....

A loud rapping woke him and he sat up, awake as ever.

Those boys from the beach now stood in the doorway, both glistening wet.

Behind them rain slanted down in the dark and troubled rumbling ruled the heavens.

He leaped from the empty pallet and pushed them aside.

Lightning streaked across the southern sky. A sizzling electrical dance. He stood there a while, transfigured by the mighty storm. And then when a mighty streak spurted a long spark from cloud to earth he suddenly began to shake and quiver, as though blasted by that fire.

Retreating from the door he fell back on the pallet, leaning toward the still smouldering fire. His teeth chattered and he shook all over.

That's how the girl found him when she returned, so thoroughly soaked through she might have crawled up out of the river itself.

"Poor boy," she said. Her eyes flashed, as if they could reflect the lightning through the walls of the hut.

"I believe I am with fever," Ben said.

"What do we do with you?"

"I read somewhere that cold water drank plentifully is good for a fever. Can you fetch me some?"

"Just the thing," she said and went out into the storm carrying the bucket.

"Ma," one of the boys said, "he's shaking like a dying dog."

She paid the boys no attention, kneeling alongside Ben so that he might drink rain-water from the bucket, and when he had finished she went outside for more.

"Oh, oh," Ben let out these moans, as though he had been struck by lightning.

He was so overwhelmingly thirsty now, despite his quakings, that he could drink the sea! Was this his reward for a meal of clams and a taste of cunt? Was it his fate to expire from fever on the verge of his great adventure, without ever exploring it further?

He kept on drinking, loosening his hold on the bucket only when it seemed his trembling arms might heave it into the air and so that the girl—woman? Mother of these boys?—So how old was she? Who was she?—could help him drink.

In the morning he awoke in an empty hut and found that his fever had left him. Pulling on his rags he breathed in the perfume of the girl and the smoke from the fire and his own familiar body and stepped outside.

Fog hovered over the nearby shore and the early light turned it the color of pearl. Starting at a sound he looked upriver to see the large head of a female deer and the smaller shapes of a pair of fawns bowing to drink where the creek water ran to the beach.

Feeling so much less fearful now, he watched as the animals took their time and when they had departed he walked to the shore, laughed at by sea-birds, enumerating his blessings of the night before: he had eaten, he had drunk, he had loved, he had cured himself of his ills.

Oh, Amboy! A place he would remember!

And now the world lay all before him.

He crossed the river on the ferry a few miles upstream and proceeded on his journey, on foot, having fifty miles to Burlington where he was told he should find boats that would carry him the rest of the way to Philadelphia.

Pip
(With Herman Melville)

A Story in Three Parts

Originally published in *Michigan Quarterly Review*

*Monsieurs, have ye seen one Pip?—a little negro lad, five feet
high, hang-dog look, and cowardly! Jumped from a whale-boat
once;—seen him? No!...He saw God's foot upon the treadle of
the loom, and spoke it; and therefore his shipmates called him
mad...*

Melville, *Moby-Dick*

1 — One Pip

With water? Everything! Always with water. From the womb to the well or running stream, always. Womb? His mother's, yes, begins.

Her people, so, therefore, his people, had made the Passage a hundred years before, lived in South Carolina all the generations since. She knew how to read and write—the doctor who made the rounds of the plantation took her under his wing and taught her, and a few others, these arts. She in turn had tried to teach her mother, but her mother remained too tired, as young as she was, after a day's work with the rice. All so complicated. They kept a small compact black idol, a seated man with wiry arms and a long neck, stowed in the back of their cabin even as they went to church every Sunday—it made a difference to them, keeping the old ways while all around them most other souls who lived in the cabins jumped up and down and sang their hearts out while the preacher shouted the name of Jesus. Sunday nights, they would set the black stone god on their table and stare at him, giving themselves over to the deepest thoughts they could muster while thinking his unsayable name.

"—"

The idol had come on the Passage from the old country long long ago, with the great great grandparents, and she believed the little man had saved them from the sickness and the storms that blasted them and battered the ship, killing so many, so many, as they sailed west.

Jesus! A god nowhere near as old as theirs! He kept them rounded up, crowded into a make-shift church every Sunday.

That's where she saw him for the first time as more than the boy he was when they first noticed each other—clapping his hands above his head, dodging this way, dodging that way.

He sparked something in her, down below, the way lightning might strike a tree on fire in a violent spring storm. Jesus! She shouted out. Jesus! Just her way of announcing to herself that she felt the desire in her.

Imagine his mother on her back, legs raised, ankles hooked behind the neck of the rowdy young fellow who had worshiped her from afar, this young stalk of a man, muscley arms, thick neck, callused hands, walking hang-dog all the days until one late afternoon, after the overseer called in the hands from the fields—it was raining, unaccountably, warm drizzle seeming almost to emerge from the air itself at every level from the clouds to the distant tree-tops to the succulent air they waded through as if through a shoulder-high creek—and this young lad seeing her—and she seeing him—worked up the courage to speak.

The loving, the only freedom they had!

Raising that raggedy hem up to her chin, feeling that good heat between her legs, oh, it made her raise herself up in spirit high as those rain clouds—the warm rain seeping, seeping everywhere—

Her blood stopped, the baby grew in her belly. The family gathered around the little black god, saying, praying. She imagined the infant, a tiny man, floating in her belly water, the ocean inside her.

In the middle of the hot season, which everyone said was as hot as home, though only the oldest among the folks in the cabin had even the slightest memory of the place, she felt the stirrings, twinges at first, and then twistings, and soon she lay on her side and then on her back, her apron up to her chin, while the wiggedy woman worked over her, helping to pull that child from its hiding place of water and blood and various other body liquors, the kind that stinked up the cabin even while the infant cried its heart out into the stale, unmoving air.

"I am here!" he seemed to announce. "Make my way in the world!"

To what?

A life of indentured labor in the rice fields loomed ahead of him in the not so distant future when he would put aside his wooden toys and wade in water up to his knees as he followed along behind his mother who stooped to shake the kernels from the mature and blooming plants.

That was the system that bound them, that was the system that, ironically, led to his freedom.

Herewith, told as compactly as possible, was how it happened: the scion of the plantation owner caught her in the barn and amid nervous, snorting, sometimes stamping horses, raped her. His young wife, nervous herself, and shouting—it was not the first time he had gone to the barn—called him out at the family dinner table the next evening. His father put the girl up at auction in town the next week and a passing dealer from Virginia bought her, along with a few other souls, and sold her to a farmer in Alabama. (The child went along with her, for a few dollars extra, a bargain to anyone who looked beyond the next five years, oh, the labor he would produce!)

The thing about slavery—that near-cosmic interlocking web of individual souls, the slaves and the free—it made anything possible. Here and there we observe notes of great heroism on the part of the free on behalf of the slaves, and here and there we see the basest, most evil acts imaginable in the human sphere of things, and so much worse than anything we observe in the natural world—rape, oh, yes, even torture and cannibalism—put on the slaves by the free. So while difficult to consider in the abstract, the chain of simple, ordinary events, in this case mostly positive, that sent this young man from Alabama to Connecticut, rings true, even if, to the unlearned observer, sounding somewhat like a fairy tale.

Simply this: a secret Abolitionist kidnapped him when the boy was only six years old and conveyed him to near-New England where he arranged for a young family to take him in. Once a wave in a black sea that broke on a white shore, now he lived as one of the few black children in a sea of white.

How many slave children could have said this was their story?

A few, almost none, perhaps just this young fellow.

This extraordinary young fellow!

One Pip!

In Tolland County, Connecticut he spent the rest of his growing up in a family who produced a son somewhat overweight, especially when standing next to slender Pippin, or Pip, as he came to be known, this fellow nick-named Dough-Boy. In outer aspect, Pip and Dough-Boy made a match--as Melville described it—like a black pony and a white one, of equal developments, though of dissimilar color, driven in one eccentric span. But while hapless Dough-Boy was by nature dull and torpid in his intellects, Pip, though over tender-hearted, was at bottom very bright… Pip loved life…In his…county in Connecticut, he had once enlivened many a fiddler's frolic on the green; and at melodious even-tide, with his gay ha-ha! had turned the round horizon into one star-belled tambourine. So, though in the clear air of day, suspended against a blue-veined neck, the pure-watered diamond drop will healthful glow; yet, when the cunning jeweller would show you the diamond in its most impressive lustre, he lays it against a gloomy ground, and then lights it up, not by the sun, but by some unnatural gases. Then come out those fiery effulgences, infernally superb; then the evil-blazing diamond, once the divinest symbol of the crystal skies, looks like some crown-jewel stolen from the King of Hell. But let us to the story…of how two boys set out together on a lark to meet their fate. One late autumn afternoon, when clouds had gathered above the dying grass on their sweet Connecticut field, they heard their mother's call from the house to come in for supper. As if he had been planning it all his young life, Pip put a finger to his lips, and Dough-Boy, as boys will, kept his silence. A cow moaned in the barn. A hawk circled over head, looking for the last mouse of Indian Summer. What if we dance along the road, Pip said, and run all the way to the sea-shore?

A light came in to Dough-Boy's eyes. What if? a boy asks. Why not? a boy says.

Off to the shore, following the weather. No dark of night fazed them. They had each other, the black boy, the white boy, walking all day, sleeping in each others' arms most of the night. A few farmers gave them passage overland. After some days they arrived in New Bedford and saw the sea reflected in the sky, a marbled display of cloud that augured troubled seas. Yes, it rained, and they huddled under a thicket of trees not a hundred yards from the shore.

Darkness settled over them before they arrived at the harbor, which seemed a place into which all light had retreated and then been covered over with a lid. Such dreary streets! Blocks of blackness, not houses, on either hand, and here and there a candle, like a candle moving about in a tomb. At this hour of the night, of the last day of the week, that quarter of the town proved all but deserted. But presently they came to a smoky light proceeding from a low, wide building, the door of which stood invitingly open. It had a careless look, as if it were meant for the uses of the public; so, entering, the first thing they did was to stumble over an ash-box in the porch. Ha! thought Pip, who had listened to his sermons in his late childhood, ha, as the flying particles almost choked him, are these ashes from that destroyed city, Gomorrah? However, they picked themselves up and hearing a loud voice within, pushed on and opened a second, interior door.

It seemed the great Black Parliament sitting in Tophet. A hundred black faces turned round in their rows to peer; and beyond, a black Angel of Doom was beating a book in a pulpit. It was a negro church; and the preacher's text was about the blackness of darkness, and the weeping and wailing and teeth-gnashing there. Pip, raised as the black oddity in a white family in a white town in a white county, had never seen anything like it. He listened, as if mesmerized by some master magician, hearing about his sins committed and his sins to come—the DARK part of you, the preacher intoned, the part that the DEVIL owns, the part that is DEAD to the rest of you but DRIVES you to commit the dastardly. His hands shook first, and then his knees, and soon he could hardly stand, leaning back against the wall that stood between him and the street. He reached for Dough-Boy's hand, but his brother had already lighted out the door, fearing such darkness as welled up inside this church.

Thus Pip had no one, nothing to hold on to, and he too wept, and he too gnashed his teeth, and felt himself falling forward even as leaned further back against the wall, and a dark face loomed up in his thoughts, and he did not know the face but knew it was his father, or, rather, his Father, God Himself, whose face glowed as dark as the light-faced Jesus he was raised to believe in, and he held out his hand—while the preacher shouted out, COME TO ME—and he felt the fingers of a hand reaching back to him—and it tugged him forward, and he shouted FATHER!

All the heads in the congregation turned around, and row upon row of black and brown and tan and near-white, and darker than dark faces opened their eyes wide upon him, and he backed out the door into the dark street that seemed almost by comparison as light as that moment just before the night ends and the dawn begins—a sliver of light sandwiched between the dark and the light...He found Dough-Boy standing with his face to the east, tears running down his cheeks.

"What's that?" Pip said.

"I want to go home," Dough-Boy said through his tears.

"Now, now," said Pip. "You have no home now, no home except with me, your brother."

He took Dough-Boy by the hand and led him toward the water, which differed only from the dark sky by the sizzling sound made by the waves. They found a small boat chained to a metal pillar and climbed down into it.

Just then a figure passed them by, tall and unusual as it stretched out at the advent of first light, jarring Pip into recognition. A man, yes, but what a man! Such a face! It was of a dark purplish, yellow color, here and there stuck over with large, blackish looking squares, as if its owner had been in a midnight brawl, got dreadfully cut, and there he was, just returning from the surgeon. But in that moment that he passed he turned his face so towards the light, that Pip plainly saw they could not be sticking-plasters at all, those black squares on his cheeks. They were stains of some sort or other. At first he knew not what to make of this; but soon an inkling of the truth occurred to him. He remembered a story told by some white boy, the son of a whaleman, about a whaleman who, falling among the far South Sea cannibals, had been tattooed by them. Pip marveled at this art work, even as its owner, after bestowing on him and Dough-Boy a jagged wink of his eye, disappeared into the shadows. They next pulled the sails over them, Pip consoling Dough-Boy with intermittent pats on his shoulder, until they awaked early and pulled sails aside and watched that slant of earliest morning grow wider and wider, like an eye gazing down at them in a long horizontal ever-enlarging stare.

The next morning Dough-Boy seemed cured of his home-sickness, and good for that. He miraculously produced some silver coins from inside his sock.

"Have you been walking on those?" Pip inquired.

"Dancing on them," Dough-Boy said.

The coins bought them a ferry-ride to Nantucket.

"So, my boys, you're going to see the world?"

The ferry-man, who wore a thick dark beard and a gold earring that dangled from his left ear-lobe, took their money while squinting oddly into the light behind them, as if he could not see the boys at all.

"I suppose," Pip said.

"I suppose, too," Dough-Boy said.

"See life and death in various arctic and tropic poses," the ferry-man said. "Well, I'll help ye on your way." And he gestured for them to board his little ferry.

Within the hour, Pip found himself looking back at the mainland receding into a flowering cloud bank. This was serious travel now, serious travel, the spat and hiss of the waves against the sides of the small boat, the lulling motion in his stomach. Dough-Boy moaned with the roll of the waves. The trip took much longer than they had ever imagined. Five days from Connecticut seemed like a lark compared to these hours on the heaving near-ocean. Slowly the light faded from the sky, the eastern blackened almost at once and to the west, from whence they had come, a gradual thinning out and covering over. It could not have been more than early afternoon but it seemed almost the dark of night.

But darker still was the face of the man they first encountered just after disembarking from the ferry, a stranger as tall and straight as a young tree, with a long steel-tipped weapon in hand.

"You come from over dere?" he said, pointing with the weapon—only later would they recognize they had seen their first, though hardly their last, harpoon in the direction of the mainland.

Dough-Boy shed yet another tear or two.

"Yes," he said, "from our home."

"Say goodbye," the tall dark man said. He stared down at Pip from his considerable height. "You, my brother, say goodbye."

"Goodbye?" Pip did not seem to understand.

"To home," the dark harpooner said.

Dough-Boy shed more tears. Pip pinched him at the elbow and shook his head. "You hush, now," he said. "We are on our way."

"To where, oh, where?" Dough-Boy tried to keep his tear voice steady but did not do a good job of it.

"Dere," said the tall dark harpooner, turning the point of his weapon toward the harbor.

Three ships stood out among the many smaller vessels, the Devil-Dam, the Tit-bit, and the Pequod. The dark harpooner herded them toward this last, using his weapon like a shepherd's crook. The Pequod was a rare old craft, a ship of the old school, rather small if anything; with an old fashioned claw-footed look about her. Long seasoned and weather-stained in the typhoons and calms of all four oceans, her old hull's complexion was darkened like a French grenadier's, who has alike fought in Egypt and Siberia. Her venerable bows looked bearded. Her masts—cut somewhere on the coast of Japan, where her original ones were lost overboard in a gale—her masts stood stiffly up like the spines of the three old kings of Cologne. Her ancient decks were worn and wrinkled, like the pilgrim-worshipped flag-stone in Canterbury Cathedral where Beckett bled. But to all these her old antiquities, were added new and marvelous features, pertaining to the wild business that for more than half a century she had followed. Old Captain Peleg, many years her chief-mate, before he commanded another vessel of his own, and now a retired seaman, and one of the principal owners of the Pequod—this old Peleg, during the term of his chief-mateship, had built upon her original grotesqueness, and inlaid it, all over, with a quaintness both of material and device, unmatched by anything except it be Thorkill-Hake's carved buckler or bedstead. She was apparelled like any barbaric Ethiopian emperor, his neck heavy with pendants of polished ivory. She was a thing of trophies. A cannibal of a craft, tricking herself forth in the chased bones of her enemies. All round, her unpanelled, open bulwarks were garnished like one continuous jaw, with the long sharp teeth of the Sperm Whale, inserted there for pins, to fasten her old hempen thews and tendons to. Those thews ran not through base blocks of land wood, but deftly travelled over sheaves of sea-ivory. Scorning a turnstile wheel at her reverend helm, she sported there a tiller; and that tiller was in one mass, curiously carved from the long narrow lower jaw of her hereditary foe. The helmsman who steered by that tiller in a tempest, felt like the Tartar, when he holds back his fiery steed by clutching its jaw. A noble craft, but somehow a most melancholy! All noble things are touched with that.

Now when the boys followed the harpooner aboard they looked about the quarter-deck, for someone having authority, in order to propose themselves as candidates for the voyage, at first they saw nobody; but they could not well overlook a strange sort of tent, or rather wigwam, pitched a little behind the main-mast. It seemed only a temporary erection used in port. It was of a conical shape, some ten feet high; consisting of the long, huge slabs of limber black bone taken from the middle and highest part of the jaws of the right-whale. Planted with their broad ends on the deck, a circle of these slabs laced together, mutually sloped towards each other, and at the apex united in a tufted point, where the loose hairy fibers waved to and fro like a top-knot on some old Pottowotamie Sachem's head. A triangular opening faced towards the bows of the ship, so that the insider commanded a complete view forward.

And half concealed in this queer tenement, they at length found one who by his aspect seemed to have authority; and who, with, as it appeared, the ship's work suspended, was now enjoying respite from the burden of command. He was seated on an old-fashioned oaken chair, wriggling all over with curious carving; and the bottom of which was formed of a stout interlacing of the same elastic stuff of which the wig-wam was constructed.

There was nothing so very particular, perhaps, about the appearance of the elderly man they saw; he was brown and brawny, like most old seamen, and heavily rolled up in blue pilot-cloth, cut in the Quaker style; only there was a fine and almost microscopic net-work of the minutest wrinkles interlacing round his eyes, which must have arisen from his continual sailings in many hard gales, and always looking to windward;—for this causes the muscles about the eyes to become pursed together. Such eye-wrinkles are very effectual in a scowl.

The dark-hued harpooner apparently having disappeared, Pip, employing his best Connecticut manners and advancing to the door of the tent (while towing Dough-Boy along behind), said, "Sir, sir, are you the Captain of the ship?"

"Supposing it be the Captain of the Pequod, what dost thou want of him?" the man demanded.

"We wish to go to sea," Pip said, surprising himself with his resolution.

"Thou wast, wast thou? I see thou are no Nantucketer—ever been in a stove boat?"

"No, Sir, I never have."

"Dost know nothing at all about whaling, I dare say—eh?"

"Nothing, Sir; but I have no doubt we shall soon learn."

"But what takes thee a-whaling? I want to know that before I think of shipping ye."

"Well, sir, we want to see what whaling is. I want to see the world."

"Want to see what whaling is, eh? Have ye clapped eye on Captain Ahab?"

"Who is Captain Ahab, sir?"

"Aye, aye, I thought so. Captain Ahab is the Captain of this ship."

"You are not the Captain?"

Pip felt the boastfulness that had been powering him give him the last burst of propulsion, like the last breeze to fill an ill-fated kite.

"Thou art speaking just now to Captain Peleg—that's who ye are speaking to, young man. It belongs to me and Captain Bildad to see the Pequod fitted out for the voyage, and supplied with all her needs, including crew. We are part owners and agents. But as I was going to say, if thou wantest to know what a voyage is, as thou tellest ye do, I can put ye in a way of finding it out before ye bind yourself to it, past backing out. Clap eye on Captain Ahab, young man, and thou wilt find that he has only one leg."

"What do you mean, sir? Was the other one lost by a shark?"

"Lost by a shark? Young man, come nearer to me: it was devoured, chewed up, crunched by the monstrousest parmacetty that ever chipped a boat!—ah, ah! In other words, taken from him by a whale!"

Pip grew alarmed by his energy, perhaps also a little touched at the hearty grief in his concluding exclamation, but said as calmly as he could, "A whale might do that?" He heard an odd noise at his shoulder and glanced around to find Dough-Boy whimpering like a child.

"Oh, now, my young boys," the Captain said. "I have frightened you without reason. While there is always the possibility of some creature stoving us in, you'll have your hands full enough serving the Captain. He's a queer man, Captain Ahab—so some think—but a good one. Oh, thou'lt like him well enough; no fear, no fear. he's a grand, ungodly, god-like man, Captain Ahab; doesn't speak much; but, when he does speak, then you may well listen. Mark ye, be forewarned; Ahab's above the common; Ahab's been in colleges, as well as 'mong the cannibals; been used to deeper wonders than the waves; fixed his fiery lance in mightier stranger foes than whales. His lance! aye, the keenest and the surest that out of all our isle! Oh! he ain't Captain Bildad; no, and he ain't Captain Peleg; he's Ahab, boy; and Ahab of old, thou knowest, was a crowned king!"

Next he led them out of the tent and into the damp and bracing air.

"Now then," he said, "ye never been to sea. Take a long look and see what you see, just step forward there, and take a peep over the weather-bow, and then back to me and tell me what ye see there."

For a moment Pip stood a little puzzled by this curious request, not knowing exactly how to take it, whether humorously or in earnest. But concentrating all his crow's feet into one scowl, Captain Peleg started him on the errand.

Going forward and glancing over the weather bow, Pip perceived that the ship swinging to her anchor with the flood-tide, was now obliquely pointing towards the open ocean. The prospect was unlimited, but exceedingly monotonous and forbidding; not the slightest variety that he could see.

"Well, what's the report?" said Peleg when Pip came back; "what did ye see?"

"Not much," Pip replied—"nothing but water; considerable horizon though, and there's a squall coming up, I think."

"Well, what dost thou think then of seeing the world? Do ye wish to go round Cape Horn to see any more of it, eh? Can't ye see the world where you stand?"

Pip looked to Dough-Boy, Dough-Boy looked to Pip, and the pair bowed their heads toward the water, toward the Captain. Within a few moments he led them below-decks to the quarters of Captain Ahab, the master of the Pequod, of whom they had never seen the likes before.

He frightened them, desperately. Behold: He looked like a man cut away from the stake, when the fire has overrunningly wasted all the limbs without consuming them, or taking away one particle from their compacted aged robustness. His whole high, broad form, seemed made of solid bronze, and shaped in an unalterable mould, like Cellini's cast of Perseus. Threading its way out from among his gray hairs, and continuing right down one side of his tawny scorched face and neck, till it disappeared in his clothing, you saw a slender rod-like mark, lividly whitish. It resembled that perpendicular seam sometimes made in the straight, lofty trunk of a great tree, when the upper lightning tearingly darts down it, and without wrenching a single twig, peels and grooves out the bark from top to bottom, ere running off into the soil, leaving the tree still greenly alive, but branded. Whether that mark was born with him, or whether it was the scar left by some desperate wound, no one could certainly say. So powerfully did the whole grim aspect of Ahab affect Pip, and the livid brand which streaked it, that for the first few moments he hardly noted that not a little of this overbearing grimness was owing to the barbaric white leg upon which he partly stood. The black boy was struck with the singular posture the Captain maintained. Upon each side of the Captain's desk, there was an auger hole, bored about half an inch or so, into the plank. When he rose to speak, his bone leg steadied in a hole…

"You will serve me?" he said to the boys.

They nodded wordlessly, and in a moment, dismissed by their new—and as it would turn out final—master, they trailed behind Captain Peleg up to the tent on the deck where another brawny leathery browed Nantucket Captain signed them both for a thousandth lay each of the profits from this whaling voyage.

Pip understood that he would become the marked Captain's shadow. But until the voyage began he slept some depth below the decks curled up in the arms of his brother, Dough-Boy. It felt so cold down here that his shivers began to shiver. He arose early and crept back up topside even before the rising sun gave him a shadow. Turning his back to the town he stared out over the quietly rippling water, where the harbor met the ocean and stood there a long while, as the sun inched quietly across the pure cream of the southern sky. If he had known the word, he would have called what he was doing meditation. (Water and meditation are wedded forever.). His mother's face came to mind, and he breathed and breathed as he studied it, her dark, springy hair, her broad uncreased forehead, the brown depths of her eyes, the beautiful flanges of her nose, her full lips, the way her tongue peeked out when she was thinking. Hello, Mama. Goodbye, Mama. Hello, Mama. Goodbye, Mama. Hello, Mama, Goodbye, Mama. He breathed in and out, in and out, in and out. Breath comes in threes. As the tide laps waves against the hull. Slapping and quiet, slapping and quiet, slapping and quiet. Cool wind. He breathed in and out. Recognized his breathing. A sea-bird caught his eye as it swerved over the mast, skidded in air, and lighted down upon the bow. Oh, Mama, where are you? In warm weather, water, bath of life, the essence of wind and wave come slapping, lapping, stillness.

Third among the harpooneers on this voyage was Daggoo, a gigantic, coal-black man, with a lion-like tread—a king to behold. Suspended from his ears were two golden hoops, so large that the sailors called them ring-bolts, and would talk of securing the top-sail halyards to them. In his youth Daggoo had voluntarily shipped on board of a whaler, lying in a lonely bay on his native coast. And never having been anywhere in the world but in Africa, Nantucket, and the pagan harbors most frequented by whalemen; and having now led for many years the bold life of the fishery in the ships of owners uncommonly heedful of what manner of men they shipped; Daggoo retained all his barbaric virtues, and erect as a giraffe, moved about the decks in all the pomp of six feet five in his socks. There was a corporeal humility in looking up at him; and a white man standing before him seemed a white flag come to beg truce of a fortress. When Pip turned at a sound and saw him approaching, the same man who had led them to the ship, he wanted to bow down and at the same time hug his giant leg and look up at him and declare him "Papa!"

"You! Squib!" the harpooner said to him, "you sign for the voyage?"

Pip nodded, finding it difficult to speak.

"Brave little black spot," the harpooner said.

"I—"

The harpooner stared him down, laying a finger across his lips.

"Never say a word on dis ship," he said. "You obey, not talk. Sing, maybe, but not talk. Dance, maybe, but not talk."

He seemed about to say more when he turned quickly, as if about to strike at an interloper, and Pip saw an odd pair of new arrivals clambering aboard the deck: a young man about average height with brown hair and wide eyes dressed in a tight wool coat to keep himself warm and that same bald-headed tattooed native whom the boys had encountered on the street, his face a patch-quilt of lights and darks.

"Shoo, shoo!" said the giant harpooner, with a wave of his instrument, "dese men don't come here on board to be stared at!"

At which, Pip and Dough-Boy scrambled across the deck and took the steps down and down and down to their private domain. There they stayed, until a seaman roused them from their sleeping entanglements and bid Pip come up to the Captain's quarters.

Much to the boy's chagrin, they were already moving.

"Here ye be!" The Captain pointed at him with a pen-point in hand. "And here ye remain!" He inclined his head toward a corner of the large cabin where lay a blanket and a pillow. Pointing with the pen, he growled, "Down dog, and kennel!"

In his place, Pip noticed that the ship rolled, the ship pitched as they headed out into the cold Atlantic, and in these early days of the voyage he learned to serve as only a servant could, being lower than low but yet still essential to the well-being of his master, who could not stand so high except for that he kept his servant beneath him.

Though stand be just a metaphor when referring to this Captain Ahab, who had lost a leg to the vindictive whale and its whiteness of being. Pip, as he followed the man about, was struck with the singular posture his master maintained. Upon each side of the Pequod's quarter deck, and pretty close to the mizen shrouds, there was an auger hole, bored about half an inch or so, into the plank. His bone leg steadied in that hole; one arm elevated, and holding by a shroud; Captain Ahab stood erect, looking straight out beyond the ship's ever-pitching prow. There was an infinity of firmest fortitude, a determinate unsurrenderable wilfulness, in the fixed and fearless, forward dedication of that glance. Not a word he spoke; nor did his officers say aught to him; though by all their minutest gestures and expressions, they plainly showed the uneasy, if not painful, consciousness of being under a troubled master-eye. And not only that, but moody stricken Ahab stood before them with a crucifixion in his face; in all the nameless regal overbearing dignity of some mighty woe.

By day Pip, doing his duties, which included everything from carrying his master's wine glass to polishing his extra leg, noticed the crew remained on alert every passing minute, because those who spoke to him, and more and more of the crew did speak to him the farther out to sea they sailed, said a whale-spout might materialize at any second, and this was their business, spying the spout, so that each man remained as ready to catch sight of it as the sailor whose duty it was that day or night to climb up the mast-head and keep a horizon-filled watch for the tell-tale plume in the distance. He craned his neck each time he found himself on deck, watching the watchers.

Some weeks out, while in an off-moment from duty during an evening he heard a young sailor, perhaps the same brown-haired man who had boarded with the tattooed giant some weeks before, reading from a note-book, aloud, to his tattooed friend.

"Whales are as scarce as hen's teeth they tell me when I am up on the mast-head. Perhaps they were; or perhaps there might have been shoals of them in the far horizon; but lulled into such an opium-like listlessness of vacant, unconscious reverie is this absent-minded youth by the blending cadence of waves with thoughts, that at last I lose my identity; take the mystic ocean at my feet for the visible image of that deep, blue, bottomless soul, pervading mankind and nature; and every strange, half-seen, gliding, beautiful thing that eludes me; every dimly-discovered, uprising fin of some undiscernible form, seems to me the embodiment of those elusive thoughts that only people the soul by continually flitting through it. In this enchanted mood, my spirit ebbs away to whence it came; becomes diffused through time and space; like Cranmer's sprinkled Pantheistic ashes, forming at last a part of every shore the round globe over. There is no life in me, now, except that rocking life imparted by a gently rolling ship; by her, borrowed from the sea; by the sea, from the inscrutable tides of God. But while this sleep, this dream is on me, move my foot or hand an inch; slip my hold at all; and my identity comes back in horror. Over Descartian vortices you hover. And perhaps, at mid-day, in the fairest weather, with one half-throttled shriek I could drop through that transparent air into the summer sea, no more to rise for ever. Heed it well, ye Pantheists!"

Dreamy, meditative talk, yes?

But nothing like the nights on deck, when the weather turned warm and the seas for a dreamy few minutes rocked the ship like an infant in a cradle.

2nd Nantucket Sailor

Avast the chorus! Eight bells there! d'ye hear, bell-boy? Strike the bell eight, thou Pip! thou blackling! and let me call the watch. I've the sort of mouth for that—the hogshead mouth. So, so, (thrusts his head down the scuttle), Star—bo-l-e-e-n-s, a-h-o-y! Eight bells there below! Tumble up!

French Sailor

Merry-mad! Hold up thy hoop, Pip, till I jump through it! split jibs! tear yourselves!

Tashtego Quietly smoking

That's a white man; he calls that fun: humph! I save my sweat.

Pip Shrinking under the windlass

Jollies? Lord help such jollies! Crish, crash! there goes the jib-stay! Blang-whang! God! Duck lower, Pip, here comes the royal yard! It's worse than being in the whirled woods, the last day of the year; Who'd go climbing after chestnuts now? But there they go, all cursing, and here I don't. Fine prospects to 'em; they're on the road to heaven. Hold on hard! Jimmini, what a squall! But those chaps there are worse yet—they are your white squalls, they. White squalls? White whale, shirr! shirr! Here have I heard all their chat just now, and the white whale—shirr! shirr!—but spoken of once! And only this evening—it makes me jingle all over like my tambourine—that anaconda of an old man swore 'em in to hunt him! Oh, thou big white God aloft there somewhere in yon darkness, have mercy on this small black boy down here; preserve him from all men that have no bowels to feel fear!

And then came a sighting, and another, and another.

Pip's work however, appeared to be below rather than above. He cleaned the Captain's cabin and washed the walk before it, and now and then helped the cook with the cutting of the meat and the mixing of the dough. (Dough-Boy, less fortunate, did not work on his name-sake but rather spent most of his waking days polishing brass and swabbing decks.) On calm days Pip slowed down, and now and then caught a glimpse of sailors he had noticed before and upon the sailing, that tattooed Islander, for example, sitting upon his bunk, his hand holding close up to his face a little negro idol, peering hard into its face, and with a jack-knife gently whittling away at its nose, meanwhile humming to himself in his heathenish way. The wash of nostalgia for a home he could not remember splashed over the young boy so that for a moment or two he wanted to burst into tears. And then he watched the ginger-haired sailor who had accompanied the larger harpooner, him sitting also, reading from a book whose title Pip, as he meandered past him, caught a glimpse of: *Metaphysics.*

It was but some few days after that a most significant event befell the most insignificant of the Pequod's crew; an event most lamentable; and which ended in providing the sometimes madly merry and predestinated craft with a living and ever accompanying prophecy of whatever shattered sequel might prove her own.

Now, in the whale ship, it is not every one that goes in the boats. Some few hands are reserved called ship-keepers, whose province it is to work the vessel while the boats are pursuing the whale. As a general thing, these ship-keepers are as hardy fellows as the men comprising the boats' crews. But if there happen to be an unduly slender, clumsy, or timorous wight in the ship, that wight is certain to be made a ship-keeper. It was so in the Pequod with the little Pippin by nick-name, Pip by abbreviation. Poor Pip! Ye have heard of him before; ye must remember his tambourine on that dramatic midnight, so gloomy-jolly, just a moment before.

It came to pass, that in the ambergris affair Stubb's after-oarsman chanced so to sprain his hand, as for a time to become quite maimed; and, temporarily, Pip was put into his place.

The first time Stubb lowered with him, Pip evinced much nervousness; but happily, for that time, escaped close contact with the whale; and therefore came off not altogether discreditably; though Stubb observing him, took care, afterwards, to exhort him to cherish his courageousness to the utmost, for he might often find it needful.

Now upon the second lowering, the boat paddled upon the whale; and as the fish received the darted iron, it gave its customary rap, which happened, in this instance, to be right under poor Pip's seat. The involuntary consternation of the moment caused him to leap, paddle in hand, out of the boat; and in such a way, that part of the slack whale line coming against his chest, he breasted it overboard with him, so as to become entangled in it, when at last plumping into the water. That instant the stricken whale started on a fierce run, the line swiftly straightened; and presto! Poor Pip came all foaming up to the chocks of the boat, remorselessly dragged there by the line, which had taken several turns around his chest and neck.

Tashtego stood in the bows. He was full of the fire of the hunt. He hated Pip for a poltroon. Snatching the boat-knife from its sheath, he suspended its sharp edge over the line, and turning towards Stubb, exclaimed interrogatively, "Cut?" Meantime Pip's blue, choked face plainly looked, Do, for God's sake! All passed in a flash. In less than half a minute, this entire thing happened.

"Damn him, cut!" roared Stubb; and so the whale was lost and Pip was saved.

So soon as he recovered himself, the poor little negro was assailed by yells and execrations from the crew. Tranquilly permitting these irregular cursings to evaporate, Stubb then in a plain, business-like, but still half humorous manner, cursed Pip officially; and that done, unofficially gave him much wholesome advice. The substance was, Never jump from a boat, Pip, except—but all the rest was indefinite, as the soundest advice ever is. Now, in general, Stick to the boat, is your true motto in whaling; but cases will sometimes happen when Leap from the boat, is still better. Moreover, as if perceiving at last that if he should give undiluted conscientious advice to Pip, he would be leaving him too wide a margin to jump in for the future; Stubb suddenly dropped all advice, and concluded with a peremptory command, "Stick to the boat, Pip, or by the Lord, I won't pick you up if you jump; mind that. We can't afford to lose whales by the likes of you; a whale would sell for thirty times what you would, Pip, in Alabama. Bear that in mind, and don't jump any more." Hereby perhaps Stubb indirectly hinted, that though man loved his fellow, yet man is a money-making animal, which propensity too often interferes with his benevolence.

But we are all in the hands of the Gods; and Pip jumped again. It was under very similar circumstances to the first performance; but this time he did not breast out the line; and hence, when the whale started to run, Pip was left behind on the sea, like a hurried traveller's trunk. Alas! Stubb was but too true to his word. It was a beautiful, bounteous, blue day; the spangled sea calm and cool, and flatly stretching away, all round, to the horizon, like gold-beater's skin hammered out to the extremest. Bobbing up and down in that sea, Pip's ebon head showed like a head of cloves. No boat-knife was lifted when he fell so rapidly astern. Stubb's inexorable back was turned upon him; and the whale was winged. In three minutes, a whole mile of shoreless ocean lay between Pip and Stubb. Out from the centre of the sea, poor Pip turned his crisp, curling, black head to the sun, another lonely castaway, though the loftiest and the brightest.

Now, in calm weather, to swim in the open ocean is as easy to the practised swimmer as to ride in a spring- carriage ashore. But the awful lonesomeness is intolerable. The intense concentration of self in the middle of such a heartless immensity, my God! who can tell it? Mark, how when sailors in a dead calm bathe in the open sea—mark how closely they hug their ship and only coast along her sides.

But had Stubb really abandoned the poor little negro to his fate? No; he did not mean to, at least. Because there were two boats in his wake, and he supposed, no doubt, that they would of course come up to Pip very quickly, and pick him up; though, indeed, such considerations towards oarsmen jeopardized through their own timidity, is not always manifested by the hunters in all similar instances; and such instances not unfrequently occur; almost invariably in the fishery, a coward, so called, is marked with the same ruthless detestation peculiar to military navies and armies.

But it so happened, that those boats, without seeing Pip, suddenly spying whales close to them on one side, turned, and gave chase; and Stubb's boat was now so far away, and he and all his crew so intent upon his fish, that Pip's ringed horizon began to expand around him miserably. By the merest chance the ship itself at last rescued him; but from that hour the little negro went about the deck an idiot; such, at least, they said he was. The sea had jeeringly kept his finite body up, but drowned the infinite of his soul. Not drowned entirely, though. Rather carried down alive to wondrous depths, where strange shapes of the unwarped primal world glided to and fro before his passive eyes; and the miser-merman, Wisdom, revealed his hoarded heaps; and among the joyous, heartless, ever-juvenile eternities, Pip saw the multitudinous, God-omnipresent, coral insects, that out of the firmament of waters heaved the colossal orbs. He saw God's foot upon the treadle of the loom, and spoke it; and therefore his shipmates called him mad. So man's insanity is heaven's sense; and wandering from all mortal reason, man comes at last to that celestial thought, which, to reason, is absurd and frantic; and weal or woe, feels then uncompromised, indifferent as his God.

Oh, Pip, this was but a portent and a premonition of things to come! Pip himself had no sense of this, but others on board the Pequod, even in the midst of their grinding work, saw a certain dark glow about him as they went about their work and mulled on the sea around them, much of that glow insidious and off to the side, like the light of a star.

Had you for example stepped on board the Pequod at a certain juncture of the post-mortemizing of a whale, with the cutting and flensing almost accomplished, and had you strolled forward nigh the wind-lass, pretty sure you might have scanned with no small curiosity a very strange, enigmatical object, which you would have seen there, lying along lengthwise in the lee scuppers. Not the wondrous cistern in the whale's huge head; not the prodigy of his unhinged lower jaw; not the miracle of his symmetrical tail; none of these would so surprise you, as half a glimpse of that unaccountable cone,—longer than a Kentuckian is tall, nigh a foot in diameter at the base, and jet-black as Yojo, the ebony idol of Queequeg. And an idol, indeed, it is; or, rather, in old times, its likeness was. Such an idol as that found in the secret groves of Queen Maachah in Judea; and for worshipping which, king Asa, her son, did depose her, and destroyed the idol, and burnt it for an abomination at the brook Kedron, as darkly set forth in the 15th chapter of the first book of Kings.

Walking up to this phenomenon, Pip could not have known all this, and yet he felt drawn to it the way he had been drawn to the smaller idol of the tattooed heathen harpooner.

Meanwhile Queequeg, who had ordered the ship's carpenter to construct his coffin, was busy with the measuring of it. He called for his harpoon, had the wooden stock drawn from it, and then had the iron part placed in the coffin along with one of the paddles of his boat. All by his own request, also, biscuits were then ranged round the sides within: a flask of fresh water was placed at the head, and a small bag of woody earth scraped up in the hold at the foot; and a piece of sail-cloth being rolled up for a pillow, Queequeg now entreated to be lifted into his final bed, that he might make trial of its comforts, if any it had. He lay without moving a few minutes, then told one to go to his bag and bring out his little god, Yojo. Then crossing his arms on his breast with Yojo between, he called for the coffin lid (hatch he called it) to be placed over him. The head part turned over with a leather hinge, and there lay Queequeg in his coffin with little but his composed countenance in view. Rarmai (it will do; it is easy), he murmured at last, and signed to be replaced in his hammock.

But ere this was done, Pip, who had been slyly hovering near by all this while, drew nigh to him where he lay, and with soft sobbings, took him by the hand; in the other, holding his tambourine.

"Poor rover! will ye never have done with all this weary roving? Where go ye now? But if the currents carry ye to those sweet Antilles where the beaches are only beat with water-lilies, will ye do one little errand for me? Seek out one Pip, who's now been missing long: I think he's in those far Antilles. If ye find him, then comfort him; for he must be very sad; for look! he's left his tambourine behind;—I found it. Rig-a-dig, dig, dig! Now, Queequeg, die; and I'll beat ye your dying march."

"I have heard," murmured first-mate Starbuck, gazing down the scuttle, "that in violent fevers, men, all ignorance, have talked in ancient tongues; and that when the mystery is probed, it turns out always that in their wholly forgotten childhood those ancient tongues had been really spoken in their hearing by some lofty scholars. So, to my fond faith, poor Pip, in this strange sweetness of his lunacy, brings heavenly vouchers of all our heavenly homes. Where learned he that, but there?—Hark! he speaks again: but more wildly now."

"From two and two! Let's make a General of him! Ho, where's his harpoon? Lay it across here.—Rig-a-dig, dig, dig! huzza! Oh for a game cock now to sit upon his head and crow! Queequeg dies game!—mind ye that; Queequeg dies game!—take ye good heed of that; Queequeg dies game! I say; game, game, game! but base little Pip, he died a coward; died all a'shiver;—out upon Pip! Hark ye; if ye find Pip, tell all the Antilles he's a runaway; a coward, a coward, a coward! Tell them he jumped from a whale-boat! I'd never beat my tambourine over base Pip, and hail him General, if he were once more dying here. No, no! shame upon all cowards—shame upon them! Let 'em go drown like Pip, that jumped from a whale-boat. Shame! shame!"

During all this, Queequeg lay with closed eyes, as if in a dream. Pip was led away, and the sick man was replaced in his hammock. Yet out on deck again with Master, not long after Pip witnessed the disaffiliation of the navigation system, with the log used to score along with the line having torn free from the ship.

Ahab saw this as the loosening out of the middle of the world. "Haul in, haul in, Tahitian! These lines run whole, and whirling out: come in broken, and dragging slow. Ha, Pip? come to help; eh, Pip?"

Pip spoke up, as if out of his own body.

"Pip? whom call ye Pip? Pip jumped from the whale-boat. Pip's missing. Let's see now if ye haven't fished him up here, fisherman. It drags hard; I guess he's holding on. Jerk him, Tahiti! Jerk him off; we haul in no cowards here. Ho! there's his arm just breaking water. A hatchet! a hatchet! cut it off—we haul in no cowards here. Captain Ahab! Sir, Sir! here's Pip, trying to get on board again."

"Peace, thou crazy loon," cried the Manxman, seizing him by the arm. "Away from the quarter-deck!"

"The greater idiot ever scolds the lesser," muttered Ahab, advancing. "Hands off from that holiness! Where sayest thou Pip was, boy?"

"Astern there, Sir, astern! Lo, lo!"

"And who art thou, boy? I see not my reflection in the vacant pupils of thy eyes. Oh God! that man should be a thing for immortal souls to sieve through! Who art thou, boy?"

"Bell-boy, Sir; ship's-crier; ding, dong, ding! Pip! Pip! Pip! One hundred pounds of clay reward for Pip; five feet high—looks cowardly—quickest known by that! Ding, dong, ding! Who's seen Pip the coward?"

"There can be no hearts above the snow-line. Oh, ye frozen heavens! look down here. Ye did beget this luckless child, and have abandoned him, ye creative libertines. Here, boy; Ahab's cabin shall be Pip's home henceforth, while Ahab lives. Thou touchest my inmost centre, boy; thou art tied to me by cords woven of my heart- strings. Come, let's down."

"What's this? here's velvet shark-skin, intently gazing at Ahab's hand, and feeling it. Ah, now, had poor Pip but felt so kind a thing as this, perhaps he had ne'er been lost! This seems to me, Sir, as a man-rope; something that weak souls may hold by. Oh, Sir, let old Perth now come and rivet these two hands together; the black one with the white, for I will not let this go."

"Oh, boy, nor will I thee, unless I should thereby drag thee to worse horrors than are here. Come, then, to my cabin. Lo! ye believers in gods all goodness, and in man all ill, lo you! see the omniscient gods oblivious of suffering man; and man, though idiotic, and knowing not what he does, yet full of the sweet things of love and gratitude. Come! I feel prouder leading thee by thy black hand, than though I grasped an Emperor's!"

"There go two daft ones now," muttered the old Manxman. "One daft with strength, the other daft with weakness. But here's the end of the rotten line—all dripping, too. Mend it, eh? I think we had best have a new line altogether. I'll see Mr. Stubb about it."

***

The coffin laid upon two line-tubs, between the vice-bench and the open hatchway; the Carpenter calking its seams; the string of twisted oakum slowly unwinding from a large roll of it placed in the bosom of his frock.—Ahab comes slowly from the cabin-gangway, and hears Pip following him.

"Back, lad; I will be with ye again presently. He goes! Not this hand complies with my humor more genially than that boy.—Middle aisle of a church! What's here?"

"Life buoy, Sir. Mr. Starbuck's orders. Oh, look, Sir! Beware the hatchway!"

"Thank ye, man. Thy coffin lies handy to the vault."

"Sir? The hatchway? oh! So it does, Sir, so it does."

"Art not thou the leg-maker? Look, did not this stump come from thy shop?"

"I believe it did, Sir; does the ferrule stand, Sir?"

"Well enough. But art thou not also the undertaker?"

"Aye, Sir; I patched up this thing here as a coffin for Queequeg; but they've set me now to turning it into something else."

"Then tell me; art thou not an arrant, all-grasping, inter-meddling, monopolizing, heathenish old scamp, to be one day making legs, and the next day coffins to clap them in, and yet again life-buoys out of those same coffins? Thou art as unprincipled as the gods, and as much of a jack-of-all- trades."

"But I do not mean anything, Sir. I do as I do."

"The gods again. Hark ye, dost thou not ever sing working about a coffin? The Titans, they say, hummed snatches when chipping out the craters for volcanoes; and the grave-digger in the play sings, spade in hand. Dost thou never?"

"Sing, Sir? Do I sing? Oh, I'm indifferent enough, Sir, for that; but the reason why the grave-digger made music must have been because there was none in his spade, Sir. But the calking mallet is full of it. Hark to it."

"Aye, and that's because the lid there's a sounding- board; and what in all things makes the sounding-board is this—there's naught beneath. And yet, a coffin with a body in it rings pretty much the same, Carpenter. Hast thou ever helped carry a bier, and heard the coffin knock against the churchyard gate, going in?"

"Faith, Sir, I've—"

"Faith? What's that?"

"Why, faith, Sir, it's only a sort of exclamation-like—that's all, Sir."

"Um, um; go on."

"I was about to say, Sir, that—"

"Art thou a silk-worm? Dost thou spin thy own shroud out of thy-self? Look at thy bosom! Despatch! and get these traps out of sight."

"He goes aft. That was sudden, now; but squalls come sudden in hot latitudes. I've heard that the Isle of Albemarle, one of the Gallipagos, is cut by the Equator right in the middle. Seems to me some sort of Equator cuts yon old man, too, right in his middle. He's always under the Line—fiery hot, I tell ye! He's looking this way—come, oakum; quick. Here we go again. This wooden mallet is the cork, and I'm the professor of musical glasses—tap, tap!"

Ahab to himself.

"There's a sight! There's sound! The greyheaded woodpecker tapping the hollow tree! Blind and dumb might well be envied now. See! that thing rests on two line-tubs, full of tow- lines. A most malicious wag, that fellow. Rat-tat! So man's seconds tick! Oh! how immaterial are all materials! What things real are there, but imponderable thoughts? Here now's the very dreaded symbol of grim death, by a mere hap, made the expressive sign of the help and hope of most endangered life. A life-buoy of a coffin! Does it go further? Can it be that in some spiritual sense the coffin is, after all, but an immortality-preserver! I'll think of that. But no. So far gone am I in the dark side of earth, that its other side, the theoretic bright one, seems but uncertain twilight to me. Will ye never have done, Carpenter, with that accursed sound? I go below; let me not see that thing here when I return again. Now, then, Pip, we'll talk this over; I do suck most wondrous philosophies from thee! Some unknown conduits from the unknown worlds must empty into thee!"

Ahab moving to go on deck; Pip catches him by the hand to follow.

"Lad, lad, I tell thee thou must not follow Ahab now. The hour is coming when Ahab would not scare thee from him, yet would not have thee by him. There is that in thee, poor lad, which I feel too curing to my malady. Like cures like; and for this hunt, my malady becomes my most desired health. Do thou abide below here, where they shall serve thee, as if thou wert the captain. Aye, lad, thou shalt sit here in my own screwed chair; another screw to it, thou must be."

"No, no, no! ye have not a whole body, Sir; do ye but use poor me for your one lost leg; only tread upon me, Sir; I ask no more, so I remain a part of ye."

"Oh! spite of million villains, this makes me a bigot in the fadeless fidelity of man!—and a black! and crazy!—but methinks like-cures-like applies to him too; he grows so sane again."

"They tell me, Sir, that Stubb did once desert poor little Pip, whose drowned bones now show white, for all the blackness of his living skin. But I will never desert ye, Sir, as Stubb did him. Sir, I must go with ye."

"If thou speakest thus to me much more, Ahab's purpose keels up in him. I tell thee no; it cannot be."

"Oh good master, master, master!"

"Weep so, and I will murder thee! have a care, for Ahab too is mad. Listen, and thou wilt often hear my ivory foot upon the deck, and still know that I am there. And now I quit thee. Thy hand!—Met! True art thou, lad, as the circumference to its centre. So: God for ever bless thee; and if it come to that,—God for ever save thee, let what will befall."

Ahab goes; Pip steps one step forward.

"Here he this instant stood; I stand in his air,—but I'm alone. Now were even poor Pip here I could endure it, but he's missing. Pip! Pip! Ding, dong, ding! Who's seen Pip? He must be up here; let's try the door. What? neither lock, nor bolt, nor bar; and yet there's no opening it. It must be the spell; he told me to stay here: Aye, and told me this screwed chair was mine. Here, then, I'll seat me, against the transom, in the ship's full middle, all her keel and her three masts before me. Here, our old sailors say, in their black seventy-fours great admirals sometimes sit at table, and lord it over rows of captains and lieutenants. Ha! What's this? Epaulets! Epaulets! The epaulets all come crowding! Pass round the decanters; glad to see ye; fill up, monsieurs! What an odd feeling, now, when a black boy's host to white men with gold lace upon their coats!—Monsieurs, have ye seen one Pip?—a little negro lad, five feet high, hang-dog look, and cowardly! Jumped from a whale-boat once;—seen him? No! Well then, fill up again, captains, and let's drink shame upon all cowards! I name no names. Shame upon them! Put one foot upon the table. Shame upon all cowards.—Hist! above there, I hear ivory—Oh, master, master! I am indeed down-hearted when you walk over me. But here I'll stay, though this stern strikes rocks; and they bulge through; and oysters come to join me."

2 — My Dream as Pip

Having completed a new novel and having sunk as I do into a middle state of light-headed being and heavy-hearted lassitude that comes with finding myself between finishing the writing of one book and the beginning of work on another, I turned to rereading some of the great pleasures of my life. Closed up in my office, seeing no one for days on end, after a week or so I finished *Moby-Dick,* closed the book, and closed my eyes. It had been a treat of a treat, with only so many pages I could take in an hour, the prose more like the finest cognac than fine wine, nothing you wanted to gulp down. As I had read it brought to the surface of my mind all sorts of thoughts and images and emotions, my father's crash landing in the Sea of Japan in 1932, shipping on a freighter with my son from the Russian port of Nahodka to the port of Yokohama, living on the ocean littoral in the summer of 1972 and every summer thereafter, a month in Hawaii in the middle of the Pacific, our older daughter's wedding at the Marine Center in Santa Cruz near the enormous skeleton of a whale. A bower in the Arsacides! One thing I certainly hadn't counted on as I read this time around was the arrival in my life of a grandchild, born in Africa, whose face kept coming to mind with every reference to Pip. I had always noticed Pip while reading *Moby-Dick* but never looked at him directly until now, let alone looked him in the eye. Melville, triumphing over a few of his own racist tics, made a wonder of him! The entire experience made me dizzy and something like inebriated, and I soon fell into a deep sleep.

I found myself leaning over the railing of a boat in mid-ocean, hoping to fish for the large golden carp I noticed swimming just beneath the surface. I leaned farther, and fell headlong into the ocean. The warmth of the water shocked me, and I called out, but my father, fishing from another boat some distance away, could not hear me. I paddled and paddled like a dog, but eventually my arms grew tired. And I sank...down, down, down, until I recovered my balance and felt the furry underfloor of the ocean beneath my bare feet. Ferns and wavery flowering plants tickled me as I passed and the air bubbles from my lips passed up in a sort of vertical musical scale—unreadable, unplayable, but still evident—up toward the faint light of the tropic sun. Was this near-dying? Was this near-death?

The currents turned me here, there, as though I were a pliant-limbed plant myself, but soon I became skilled in walking along the seafloor in that whip-lash fashion, shoulders twisting, legs lifted by the undersea streams so that I had to concentrate on placing one after the other after the other and continue on my way.

I saw what seemed to me as wonders—though I don't remember them well enough to describe, as often happens in dreams—while I pushed myself along. Some distance above me, a shaft of bright sunlight veered down at a slight angle from the surface of the sea, silvery-yellowish light that reminded me of the color of old gold. Immediately in front of me the water swirled with all sorts of flotsam, from the tiniest specks of sea-life to torn patches of plant. Beyond that the brownish-darkness of the sea-floor's false horizon loomed in the distance.

Half-sighted, half-blind, I moved along, to what destination I could not have said, except that I felt myself pushed by the current at my back in that murky direction. Murky! Oh, I did not know the half of it! Because now in the distance, across and through the waters, I heard music, the thump and tinny notes of a country band, the cheers and whistles of a crowd.

Oh, here he was, here was Pip! Dressed in a top hat and long coveralls colored stripes of American red, white, and blue, he led the band, and danced in place as he conducted the music, looking as alive and as sprightly and as engaged as I had first imagined him while reading *Moby-Dick*.

I listened a while to the music—you know how it is in a dream, when everything comes together and nothing seems impossible—a version of The Stars and Stripes forever, a Dixieland tune, a Christmas carol, as though the drifting bits and pieces of plant and fish in the waters surrounding us might have been snow, and then a Motown ballad and a Bob Dylan song.

"All along the watchtower," he sang along with the music.

"Pip, my young man," I said, not paying any attention to the fact that it is impossible to speak underwater, let alone sing, especially at the depth at which we found ourselves, "that is a modern tune or two. How can you know these?"

"Oh, Alan," he said (yes, he knew my name! As if he might have learned it because I was reading about his life and fate, we had that kind of intimacy between us), "you learn a lot new about time here beneath the waves." He set down his conductor's wand and gazed at me. "The sea runs round the world, the same sea covering all the earth, and when you study it, as I have now in these amazing years of my days, you see the link between oceans and time, the way time rolls round our lives in similar fashion, making a steady stream of events that sometimes runs in currents, swirling back on themselves, as in our little colloquy here, or surging ahead, as we will in a moment. Me talking to you, you talking to me, all of this underwater in a dream! Who could have imagined! Oh, for a life beneath a bower in the Arsacides! But then I am content to remain beneath the waves, this bath of life so vastly unexplored by all of you who live above the surface."

"Oh, Pip," I said, "young Pip, Master Pip, Mister Pip—"

"Just Pip, as always," he said.

"I agree. Who could have imagined? I read a book, a dream made out of language, and then dreamed this dream where we meet, but only because your master made the book in which you lived—"

"No past tense, sir, because I am still alive, in these parts, these pages, in your dream, and in your story made a dream of a dream..."

"But Pip...?"

'Yes, sir, you, Alan, what may I tell you?"

Now he had drifted closer to me, and though quite short compared to my own height, he exuded a confidence you rarely find in the living, no matter how tall, and a sweetness, too, which reminded me of my new grandchild as well, the sweetness you can see in the young child when you are one generation removed from the grueling daily round of caring for them, grueling, no matter how much you love them, of course.

Feeling this bond with him, and yet free of a certain responsibility I asked him a question that came immediately to mind. "Down here," I said, "do you see any of the other good men who went down with the Pequod?"

He smiled a smile so bright it lighted up the darker places where shadows surrounded us in the sea.

And then he began to speak again.

3 — Pip, Redivivus

The first I saw was the mate, dear Starbuck, who had been a lamp-light to me in the darkest moments of our voyage, his ever-glowing strength of character a guide as I navigated the ways of the Captain and his mad quest. (Mad! Nothing so American as a white man obsessed with embracing what he cannot ever have! Black Americans, including now ever-young yours truly, see things differently. We want to keep what we have, we want to have as much as we can, but our obsession, if you can call our thirst for freedom by that name, remains only with an idea. But then this is a child's-eye view, not that my old master Captain dignified an adult-eye view, not with his madness about capturing the whale that had taken his leg.

Ahab did not have a quest, though, did he? He had a love affair with a part of Nature he could never embrace.

Stubb, Flask, these were not so important to me in my way of seeing, but Dough-Boy, a boy I loved as my brother, gave me comfort in odd and difficult family moments, so that when he floated past me as our ship went down I reached over to him and held him by the hand and righted him, and we sank down brother-to-brother together. The difference between him and me became clear when I spoke to him and he did not blink, his open eyes gazing like a seal's toward Paradise.

The dark-complected and tattooed harpooners danced around me in fast-moving currents as we floated toward the sea floor, their weapons gone but their long arms remaining, wavery, like long strands of sea-plant and weed.

Daggoo!

Tashtego!

Brothers, brothers!

And my, yes, beloved Queequeg! And was there a boy as lucky as I, who would meet his fate so young, who had ever been so blessed as to know this Polynesian prince before we all sank down?

And the Manxman, and others in the crew, and Sinbad the Sailor and Jinbad the Jailer and Minbad the Mailer and Winbad the Wailer...

Along alone...

Oh, a watery death, full fathom ...

I watched these others of the crew sink around me, some upside down, some right side up, some sideways, some with their pockets of their britches turned out, some with hair flaring out around them.

Chunks and bits and parts of the ship came down with them. Oh, I had never been so deep, I swear, not even when I went overboard and suffered that vision of God's Feet on the treadle of life!

Here was intense pressure all around us, our weight carrying us into it even as we left the light behind. One last glimpse I had in the growing dimness, that of the large oblong object floating slowly back up past me toward the surface, and clinging to it that young fellow I had first seen in the company of the Polynesian prince, the man from the prov-inces beyond where I had lived, who seemed to be the only one alone who would survive to tell the story.

I reached up and caught hold of his heel, which pressure he could not have felt given all the water pressing around him. And up he towed me, or heeled me, I should say, to be exact, to that point near the surface when light streamed down but not yet the air that would give me back my life to live. When something struck me from below, and turned me over on my belly, at which a long sleek fish of the air-spouting variety, no whale, but something modeled on a whale, turned its head and then a fin in my direction and I caught hold of that fin, and rode the fish up to where we broke the surface some many yards away from where the last boilings of the vortex that took the Pequod down had smoothed out into the rolling waves as before.

So amazed I was that I had been saved that I forgot entirely that I had not been breathing air and now I was, taking in huge gulps as a thirsty fellow would take in water or beer, or a guilty man might wish to gulp down the famous wine which good Christians purport to stand in for the blood of their Saviour.

My Saviour in this instance was a fish!

Not a whale, of course. Because I was not a Jonah but only myself, a Pip, whose story you know shows how innocent he was, and how much a victim of accident he was, beginning with the complected quality of his skin. Pure chance, born this black! But not a chance, or a chance of a chance, that the Fish that saved me had only been accidentally passing by.

It saved me for further things, for a life beyond the brief years I lived within the shores of that whale story. It carried me, this fish, along until I had caught enough air to gain my strength and then I stood upon its back and rode it, rode it all the way through another day of sun and then a day of light storms, and then more days of sun, until we reached an island—a chain of them, as a law abiding man might call it, or a necklace of them, as someone more attuned to the beauty of the world might proclaim. There I disembarked, to be met by local men and boys who had been fishing near the white-pearl beach, men and boys whose complectedness seemed quite close to my own. And in this world of darker hue, I found my welcome, and learned the language, married the daughter of a chief who reigned some distance inland and desired a husband for his lovely daughter whose own people came from farther away rather than closer, the better to make, as the local shaman-doctors would have it, a better combination of peoples than if she married someone closer in.

And so I married, and grew to become a skilled hunter, and negotiator, and husband, and father—and to dance and bundle and sometimes snuggle and nip the light-tinted ears of other dark girls with whom we all laughed—laughter being the prime motive of all life in these watery parts of the world. My own little boy, the first of my children, I call Little Pip, and after him a Pippa and then another Littler one of myself, and all of us laughing our way to the depth of things and back to the airy part of the world.

When I first arrived here, before I learned the depths of the ways my new people lived, I would upon occasion feel a certain longing for my home state, and a certain regret, feeling it as a wincing tinge around my heart space, that I would not ever return to that country from which I had first set out. But this I conquered with a large lotion of laughter and the necessity to make the others around me live and laugh. Only once, in fact, did I ever see another former countryman of mine, when a raggedy old bearded white man in a stump of a boat was washed up in a storm upon our beach. I stayed apart from him, while cousins by marriage tended to his needs. One night I stole up close to the hut where he was living, and heard the sound of his voice as he talked to himself amidst what turned out to be the heat of a raging fever contracted while floating his many weeks upon the ocean, and it was a kind of music to my ears, thought it meant not much. Raven, he called out, quoth you what? come hither and dance with me. Raven? Do you know the way to Baltimore? Is my grandfather alive? How will I know him? How will I know him? Oh, say, can you see? Oh, say, can you see? Over and over again, and within a week or so the poor pale-skinned wretch succumbed to that fever.

And after him, no other American crossed my sights.

Until now. Until we met. In your dream.

Or is it a dream? Or simply another permutation of the world as we know it, whether in sleep or in the vivid territory of the imagination. I had gone out for a ride on my ocean board, which I learned to negotiate with a steadiness I learned from that first long journey on the back of the dolphin, and a huge rogue wave slapped me from my perch, and I sank a while, down to this level—or was I floating up? Whereever we are, wherever we have met to make this gam, to salute each other, as one passes one way, and another the other the world has been ours, and the world will be ours again, if not in our own lives but in the lives of others.

And now, my last words and thoughts, oh, that water is best...

Yours truly, I call out to you across these surging flows, some slow and some fast, some cold, some warm, where the fish fleet sails and the currents within me match the currents without,

And here, he said, bidding a familiar man come forward out of the darkness of the distant waters, not a drowned man but a man who had died, I don't know how this happens, Pip said, but it does.

Father! I said aloud into the waters. To see you here! Even if it is only but a dream!

Holding hands, the three of us made a circle beneath the flood, and we danced, in tune with the currents, we danced around and around and around.

Days Given Over to Travel

Originally published in *Prairie Schooner*

When Mama came for me, my older boy was sailing off the coast of Brazil. I'm not kidding. My boy, sailing off the coast of Brazil. Of course, I always think of him as little but he wasn't so little anymore, he had a wife, a family and they were grown, and he was a grown man enjoying a big fancy trip on a big boat. A ship, he called it. The kind our people never traveled in, not even in the old days when my father first came to this country from the old country. (He crossed in steerage, just the way you see in the movies, below the deck, the cold Atlantic beating against his wall, the inside of his stomach beating against the wall of his chest.)

So it was still a thrill for me to hear about, my son, local as he was, going where he was going, because he came from here, from Jersey, where we all came from (except his father, who had to come a longer way to get here and always had mixed emotions about where he had arrived, by boat, all the way from China to San Francisco, the long way around from Russia, where my father, the Atlantic crosser also came from) and if you came from here, it's my thought about it, that as far away as you can go you can never get away, not that you should want to.

Ten days before my son left he told me about it. Not that he told me everything about what he was doing, I wasn't so dumb I didn't know that he told me almost next to nothing about what he was doing, ever since he was a boy, but I took that as a compliment, as his respect for his mother, not to tell me, because so much a boy does is frightening for a mother, the way he goes out into the world, the things he wants to do, the things he has to do.

(I know this from my brother's life and from the stories my husband always told, maybe even, may he rest in peace, too often, but these are other stories for another time, if there is one. Will there ever be? Don't think I don't wonder, even now....)

Ten days before all this, my son told me, at the wedding in Connecticut where we all had gathered, my cousin Marvin's daughter's wedding, which makes it sound like a distant relation except Marvin was always like a nephew to me. He and his wife Phyllis, they made a nice wedding for their daughter Susan and her fiancé. The weather was cooperating. A cool night, but it hadn't snowed yet so it still seemed like autumn, not winter, no matter what it said on the calendar.

The food was delicious, the music was playing, I was waiting for dessert and coffee. In my wheel chair, where lately I had decided to sit, it wasn't all that comfortable. My companion, Irving, went to the bathroom. My older boy was bringing me a fresh drink, he was always so polite to me, asking if I needed anything (and I wish only if he could do it all over again he could have been so polite to his father, oh, it was awful, the way they fought, and fought and fought...on politics, about religion, about this, about that...).

"Here's your scotch, Mother," he said, handing me the glass.

I was leaning to one side in my wheel chair—what a lousy contraption, that I should ever have to ride in one! The music was nice, old songs, "Strangers in the Night," "Slow Boat to China," and old country music, freilichs and whirling around, all the young ones even they knew them, jitter-bugging, and the lindy, and the dancing in a circle while the clarinet sounded like a sad child wailing for its mother. And a fiddler, too, but this one not on the roof.

"Thank you, darling," I said, taking the glass from him. I was staring at him, but a mother can stare, right? His curly dark hair reminded all of a sudden so much of my mother's beautiful hair I wanted to cry. "The dancing is nice, you're going to dance?"

"Of course, " he said. "But I wish you could get up and dance."

"Maybe one," I said, "my current limit for the night."

The music had turned slower, and so here was our chance.

"Mother?"

Oh, I loved the way he called me that, not Mommy or Ma, certainly not by my first name. Always mother. Nothing but mother. The way it should be, now that he's grown. And for all of you listening—whoever you are, wherever you are, I don't know you, but something tells me someone somehow might be listening—I wish you all the same happiness.

"Come," he said, offering his hand.

"Just a minute," I said. "It's very uncomfortable, getting up."

I told him what I felt, I felt like a prisoner in that chair.

"I feel like a prisoner in this chair."

He laughed—such a nice laugh he has, but he hardly ever uses it—and helped me to my feet.

The slow music was still playing, music, of all things from the movie "Around the World in Eighty Days," a movie I liked a lot when I first saw it though it's been years and years.

"How old is this movie?" I asked him as he led me to the dance floor.

"What movie, mother?" he said.

"The music, the music from the movie!"

"I don't know," he said. "Forty years old, fifty years?"

"I was just a kid back then," I said. "You were little yourself." I reached up and put my arm around him.

"You smell nice," I said.

Again, he laughed.

"After-shave," he said.

"You have a beard and you use after-shave? Who ever heard of that?"

I said things to him nobody else said to him, because I am his only mother. And he sometimes, as just now, he said to me things he didn't say to other people.

"I shave my neck, just under the beard line."

"Oh," I said. "I didn't know that. See, you live and learn."

The music was beautiful, clarinets and marinets, or whatever you call them, and a piano, even if it was electric, still it was a piano, and a trumpet, and drums. We moved around, slowly, but we moved, me a tiny white-haired lady, with him nearly twice as tall, dark-hair, dark beard, nice wire-rimmed eye-glasses, leaning down toward me. Other people at the party, his brother, my nephew, his wife, they were all making way for us, staring at us, cheering us on, oohing and ahhing.

"Why are you staring?" I said to them, "it's not my wedding."

And they laughed, and he led me gently into the rhythm of the music, such a nice boy—a man now, I have to keep reminding myself!—and he knew how to dance.

(He married a modern dancer, a Southern girl, always the modern, the foreign, the exotic! As if I didn't know why—he wanted to get away from home, he always did. Jersey was never good enough for him. And other mothers could take this as an insult, but not me. I never felt insulted. Other things insult me. But if your son is happy after a number of marriages why should you feel insulted? She wasn't from our tribe, but she was lovely and she made me feel as though she cared for me, so why shouldn't I be happy if they're happy. ("Tilly," she said when Irving wheeled me in to the ballroom, "your dress is so pretty!" She meant well, but what could I say? I said, "What can I say? I can't hardly walk anymore. I'm glad you like my dress." What I wanted to say was, all these dresses, I used to care, but what's the use, the way I'm feeling now. But she meant well and why should I hurt her feelings?))

Around the world I searched for you….

I remember those words, and I sang while the music played.

"You have a nice voice," he said. Nice is what he was for saying this. My voice is light and easy, it always was, for whatever reason, I can't say, because I never had any training. My aunt Bess, Marvin's mother, now she had a lovely voice and she sang whenever the spirit came to her, except for those years when she was so depressed.

But—another story that is, too.

Meanwhile, I'm dancing with my oldest son and he's turning me slowly around, and he says,

"We're going to Brazil. Did I tell you that?"

"No, you didn't. You never tell me anything."

"Next week," he said. "For about two weeks. They fly us to Rio and we board a ship there and sail along the coast and then up through the islands."

"You're paying for this?"

"The cruise line pays our air fare and gives us a free trip," he said. "In exchange, I give a couple of talks."

"You see," I said, "you were always good at talking. You should—"

He cut me off, laughing.

"I should have been a lawyer."

"Yes," I said. "You should have."

I could hear my own voice, the mix of anger and respect, but I don't know what my face looked like when I spoke that way, and I know I've said it to him before, and who knows? I might say it to him again. But it felt— my face—like a pond or a lake when the wind blows across it, hot and cold, parts of the water one temperature, parts of the water another temperature.

Something was on my mind, in the back of it, so it didn't come to me up front right away. I kept on talking.

"Tell me," I said, "if you don't mind my asking, where exactly is Brazil?"

He laughed and gave me a quick geography lesson.

I laughed back at him, at myself. What's a smart son for, if not to talk to you about geography, where things are and where they're going. At least the first part he knew.

And then all of a sudden the other thing came to me, what I was thinking (I suppose, thinking back on it, if this is what you'd call think-ing, because of his telling me about his trip), not like a voice, not like a picture, no words for me to read, either, just a kind of message or a movie, water moving, waves high and white with froth, like the froth on a wonderful glass of beer, the kind I used to drink when I was a girl and my father would offer me one, fresh and fizzy, right out of the keg from the saloon on Smith Street where we strolled sometimes on Saturdays after shul, oh, and how the past pulls at me, tugs at me the way a child pulls at his mother's skirt, it wants my attention, it wants my full attention, I can see the bubbles in the beer, I can taste it on the tip of my tongue, and I can feel the pressure of my papa's hand around my own small hand, the way it was in Amboy in those days when I was just a little girl—and it's like a wind catches me up and carries me along just then while we're still dancing, I'm in the present but I'm in the past and the present feels like it's already over and the past, all those days gone by feels like it is just happening at that moment, and so I have to say it feels like the present, not like a movie about the past but the present itself.

Can you be in two places at once? I was dancing with my son and I was walking along Smith Street in old Perth Amboy holding my father's hand. He was a short man, with slender shoulders and his dark hair slicked back from his forehead and brushed back on the sides.

"Taiby," he said, calling me by my little nickname, "you want a piece of candy?"

"Yum," I said.

Maybe we were going to the candy store, I thought. But out of his pocket he took a sugar candy and popped it into my mouth.

Um, yum!

The strong sweet taste of it, my mouth is watering.

It was a warm day, not cool like today, and from the Arthur Kill, the mile-wide stretch of water that separated Amboy from Staten Island, the breeze was blowing, a slightly salty odor, like the iodine later in life we put on cuts except I couldn't have said it then.

Except I could taste it, the way I was tasting the candy.

My father squeezed my hand.

"Listen," he said, "it's your Mama's birthday coming. What are we going to do?"

"A surprise," I said. "Let's make her a surprise."

"So what surprise?"

"The boat," I said. "We'll take her on the boat."

"The ferry?"

"Yep," I said.

"Such a smart girl," he said. "You got good ideas, maideleh. That's what we'll do, the ferry. We'll take her on a ride. For an afternoon, I'll get someone to run the store."

Mama' s birthday wasn't until the next week and I don't remember what I did in between, I was so excited about our surprise. It was all I could do when we got home not to pee in my pants. There she was, in the doorway, her dark eyes, her dark hair, her pillow-like breasts, so comforting to me when she pulled me to her and hugged me, kissing the top of my head.

"Taiby," she said, "you been a good girl?"

"She was good," Papa said.

From the back of the little house I could hear my brother talking to himself while he played.

"I know something," I said to him just before supper.

"What?" he said.

"I can't tell you," I said.

"Tilly, you tell me," he said, grabbing my arm.

I was older but he was stronger and when he squeezed I cried out.

"What is it?" Mama called from the kitchen.

"She hurt me, Ma!" my brother called back.

"That's a lie!" I said at the top of my voice.

"Children, please," Mama said, "I'm cooking, I'm cooking."

See, she didn't like to cook, it was just something she knew she had to do because she had a family. It was plain food, boiled beef flanken, potatoes, chicken from the market, sometimes fish from the fish market and we ate and we got full and we stayed healthy.

Except when Meyer, my brother, ate all the pickles from barrel in the pantry and got such a stomach ache and cried and cried, and I wished him dead because no one paid any attention to me. I took his marbles and threw them in the bushes, and for that I never asked anyone to forgive me, something I never thought about for more than seventy years.

"What is it?" he said over and over again all through supper. "What is it? What is it? What is it?"

My father, a gentle man, nearly clopped him one with an open hand.

"Enough," our mother said, "we're finished. No more noise."

"She won't tell me," my brother said.

Papa reached over and touched the tip of his longest finger to my brother's rosy cheek.

"You have to be big to know these things. Next week you'll be older, we'll tell you then."

That night I couldn't sleep right away so excited I was with my secret. Every time I started to doze a funny taste came into my mouth, the sour-brine flavor of those pickles my brother had eaten—and I had never even had a bite.

"Your breath smells funny," Mama said when she came in to wake me. "Have you been eating those pickles?"

"No, Ma," I said. "I don't like them."

She gave me a queer look and it made me feel even stranger, the only thing keeping me from saying anything about our surprise.

Oh, it was a hard week, keeping my mouth shut. I was so glad I didn't say anything to my brother. He had just started school and in the afternoon walked over to the candy store and pretended to work behind the counter with Papa, though all he did was pick sweets out of the trays and eat them. Sweets and pickles! It makes my mouth water just to think of them separate, let alone together.

The time went by—oh, how it goes! One minute you're walking along talking to your father, thinking up a surprise, the next minute he's arranged for a man he knows to watch the store and you're getting dressed for the big event. (Dressing in a dress, I was, a pretty white dress Mama had saved up to buy for me.) And walking there, under a bright sun, your little brother dragging along behind looking for stones to throw over the rocks into the river.

"So where are you taking me?"

Mama had been going along with our invitation, but now, blocks and blocks later on our travels from one side of the neighborhood to the other, from where the railroad tracks made a border between us and the trash heaps to where the beach of dirty sand and rocks took the waves from the water between us and Staten Island, she was getting annoyed.

"Where? It better be good, you asked a man to run the store. What does he know about money?"

"Taibeleh," my father said, pointing to the water, "what do they call this, a river?"

I told him. It had a Dutch name, I knew that, they taught us in school—the Arthur Kill. First, the Indians lived here. Then came the Dutch. Then the English. Then the Americans. Then the Jews. (Better late then never). See how much I know?—I learned my lessons.

So where are the Indians? he asked and made a little laugh, like a cough, in his throat. All gone, gone. Only my little brother Meyer whooping and hollering and running and skipping along, first ahead of us, then behind, and then ahead again, a Jewish Indian.

"Where is he going?" Mama said. "Where are you taking me?"

"Why do you think we're taking you some place?" Papa tried to keep a straight face, but when he looked down at me he couldn't help but smile.

"It's a trick," Mama said. "You made me fix my hair, you made me get dressed up."

"You look beautiful, Mama," I said.

Her dark hair oiled and curled, her eyes with the black mascara beneath, making them into deep wells of looking—her looking out, us looking in. She was a big boned woman but thin, thin, and I wanted to look like her when I grew up. It was all I wanted, back then, just everything.

Other families were walking, but no one we knew. It was all Gentiles over on this street, and they were coming back from their church just as we were going on our birthday outing. The women looked pale to me compared to Mama, and the men, so stern in dark suits it hurt my eyes to look. The children seemed the same as me and Meyer, girls walking straight-backed, pretending to be older than they were, little boys scurrying around like squirrels.

The houses they lived in, these big white wooden buildings with pillars sitting up on the hill to our left as we walked along, were different from ours. You could see all the way across the bay to the ocean from one of these houses, I was sure.

I said that to Papa.

"And in winter, who wants to live in such a big place? You'd have to have a stove in every room and they're so many rooms. You want to freeze, like in the old country?"

"I wouldn't mind," Mama said.

"What's the matter?" Papa said. "Where we live isn't good enough?"

"There's no water to see," Mama said. "No ocean."

"Mama," I spoke up, "it's not the ocean, it's Raritan Bay and the Arthur Kill."

"A smart one," Mama said, reaching down and patting me on the head. "But how smart, one day we'll find out."

"The hill, the hill!" my brother shouted out.

The corner of Water Street and Kearney, where in winter the children came to sled down toward the Kill. How my little brother ever walked this far, I couldn't say. He didn't have a sled, like some of the other boys. I didn't even know if he asked Papa for one, so maybe Papa said no or maybe he didn't say anything. So what did my brother sled on, garbage can lids? Who knew? He wasn't talking. Just shouting.

"This is where you're taking me?" Mama said over his noise. "Shash!" she called to him. "The water looks beautiful enough to drink." She took my father's arm as we walked down the hill. A few small sailboats bobbed up and down in the Kill. Even from this distance you could see one or two men walking around on the decks. It was the Gentiles who traveled on these. Who ever heard of Jews with sailboats?

"Where do they go, up and down the water, up and down?" Papa said as if to prove my point.

"They have fun," Mama said. "They don't work seven days in a candy store."

"You're working today?"

"You let me out for good behavior."

"What?" Papa didn't get the joke. He grew up in the old country and didn't arrive here in time to learn all the American jokes. He sighed and kept on walking.

The water of the Kill looked silvery in the sun, rippling and rolling, and the closer we got it smelled more and more like itself. It made me so happy to see it, because we were giving Mama all of it for a present.

"All right," she said as we walked toward the dock where the ferry boat sat waiting, "what's going on here?"

"Happy Birthday, Mama," I said.

"What? What?" My brother didn't want to miss a trick, he was running circles around us but he was listening.

"For your birthday, Sarah, we're taking you on a trip."

As if the captain of the ferry heard us talking, he blew a whistle, and it made me jump.

"I love you, Mama," I said, squeezing her hand.

Papa led us to the dock. We waited while he went to the office and bought us our tickets.

"You thought of this?" Mama said.

"Me and Papa," I said.

"Me, too," my brother said, and I pulled my hand loose from Mama's to try and give him a swat, but he danced away.

"No fighting, children," Papa said, returning to usher us up to the metal plank that joined the dock to the deck of the boat.

"Climb on," he said.

My brother jumped aboard, landing flat-footed with a loud splat and turning to face us. I ate all the pickles! his smile said and now I'm the first on the boat.

"This is quite a surprise," Mama said.

"Taiby and I have been planning it all week," Papa said. "Right, Taiby?"

"Oh, yeah, Mama," I said. I was nervous, bobbing up and down on my toes like one of the boats in the water. "So let's go already."

"Sure," Mama said, and taking my father's arm with one hand and holding me by the other led us across the gang-plank.

I knew I didn't like it, the minute I climbed aboard. One minute I was standing on solid ground, the next the deck is moving under my feet, making me very nervous.

"Mama," I said, "it's going."

"It's not going yet, but it's moving. Isn't that what you wanted?"

"I wanted to make you a nice present," I said.

"We're making, we're making," Papa said. "Didn't I tell you—"

The whistle blew, making me jump.

"—about me crossing the ocean?"

"A hundred times you told them, Izzy," Mama said.

"I'll tell them one more time," Papa said, "it can't hurt them. They should remember how their father came here, all the trouble, all the traveling."

But just then the deck moved again and before I could blink we were sliding out of the pier into the Kill.

Talk about sledding! We didn't need any hills! It was like sliding on a straight piece of ice, riding over the water was! Suddenly the wind started up, blowing my hair about my face. It smelled like a mix of salt and sweet, the ocean water rushing in from the bay. Back then I didn't know about tides, but the outgoing tide was pulling, pulling. I felt a little chill that comes with being scared.

"Meyer?" Mama called over the roar of the motors, "where's Meyer?"

"Don't shout, I can't hear you," Papa said, looking around.

"There he is," I said, seeing my brother leaning over the chain that kept people from walking onto the front part of the deck.

"Meyer!" Mama called to him.

"You think the water is rough?" Papa said.

"I don't know," I said.

"You should have been on the boat we crossed over the Atlantic."

"Hush, Izzy," Mama said. "She's heard the story." She took a deep breath.

"Meyer!"

"Good stories you can hear over and over," Papa said.

"Look! Look!" my brother turned around and shouted back at us, except you couldn't hear him, but you knew from the way he was waving his arms and pointing he was saying it.

He meant the land sliding away behind us, the water rushing alongside us, churning like a bath when you splashed your arms about, and he meant the beach and green strip of trees on the far shore and the houses nestled in the trees—the village of Tottenville, part of the borough of Richmond, one of the five boroughs of New York City—pulling us toward it. I'd never been there. I felt a little better. My feet danced, my heart rolled. We were on a trip to another world!

It was a short distance we had to go. I didn't have much time to look around, but I saw the captain, a moon-faced man with a thick dark mustache, looking down at us from behind the large glass window high on his deck, and I saw the other passengers, mostly Gentile families going who knew where, or from what to why, to church? from church? I didn't know how Gentiles lived out a Sunday except for that.

Over in a corner on a bench by himself there was a tall black man who worked at the fish market, his dark skin looking to me like the hide of some strange fish. (One day he came in to our store while I was sitting there with Papa and he bought cigarettes, and didn't pay any attention to me except just as he was leaving when he turned and winked and I turned my back, a little chilled in a fright.)

And one other Jewish family, the Torpers, but they were Conservative, from the Temple that had just opened at High Street and Kearney, so we just knew who they were but didn't know them. (And did they know us? Because the Mrs. nodded when I looked her way, I thought maybe yes.) We were all Jews, but look how different they were from us. The father was beefy and wore a mustache. He waved his hands about as he talked—a doctor? a lawyer? The mother wore a fancy green dress so much nicer than what Mama was wearing I had to look away. (All her clothes money went to dressing me!)

I looked up at the sky. It wasn't moving. We were moving.

Then I looked back at the Torpers, to look at their children, a girl with long curly blonde hair that whirled in the wind off the water and a boy with a little hump on his back, who stood close to his mother

Not like my handsome brother!

Who came rushing along the deck.

"Indians!" he said.

"What?" Papa said.

"Smoke signals!" Meyer's face turned red from the excitement of the game he was playing.

"No Indians," Papa said. "That's New York. Even a greenhorn like me knows for Indians you have to go in the other direction, west, not east."

"Let him think Indians," Mama said. "Why not Indians?" she said to Meyer.

There wasn't any time for an answer. Such a short trip! It was over nearly before it began! One minute, it seemed like one minute! pushing off from the dock in Perth Amboy, a few minutes later, sliding in to the dock at Tottenville. The captain blew the whistle! I jumped again in my skin.

"And now?" Mama put her hands on her hips, the way she did when she wanted something from Papa, and wouldn't give up till she got it.

"That was half the birthday," Papa said.

"You're not taking me all the way to New York?"

"We don't have time," Papa said. "I got to get back to the store by tonight."

"So what's the other half of my birthday?" Mama pursed her red lips at him, almost pouting. Sometimes you could forget, if you knew it to begin with, just how young she was, but not at a time like this.

"We ride back," Papa said.

Mama gave him a look, silent, I didn't even know how to describe.

Meyer reached up and tugged at his hand.

"Can we get a soda?"

"Soda you want? We got a store for that."

"I want a soda now," Meyer said.

"I'll give you a soda," Mama said, taking a handful of his skin at the back of his neck.

"Yow!" he said.

"You sound like a cow," I said.

"You're a meanie," he said.

"Me?" Mama said.

"Taiby," Meyer said.

"I'm not a meanie. You're a weenie."

Mama let him go and turned and grabbed me.

"Young lady, watch your mouth."

I began to cry.

"Please, please," Papa said, "come, we'll stroll around. It's not such a big deal, this place, but we can walk a little before the ferry leaves."

Mama tried to get in to the spirit of things, allowing him to take her by the elbow as we strolled off the dock and onto the land and wandered along toward the south side of the little village where large white houses stood just above the beach. It was something like Amboy here, but different, a place that seemed older to me, like something out of a story book. And it was greener. There was a big green tree-filled street, as nice as High Street and Water Street back home, the sky leafy and bright above us. And from there, in front of those houses, we looked back across the water to home, and I was thinking—I remember it so well—that only an hour or so ago I was staring at these houses and now I was staring back—and what did it all mean?

"It's a hick town here," Mama said. "How can it be part of New York City?"

"It's nice," Papa said, as if he had given her the place to keep and didn't want her to think it wasn't good enough. "It's got the water."

"And we don't have water in Amboy?" Mama said.

The mention of the water perked my brother up.

"Let's go to the beach," he said, pointing to the little strip of sand and rocks just on the other side of the narrow road.

"No beach," Mama said. "You're all dressed up."

"Beach, I want the beach. Taiby does too."

"No, I don't," I said, glad to be able to make him feel bad. Pickle-stealer, noise-maker, trouble-stirrer, my little brother bothered me and bothered me. "I never want to go to the beach."

"Yes, you do," he said.

"No, I don't."

"Yes, you do."

"No, I—"

"Children," Mama said, "it's just for a little while."

My brother was already on the run, skipping along the sand and leaping over the big rocks and arriving at the water before any of us could say another word.

"Bum," I said.

"Watch your language," Papa said. "It's your brother."

"Meyer!" Mama called to him, "you come right back."

But he didn't come back for a long while, running along the water's edge, shooing sea-gulls, bending and swooping at rocks that he picked and hurled toward the water without stopping. Maybe in a story a big wave would have washed up out of the ocean and pulled him out to sea. If my son were writing this story instead of me telling it, who knows what might have happened?

We walked gingerly along in our Sunday clothes, hoping to keep our shoes dry. Now and then I noticed a pretty shell and picked it up, sniffing its odor, iodine, nothing I liked. I admired the color, a creamy white, with a silvery underside, reminding me of the color I was wearing. I held it up to my sleeve, but not touching it there for fear of leaving a stain. Mama talked, as usual, and Papa listened.

"I'm worried," she said. "About Harold...You think it was safe to leave him in the store...I know, I know, you don't have to say...he's my cousin. But what does he know about business? They could be robbing him blind...or he could be robbing us...Oh, I know, terrible, to talk like this about my own cousin."

Seagulls floated overhead, as though the air were water instead of just plain wind. Another shell caught my eye, this one a faded pink, with flutings along the edges like a pastry perfect from a bakery. Gulls cried out, asking to be invited.

Suddenly, Mama's anxious voice broke through their chorus.

"Where's Meyer?"

We looked up, we looked around. He was nowhere to be seen.

You can imagine—she sent me and Papa around the curve of the beach, but we didn't see him up ahead. Only the small waves lapping at the dark blonde sand, only the gulls drifting—and laughing—in the pale blue sky above.

"That stupid boy, I'll kill him!" Mama raised a hand toward the sun. "Meyer!" she called out.

Papa rose to the occasion.

"You wait here," he said to Mama and me. "I'll get help." He set out along the sand around the curve of the beach.

"I know he's drowned," Mama said, her eyes suddenly swelling.

"No, Mama," I said, tugging at her hand.

She leaned down and embraced, our faces touching, and I could taste the salt of her tears.

"He's drowned," she said, her voice scarcely a whisper over the sound of the (quiet) surf. "On the boat he nearly fell over, and now he's gone."

Oi, oi, the worries of a mother! My mother, your mother, me!

A minute later Papa appeared around the curve of the beach, dragging him back to us by the hand, Meyer with his pants stained at the knees and his hair all messed and his hands sandy and his pockets bulging with stones and shells, and smelling like the sea, which was a little like the briny, salty odor of the pickle barrel he was so fond of.

"Ma," he said, "I was captured by Indians!"

Such a swat Mama gave him on his behind he wailed and wailed half the way back to the ferry dock. When the ferry engine rumbled, he clung to Papa's hand, sniffling quietly while the waters splashed and hissed against the sides of the boat.

So that was that, nearly the whole ride over and back, so quick it almost didn't happen. Eight nickels it cost Papa, and cheap at the price, or just right, given how long it took each way. Except for one thing. I always think about, I always remember. I'm standing on the deck, feeling the boards rumbling under my feet, and the wind picking like a child's fingers at my hair, and looking up at Mama—Papa stood over by the railing with Meyer, holding him so he wouldn't, God forbid, fall overboard—and we're rushing through the water toward Perth Amboy so fast I didn't have time to think about what we would do when we got home—and Mama says, out of the blue, "One day you'll remember this trip. I'll be gone. Papa will be gone. And you'll remember."

I didn't know what she was talking about.

Then.

And now as my son is spinning, not all that fast but still spinning me, around the dance floor, Mama's voice comes back to me, and for a second or two everything goes black for me and she says, *"Taibeleh, it's time...."*

And I sink.

And my son says, "Mother, are you all right?"

"Please," I say, "I'm a little dizzy, can we sit down?"

"Brazil," he says, I hear the word, and "flying down to Rio," and I even hear myself sing a little bit of that song, "Rio, Rio, flying down to Rio," but my legs are so weak I stumble and he catches me, and leads me like I'm a little child back to my chair—his brother comes running over, saying, "Ma? Ma? You all right?"—nice boy, his brother—and I am all right except I have to close my eyes, and Mama appears to me again, looking as young and pretty as she did on that day we took her on the ferry, and she says to me, *"You'll never see him again in this life."*

"Him?" I say. "Not him?"

"Ma?"

"Mother? What is it? Here some's water. Please take a sip."

"Not him, he should have a safe trip…."

"Mother?"

"Not him," she says to me. *"Not him, no—you."*

I hear this with relief, that my son will be safe. And with fear, because of what it means for me.

The evening wasn't over. I tried to be cheerful and drink my Scotch and eat some wedding cake and sip a cup of coffee. But who could be cheerful after seeing what I saw and hearing what I heard? My son was going to Brazil and I was going to take a trip myself.

"What is it, Tillie?" Irving said to me after all our goodnights with the family were finished and he was pushing me in my chair back to my room. "You don't seem like yourself."

Irving, Irving, so dapper—a word that rhymes with flapper and makes me feel just as gay—in his old tuxedo and fancy black bowler, a hat he wears only for the most special of occasions—he's buried two wives and he's been romancing me for so long now I can't forget it, let alone remember. He's short and stocky, a strong face, built like Phil, my first and only marriage.

Will I get to see Phil? I should have asked Mama. But if I saw her, why shouldn't I see him? So maybe it won't be as bad as I think.

But I think. Think. Think. Worry. Who doesn't? Who wouldn't, after her mother dead so many years it's not even worth counting, appears to you at a wedding and you've only had a few sips of Scotch?

"Tilly?" Irving has delivered me to the door of my room. Inside, he won't go, because he's too much of a gentleman, and besides, in all these last years we've been together I just couldn't bring myself to invite him. Cuddle on a sofa? Yes. Spend the night in my bed? It's too private, especially when it takes such an effort for me to get in and out. What a gentleman! He respected that, he respected me. I make a joke to myself sometimes. When you're young, you want a night. When you're old, you want a Knight.

And if for some people it's just the opposite, good for them. I'm just thinking about what it's like for me.

Which was sad, after all that I heard and thought about at the wedding.

Ten days go by—traveling home to Jersey, seeing my doctor, who said he didn't detect any changes in me, no matter what I was worrying about—which tells you just how much doctors know—and in the meantime, or inbetween time, as we used to sing when we were young, my son and his wife take their trip to Rio.

(All this traveling, I've already taken my trip and it tires me out to think about it, let alone tell about it!)

But here they are, my older one and his beloved wife. It takes them hours to pack, or at least it takes his wife that long. My boy is a man and so he packs like a man, throwing things in to a suitcase at the last minute. Except for the tuxedo. He had to get his tuxedo cleaned and pressed, because on this ship they're traveling on every other night is a formal dinner, and they're scheduled to be on board for almost two weeks. Such a fancy life my boy leads!

Here's the route: to Rio they'll go, and then sail along coast of Brazil and up (or is it down? I never did good in geography!) to the mouth of the Amazon and then in and out around the islands in the Caribbean before reaching Miami. A nice trip. Who wouldn't want such an itinerary, especially when it's free? Because my son, the talker, will give some lectures in exchange for all they give him. The flight. The trip. The ports. The food. The return home. (And think how much more he could have made if he had gone to law school?)

In that week it made me tired even thinking about his wanderings. His father and I had traveled some in our last decades together. To California once. To Israel and Italy. To Phil's native Russia. It was interesting, sometimes even fun, but to tell you the truth the only thing better than going away was coming home again.

But here I was, getting ready for another trip. At the same time as my son and his wife.

After putting the dog in the kennel—all the grandchildren are grown now and he and his new wife were having too much fun to have more children, something I can agree with—they flew to Miami, waited for the late-evening airplane to Rio, and then took off. All night they flew high over South America, something when we were little we never could have imagined. There was the Wright Brothers, but they went close to the ground. Which is how I always wished I could go when Phil and I took our trips. Who likes to be thirty thousand feet up when you could just be ten feet, just above the tops of the trees? But here it is, flying over countries, over some of the world's longest rivers and highest mountains. My son, fairly tall, felt uncomfortable, scrunched up in his seat. His wife, she sleeps anywhere, and on this flight she's out like a light. I'm beginning to see this from a different way, from a distance, their plans, and mine. (Except I didn't make mine, did I? Or didn't I? You tell me.)

He can't sleep. The turbulence, the bumping around. It's just like rough water on a river or at sea, he always tells himself, to keep calm. And whoever heard, except in the roughest water, a boat has capsized? He reads, always with a book so not to worry. What did he bring on this trip? The Washington Post. The New York Times. The Miami Herald. Newspapers, always newspapers, but he was finished with those. After a while all the news seems to blur. Every day a new front page, every day you throw it away. The next day, a new front page. For the rest of your life if you keep on looking. And after you're gone, the same thing, over and over. He read the newspaper every day, but he never expected to find anything new.

Books were different. Each book was different from every other book. Because every book had a different writer. Because it took a year of days to make a book and so there was a lot of different things that went into making a book. Because over a day nothing changed but over a year a lot changes.

He brought poetry with him, too, a book by Borges. He liked reading this man's poems. Something he wrote in a poem called "A Reader," saying "I'm not as proud of the books I've written as I am of the books I've read…." Oh, my boy was a reader! Ever since the day he went to the public library and got in a reading contest with little Spiro Georgiu, a Greek boy from his sixth grade class, he read and read, almost like a drug addict, God forbid, or an alcoholic.

Also, he brought a book by Carlos Drummond de Andrade, a writer from the country he was flying to. And he carried novels, two of them stuffed in his carry-on bag, more of them packed in his suitcase. He wasn't going to be caught without a good novel to read. That, for him, would be frustrating, hours, a day, wasted. That's why he always carried with him many more books than he needed, because at least one or two of the books he chose would turn out to be not to his liking and he would discard them. He was like that—and I hate to say it because I'm his mother and always will be, wherever I am and wherever he is—with women. All his boyish life. You go out with one girl, and that doesn't work. So you call another the next day. And you don't like her so you leave her before you get to her. And you marry and that doesn't make you happy so you divorce and then you marry again.

And again.

And it turned out one of the novels he hated after five pages and set it aside and another one he read a chapter and put it away and had to go into his carry-on bag, while his wife slept soundly in the seat beside him, to take out a new copy of one of his favorite books, stories by Hemingway, and a novel by Thomas Hardy, and this kept him happy for a few more hours into the night flight, while cities and jungles and mountains passed tens of thousands of feet below, and the roar of the jet engines rose and fell, rose and fell, like the breath of a huge weary giant out of one of his childhood nightmares. (He always had nightmares, I'm afraid, ever since he was a little boy, dreaming whatever terrible thing it was he dreamed and waking himself up with a grunt or a shout or every once in a while a scream. His wife knew this the way I knew it—because she was the one now who had to shake him away and calm him, and because she has such a funny way with her when it comes to things that seem serious but are not really serious, and makes him laugh.)

He read and flew more than half the length of South America, not thinking at all about the rain forest below but caught up in the world of the novel he was reading, the old green world of Thomas Hardy. And if I had said to him that this was the way all life was, passing by while we thought about another life, one real, one made up and how to tell which was which, what would he have said? Would he have laughed at me, his own mother? How could I know so much? Even as much or as little as I know? Is it magic? Is it God? Who knows? I'm feeling what I'm feeling and I can't describe it, but along with the feeling comes these things I knew or thought I knew or know now that I have left it all behind.

His books, his journey. (Journey? See, I never even used that word before all this happened to me after the week after the wedding.) Traveling all the night in his books, which means in his mind, in his imagination, not the imagination that creates these things but the part that makes them come alive, and so, come to think of it, which is what I'm doing right now, it makes for a complicated brain, doesn't it? We have the means to recreate, to think, and we have the means to create or make-up, invent, imagination, and if I didn't know where I was, if being somewhere is what I'm doing right now, I might think I was making all this up, all that I'm saying here right now and what I've said just before.

(All of this so complicated, you wouldn't think of your own mother thinking all this, would you? But then she might just go ahead and surprise you with what she thinks. Even before she gets too serious thinking, the way I'm trying now.)

And then he looks up from his book and sees the sky alight, faint first and then suddenly flooding in through the narrow port, as the airplane glides into its descent, the land below seeming to rise to meet the windows of the cabin, and he looks out upon a part of the world he's never seen before, the green of its mountains and hills glowing in the new morning, the width of its rivers overflowing the banks, the light beyond the horizon leading his eye toward infinity.

He touches his wife gently on the shoulder, and she awakes and shares this world with him.

A smooth landing at a rinky-dink airport. It's a big country, you think they could do better than this old tarmac and these dilapidated buildings. (This is me saying this, not him. He looks around. He's interested, ever since he was a baby he was interested.) Passing through customs in an old terminal. Rattletrap shuttle bus to the ship. It's humid here, with a sea breeze. Palm trees. Big clouds overhead. Gold beaches glimpsed on the way to the harbor. A lot of people and cars zig-zagging around town. Mountains rise within the city, haunting the eye. The poor build all the way to the top of the hills. Where we come from, the higher the better. Here the opposite is true.

Another country.

And a beautiful ship to see it from. Yes, so many decks. And from the top you can see the tallest mountain, with the statue of their Jesus, his arms outspread, as if he's about to fly away. So why doesn't he? A good question. I've always wondered. Maybe now I'll find the answer?

Inside this big boat, so many people to take care of you, wait on you, help you out, help you up, clean up, stand on, watch. Their room is very nice. Big bed, nice view from the porthole—they're just above the first deck. The bathroom is spotless.

They're here a day and a half, so they take a trip to the beach— the beaches, actually—so many beautiful beaches curving around on the east side of the city, a city that is spread out along the ocean, interrupted by lagoons and parks and a mountain or two. In the middle of all of their looking around, he turns to her and says, "You know what mother would say? It's not like Jersey!"

Would I say that? I suppose so. Because it's *not* like Jersey. Not that I don't—excuse me, *didn't*—like Jersey, the place I call(ed) home. The people, the streets, the stores, the river running past our little sandy beach at the south side of the town—it wasn't as bad as he makes it out to be, because home is home and you feel it in your bones as a place you love. One day, he'll find out—you can fight with your parents and you know you love them, and you can say you hate where you grew up but it's still a place you call home.

As the day fades they stroll around the deck, and the lights of the city wink on, a million fire-flies.

That night, a delicious meal. Exotic fish. Delicious, soft, creamy, not a fishy fish.

And at ten o'clock in the theater-night club down below, a show begins, samba dancers, and my son has a thrill of a lifetime.

First the drums, of all sizes, the drummers nearly naked men, their skin the color of milk chocolate bars from my parents' old store. (Hershey people, I think of them.) And then the women dressed in masks and high hats and skirts that flow from their waists like big clouds of smoke.

My son and his wife—she's a dancer, remember, so she's excited about all this, too—they sit at a table near the stage. Well, sit is not exactly right. Because with the drummers pounding out a rhythming beat they're bounding in their seats, they're nearly on their feet.

And next come half a dozen tall women wearing nearly nothing whose bodies, chocolate, chocolate, chocolate, move to the drums—just added—flutes and trumpets—like they were part of the sound itself.

"Goddesses," says my daughter-in-law over the sound of the music.

I should have thought of that, because they look that way, like living, liquid statues moving to the beat, and I like to dance as much as anyone else but the way these women moved, they should be given speeding tickets, parking tickets, beauty tickets, their bosoms, their arms, their legs, their hips, and hips, their behinds, worlds in themselves.

To the beat, to the beat, to the beat, to the beat....

To the beat, to the beat, to the beat, to the beat....

My son is speechless! Imagine! Mister Talker and he finds no words!

As one of the dancers shuffles over to their table and reaches toward him—

And he's on his feet! Moving to the drumming, dancing along with her, hands on her hips, to the beat, to the beat, to the beat, to the beat....

Chocolate dancer! He could eat her like candy!

And then up leaps his wife, the dancer, and she's dancing, too, while other people in the audience flee the room (too much flesh, too much bouncing, to the beat, to the beat!)

They're bouncing, they're laughing, they're sweating, they're cheering, they're chanting—

Long after the music stops, they're liquid in each others' arms.

Such a night, every mother wants her son to have one! And many more! Many more! To the beat, to the beat, to the beat!

Up anchor the next morning, and they glide out of the harbor, skimming past those golden beaches, the mountains behind them, fading into the distance as the captain steers the boat out into the heaving ocean. The ship is so big. It's like a small town, almost like a world in itself. The restaurants, the theaters, the gym, the shops, the bars, the clubs. Amazing, it moves so smoothly. You hear the engines only as a constant low rumble, like thunder that never stops far, far off on the horizon. The boat cuts through the turbulent water, making a noise like loud steam escaping from a hose that's on the loose.

Days and nights go by. They eat, they sleep. They dress up for dinner, they undress to relax. My son goes to the gym and walks on the treadmill, which gives him pause to think to himself about how many ways he is moving, trodding along on the belt beneath his feet while the ship churns northward along the coast—which you can't see except as a smudge on the horizon during the day and as twinkling lights during the night—and the ocean lifts and swells, and the moon pulls at the water or lets it fall back, and the earth rotates around the sun, and the sun drifts—he's read about this—as the galaxy floats and everything's shifting and moving toward some point we'll never know let alone see ourselves. This life, this life! Even when you're standing still, you're moving. Even as you're thinking about moving, you're moving. When you're talking about moving, you're moving. When you're reading about moving, even the book you're holding is moving with you as you move. Nothing stands still. Nothing.

The ship churns along, heading north.

At night the ocean lights up, with the lamps on the small fishing boats that put out to sea after dark—fishing all night in the deep waters, what a kind of work that is, so lonely, so dangerous, so difficult, so beautiful to notice, and when dawn comes up you see them heading back to land, the boats so small you can hardly imagine how they survive out here where the land has disappeared and there's only the rolling sea and the stone blue sky, with passing clouds to shade the light of the moon. By day you notice clouds that might be ships themselves sailing above you while you're moving forward in the sky, so upside down you think you're rightside up.

Along, along, the cruising ship cruises along, a little world unto itself.

My children, they eat, they walk, and they talk. So many people on this ship who want to talk, about their families, about their other travels, about their lives, just the thing my son doesn't want to do, he's such a private person. But then it's his business to listen and he knows it, so he listens. Also, they read—here's another funny thing, if you think of it, about a kind of traveling, what reading does. Here he is my son, sitting on one of the upper decks in a comfortable lounge chair while his wife splashes about the swimming pool, reading about England in another century, that old green world, just when it was turning away from the country to the city.

"Where were you today?" his wife asked at dinner.

"In an old Roman ruin," he said. "A bull charged me. I've been there before."

"You're cute," his wife said, raising her wine glass. "Where are you going tomorrow?"

"Bahia," he said. "And Mars."

I forgot to say, he likes to read his science-fiction, too.

"Once you pick up a book you're traveling," he said. "So why not go to Mars, or somewhere else, another dimension, if you can?"

"I'd like to go there tonight," his wife said.

"Mars?"

"Another dimension."

She's cute, too.

That afternoon, my son the talker gives his first talk.

In the little movie theater in the center of the ship a small crowd gathers, mostly women old enough to be his mother, a few younger ones, a few men, who come along with the older women. These are readers, these are serious people.

Ladies and gentlemen, he begins. (Oh, and I could see him so much as a lawyer it hurts me even to think about it!—but I'm happy, too, that he gets to do what he wants to do, because otherwise, would he even be on this ship sailing off the coast of Brazil?) Today I want to talk to you—talk, my son, talk!—about the origins of the idea of the tropical in western culture. (Such a thing! Such a topic! What a way he talks about it!)

And he reads from a letter by Christopher Columbus, who discovered all this (all these places people are still coming over from Europe to see, my grandmother and my own father included!). And he talks about the Indians Columbus found when he got here. And he talks about Greeks, and a story an Italian poet tells about the Eden on top of an island in the South Pacific, Paradise! And sailing west to find the east! A lot of this I never heard of before, some of it I heard in school, or heard about later. (And did you know some scholars think Columbus was a Jew? Imagine, a Jew discovers America! First him, then years later along comes my father, stepping off the boat in New York and doing the same thing as Columbus, except he didn't find Indians, only years later, my brother Meyer masquerading as one.)

Well, the talk goes on, more about Columbus, and then Cortes and Coronado and the Aztecs and the Mexicans and the weather and the geography, El Dorado, the silver mines, a whole new world for me to hear about it, I'll tell you, and it's wonderful, and the people applaud, they've learned so much.

This ship, it's like a school—but mostly it's like a party, they tell you what to wear—one night, it's casual, which means for men, coats and ties, for women, dresses or blouses and sweaters, no slacks, and some nights, like this one, it's formal. My son puts on his tuxedo, so handsome he looks! And his wife, the dancer, she wears one of the many outfits she's bought for the trip, a dark silk skirt and top with sequins and stars, crescents and clouds—she looks like what she is, a beautiful dancer!

They eat, they drink, they have a good time, sliding over the ocean waves....

And after a day or two, they dock at Bahia, where they spend an afternoon walking around in the upper city, enjoying the pastels of the crumbling facades of houses and churches nearly five hundred years old, standing at the hitching post where the slave auctions were held and trying to imagine what that was like, those terrible events that happened here every day under this beautiful sky, sipping fruit drinks in the courtyard of the Hotel Pelourinho, where the wonderful Brazilian writer Jorge Amado lived for a time and wrote his first novel, talking about this antique—think how many antiques are here!—New World city, about the stunning women (my son talks about this subject at the drop of a hat and his wife, I think, enjoys him enjoying himself, as long as it's just talk!), so dark, like licorice, some of them, and others as light as caramel, the fruits of slavery.

On board the ship they were moving and here on land they're moving even as they sit, because time is always passing, or maybe time is standing still and we're moving past it, I don't know. They talk a little about this, they talk about how fast the time goes, or slow, how they watch their watches and it goes slowly and they follow the sun across the sky and time seems to stand still, but then they get caught up in reading or talking or walking or swimming or taking a nap, and the next time they think about the time it has passed—gone—departed—they talk about how much time has gone by since they first met, and yet that seems like only a short while ago—and they talk about all the time they lived before they met—and how sometimes, because of his children, this seems for him just like yesterday (yes, yes! Every parent knows that about time, how nothing stands between small children and grown children, and I wonder if my own mother knew that, she never said anything about it, I never even knew if she thought about such things, but then she went and said what she said at the ferry boat dock and so I think she must have had this same sense—and does God Himself think, if he thinks in the same way we think, and why not? Why shouldn't he, if he made us in His image? And does He think about how little time has passed between making the universe and right now?—these are some of the questions on their mind on a bright sunlit afternoon, perfect temperature, a little breeze off the ocean, in Bahia des Todo Santos, Brazil, between my son and his wife—and—and, God bless them, they talk about me, about how wonderful I looked when I was dancing with him at the wedding, how charming in his own way Irving looked in his tux and bowler, and how everything seemed as good as it could be, given my health, and what did they know, what could they know, about how I felt when we danced at that wedding, the thoughts I was thinking, how when I heard about their boat trip I got carried back in my mind to that ferry ride all so long ago, when we almost lost my brother and my mother said those words to me, those words I've been thinking about so hard ever since the night of the wedding, *One day you'll remember this*...and it was true, and the thing she said to me on the night of the wedding, *You'll never see him again in this life.*...

And that was turning out to be true, too, because back in Jersey, far far north and far away from the pastel city of all the saints on the bay called Bahia, I was failing, falling fast. Even at the beginning, congestive heart failure is no picnic, but at least there's medicine to help control it. But after a while, if you're as old as I was, your valves leak too much, your blood clots too much, your lungs strain too much, and you just get so tired you want to sit and rest even before you get up to do anything. At least that was what was happening to me.

I was so tired I needed to rest from resting. And after a while, after coming home from the wedding and going to bed, I felt as though I needed a rest from living. You don't know how it is until it happens to you. Imagine, you wake up after a hard day of work the day before and you don't want to get out of bed? So it's like that, except after a hard life you don't want to get up one more time.

Awful for me to talk this way, because I loved life! Nobody loved life more than me! I loved my husband, I loved my children! Eating out, taking a drink now and then, my coffees and my pastries, all of that I loved. And dancing, even when I was mostly in a wheel chair, I danced. Look at me at the wedding, only ten days before.

And look at me now.

"Til," Irving, dear man, says to me on the telephone, "how about dinner tonight?"

"Oh, I'm so tired."

"Come on, come on," he says. "You got to eat."

"I got to die, too, and you don't see me getting up to do that."

"What are you talking about?"

"I don't know, I don't know," I say. "I'm feeling so tired I'm even too tired to be confused."

I held the telephone receiver away from my face and yawned a big yawn, not wanting Irving to hear me.

But he won't take no for an answer and so at three o'clock in the afternoon I drag myself out of bed and start to get dressed. God forgive me, I was too tired to take a shower, so I put on plenty of powder and some perfume and by five o'clock when Irving arrived at the door I was almost ready.

"You look pretty," Irving said.

"I look like I'm dead already," I said.

"Don't talk like that," he said.

"You want to know something?"

"Tell me something. What?"

"Let's get to the restaurant and I'll have a drink and I'll tell you."

"We're on the way," he said.

Even though it took what felt like ten minutes for me to walk from the house to the car, I could hardly move my legs.

And the same getting from the car to the restaurant, our old favorite, Jack Cooper's Celebrity Deli in Edison.

(Look at this, look at this, the world, the world! My son and his wife are sitting in the patio of the Hotel Pelourinho in Bahia and Irving and

I are at Jack Cooper's Celebrity Deli in Edison, and the planet is turning and everybody else is where they've been and where they're going....)

"Now what's your secret?" he said when we finally sat down.

"I should have a drink."

"Have a Coke," Irving said. "Or a coffee."

"I'll have a coffee." "And then what'll you tell me about?" I couldn't keep quiet about it. Ever since the wedding I wanted to tell somebody, and I couldn't tell my oldest because he's traveling and I couldn't tell his brother because I didn't want to scare him. So here I am, bursting with this bad (?) news.

"My mother," I said.

"What about her?"

"She talked to me."

"Your mother talked to you?" His voice slid up into the lower part of the upper registers. "How long has she been gone? Forty years?"

I stayed calm, because no use in getting upset.

"The night of the wedding. At the wedding. I heard her voice."

He asked me a little more, I told him a little more. And he listened, very understanding. (And why not? He's already buried two wives. He knows how to listen, he knows what to do. And at this stage in my life, I needed a man like this.)

"Til," he said when I was finished. "This worries me a little."

"So join the club."

"I never heard my mother's voice."

"She's never spoken to you."

"My father I heard. But not my mother."

"You never told me. When does your father talk to you?"

"Late at night, sometimes. You know how hard it is for me to sleep. I'll be up doing something, vacuuming the rug or cleaning the blinds. And I'll hear his voice. 'You little jerk,' he says. 'What are you doing, womens' work?' As if he doesn't know I'm alone and my wife is gone."

"I'm sorry," I tell him.

"Don't be sorry. Who cares what he says? I'm a grown man. I don't need his advice."

"You are grown," I tell him. "You're almost as old as I am."

"Not quite," he says, and then made what was between us an old joke. "You got yourself a younger man."

"That's what all the girls tell me. How lucky I am." Making a big effort, I reach across the table and touch his hand. "I am lucky."

But I'm tired. Oh, am I tired. The food arrives, baked chicken, a plateful of brisket. I can't lift a fork.

"Till," he says, "you got to eat."

"You want to feed me like a baby. I can't eat. I got no appetite."

"Not even for dessert?"

I shake my head. So he knows how really tired I am if I don't want dessert.

"Not even a milk shake? Maybe a milk shake? You don't have to lift it, you just suck through the straw."

"I know how to drink a milk shake," I say.

"So how's about one?"

I shake my head.

"It's time to go home."

"Tilly," he says, staring me right in the eye, "I want you to come home with me."

"What?"

He's always been such a gentleman—so what kind of thing is he asking?

"I'd love to," I say, "but I'm too tired."

"Trust me," he says.

And I do, so that when he helps me out to the parking lot and into his car and starts driving, I don't think another thing about it. The roads, the stores, the streetlights, the traffic lights, the other cars, the trees, the sky, all these things everyone in my family came to America to find, all these things I've looked at all the years I've been alive, they attract me, I keep looking, almost like I know I'm never going to see them again, soon. As if I want to remember something I might not ever be able to forget. My town. My state. My country. My world. My life.

I'm hypnotized, almost, by the world I'm alive in, and not even worrying anymore about what could happen to me if I die.

So when he passes the turn for my house, I don't pay any attention.

And when he keeps on driving—he's a crazy driver, a short man behind a big steering wheel, but a long time ago I gave up that kind of worry, too—taking the road to Carteret, where he lives, I'm thinking about other things. My past, my children, the boat in Brazil, wondering what it looks like, big and high in the water, like pictures I've seen? So much bigger than a ferry....

"Here we are," he says when we get to his house.

"Irving," I say.

But he won't take no for an answer. As tired as I am, I'm coming in. And he helps me make a comfortable place on his spotless sofa in his spotless living room in his spotless house—the air is a perfume made of cleansers and fake flowers—all of the cleaning he does all day to keep busy, this clean man, even when his father tells him not to do it—and he disappears into the kitchen where, while I'm sinking in and out of sleep, I hear him banging around in the pots, using a blender, talking to himself.

"Tilly?"

I must have dozed off because here he is standing in front of me with a tall glass full of milk.

"A milk shake," he says, as if he's correcting me in my mind.

"I told you I don't want it," I said.

But he's so insistent, I take the straw he hands me and while we hold the glass in front of me together, my cold hands, his warm hands pressed together, holding the glass I take a sip. Malted milk, cold and sweet, with the old flavor I remember when I was a child. If I had the strength, I would have laughed. As it was, it was all I could do to take a few sips. And take a breath. And rest. And sip again. And take a breath. And rest. And sip.

When the glass is half empty he takes it from me and sits down next to me on the sofa.

"It's your fault," I say.

"What?"

"My heart condition. If I hadn't gone with you to your cardiologist to keep you company when you went for your checkup and if he hadn't taken my blood pressure when he took yours none of this would have happened."

"Not this way, that's right," he said.

"And now you're healthy as an ox and I'm the sick one."

"Ox I don't know," he said. "Maybe an owl. I'm healthy as an owl."

I would have laughed at that, too, but I was already going, half in sleep, half out of it, leaning against him, enjoying the hard shoulder of a man for a pillow, thinking of all the years I lay in bed next to Phil, listening to him breathe in his sleep, feeling his bones, and wondering at the little heat rising up in my chest, a certain kind of gladness, that before my life ended I found Irving, who as bad as I felt could make me feel so good.

"You'll stay over?" he says.

"I can't," I say. "I couldn't. But I'll stay like this a little while longer."

"I'd like you to," he says.

"So, I will."

I close my eyes—and when I open them he is touching his dry lips to mine. His breath smells like brisket and coffee, milkshake, and life.

When he drops me off, it's not even seven o'clock, but to me it feels like three or four in the morning. I've been going in and out of sleep, in and out of worrying, the what ifs, the what ifs, especially what if wherever I go Phil is waiting for me and later Irving comes along and we're all three of us together, what am I supposed to do? and back in my own house I would have stood there a long time thinking about this problem, but I was so exhausted I had to sit down on the sofa, too tired to get up again and go to bed.

That's where my other son, the one who lives with me, found me when he came home from work.

"Ma?" he said. "Ma, are you all right?"

But I wasn't all right, not the way he meant it.

No. By the time he found me she had already come for me, my mother, taking me by both hands and lifting me from my body the way you undress a sleepy child at bedtime. I never expected it would be like this, but then I never thought much about this part of life, only the rest of it.

Mama, I said, I have to go back.

You can't, she said. That's all. Now hurry up.

She spoke to me as if I was still her little girl, which makes sense to me, when I think of the way I spoke to my children. No matter how big, you always see the child in them.

Where are we going? I asked her.

We're taking another ride on the ferry, she said.

At the same time this happened—the last time I would be in the same time as them—my older son and his wife were asleep in their cabin on that boat sailing off the coast of Brazil, the sound of the waves churning them further and further into sleep, and into dreams of floating and sailing in their own bodies, well, my daughter-in-law was sailing, lucky girl, and my son was dreaming one of his occasional dreams about a bicycle trip with friends to the road below a large bridge, something like the highway bridge across our Raritan River except seen from the south side, not the north, a dream I know now (and of course not before because he never told me) he had been dreaming ever since he was a boy, so even though the boat was carrying them north, this was the farthest point in their trip from care and worry. But oh, look at how even in sleep he's still moving, in his dream on the bike, in bed tossing and turning, the ship moving through the ocean, and the earth turning, and the solar system gliding and the entire universe drifting toward whatever it is, and maybe one day, now that I am where I am, I'll know, or maybe when I see Phil, who always had an interest in these things about the stars and the like, he'll already have found out and he'll tell me, though I haven't seen him yet....

RING, RING....

What?

RING, RING....

The telephone in their cabin woke them out of their dreaming.

Into what they felt as the nightmare of my going.

If only I could have explained it to them.

But this is what happens with life on earth—you get a message from your brother and you're shocked into sorrow and by the time light swells up over the billowing ocean you've already called your children— the signals going out, bouncing along the satellite trail and back down to earth again, north of where you're moving—and you've packed and told the purser that you need to disembark.

It's all timing, isn't it? Because at eleven that morning the ship is scheduled to sail into a port called Fortaleza, a beach town where they were scheduled to spend only a few hours before heading out to sea again. So Fortaleza it is. And though the afternoon and evening they spent there before flying out the next day seemed endless in the worst way when they look back at such things they're nothing, no time at all. Except for the terrible spasms of weeping my daughter-in-law endured, crying for me, crying for me, crying for me. And he started crying with her. So they wept in the hotel room and ate a bad meal—he can still taste the dry fish, the not-so-fresh salad if he thinks of it, the way he sometimes remembers my cooking for him when he was a child, which, I admit, was not the greatest, but you can't be everything and I was a very good mother, if I have to say so myself—and bought their airline tickets—and they flew south all the way to Sao Paulo before connecting to the airplane that carried them back north through the night to Miami (another uncomfortable flight, but this time my boy paid little attention to it, his sorrow was so great), and then their home in Washington, D.C., where they unpacked and packed again and drove farther north to my funeral.

Which is where we all are now, me and Mama and Papa (he just showed up) and Phil, my darling, scowling at me a little because of my late friendship with Irving but that's his Russian temper, which was, I have to say, always trouble and always attractive, and my grandmother, and all the cousins, dozens of them I never met, but it seems to be the way they do it here, everybody crowding around, crowded up against the railing of the ferry, looking down to see—

The grave-diggers digging....

The rabbi praying....

The little children running about the grave-site....

The grown-children huddled together, as if they could actually see us all on the deck of the boat, looking back at them....

My sons—I feel so sorry for them, they can hardly speak....

It hurt me to see such sorrow and unhappiness...the joy you feel when your children are born is matched only by the misery you feel when your parents go...a balancing act, life, is what I think...you can't have one part without the other...and you can't prepare for it either....

Listen to what my son was saying to his wife, the dancer....

"My father had been sick, I knew he was going to die...." He's speaking this in a whisper while the rabbi is saying some words over my grave. "And when the news came it hit me like a sledgehammer. You can think you're preparing, but you're never prepared. And now this...." His voice cracked a little. "I wasn't prepared. The way she was at the wedding, dancing with me, staying up to drink her scotch and her coffee and eat her slice of wedding cake...."

"I know," his wife says, such a good wife. (At last! Someone he can live with, and may they live long together before the ferry comes to take them on their last trip! Boats and water, boats and water! How do people who live in the mountains go? How do they move along from one place to the next? On mules? On horseback? And is their last departure a round-up of horses, heading north? And in the south, the South Americans, do they mount llamas? Do they catch the wings of those big birds the condors and glide up with them into the thermal drafts that lift them all the way to where we're going? I don't know, and I don't even know how I know to ask!)

The mourners begin to recite/chant/mutter/mumble the prayer for the dead.

(And it gives me a little shiver, which surprises me that I can still shiver, but I do....So how can I still know things and feel things? I don't know...but I'm happy to know, except it makes me sad to see my children so miserable in their grief....)

But now they have some work to do, and this will help with their grieving…they pick up shovels, my sons, and dig in to the pile of dirt at the edge of their grave and lift and throw the dirt onto the coffin in the hole….

Thunk!

The noise of the dirt hitting the top of the coffin—no sound like it! It chills you, the way the noise of a baby's first cry thrills you, this chills you.

Thunk!

The older one, the one who went away and had so far to travel to return here, finds the suit-coat he's wearing constricts his arms. (A suit! He never wears a suit! I haven't seen him in a suit since Phil's funeral.) But he stretches, and keeps on working.

And—thunk!

After a few more shovels-full it's just dirt on top of dirt, not the same sound anymore, and the grave fills up quickly as the rabbi and some of the other men gathered there pick up shovels and pitch in to help finish the work.

And then it's nearly over, and the crowd—so many friends, I knew I had them but I never thought I would look down on them and count!—drifts out of the cemetery, going to cars, driving back to the house.

My older boy lingers a moment, stands in front of the grave, sobbing, sobbing…and his son, good boy, too, walks back to him and puts a helping arm around his father's shoulder.

All the family, the mourners, driving in their cars back to the house, the wind beginning to blow strong from the north, the earth (of course) turning, the solar system, etc. moving, all of that….

I look to my side and there's Mama and she takes my hand.

Now? I say.

Not yet, she says.

A week went by for them, and one afternoon after the official mourning has ended, my daughter-in-law goes through my closets, pausing more than she should if she wants to get the job done in one day, to touch a dress, a sweater, a skirt, these things I used to wear. My clothes, not expensive, but beautiful to me, my mother had to skimp so much to buy me dresses. She and Irving lay them out in piles on the bed and on the floor and then stuff them into large green garbage bags and load them in the car. The work goes quickly except for one moment when my daughter-in-law holds up the dress I wore to the wedding and Irving says, "I'd like to keep that."

She nods, folds it carefully, hands it to him, and continues her work while he goes off to one corner of the room, clutching my dress and sobbing.

"We'll do it all in one trip," says my son, his eyes tired from all this we've all been through. He's packed the car, the trunk, the back seat.

They drive in to town, Irving following in his own car, to the synagogue and there they haul the bags into the foyer where the head of the charity giving says he'll make good use of them.

All of a sudden Mama says, Now, squeezing my hand.

It surprises me, though I expected it, and I feel like a bird about to fly, wings fluttering, heart fluttering.

And we walk together, the two of us (where's my father? Will I see him, too, soon?) down the street to the water, to the river, and board the old ferry, empty except for the two of us.

The boat gives a shudder, as though it is as alive, or whatever it is, as I am.

And I look back from the railing as we sail away, engines churning, trying to keep my eyes open, but having to squint and squint, until all this fades from view over the receding horizon. And then I turn to see where we're going, the warm wind blowing gently in my face.

What's over there? I can't see well yet in that direction. It's a little foggy. And then trees! And houses! Tottenville? Is Tottenville heaven?

About The Author

Alan Cheuse, National Public Radio's longtime "voice of books," is the author of five novels, four collections of short fiction, the memoir *Fall Out of Heaven*, and the collection of travel essays, *A Trance After Breakfast*. As a book commentator, Cheuse is a regular contributor to National Public Radio's "All Things Considered." His short fiction has appeared in *The New Yorker, Ploughshares, The Antioch Review, Prairie Schooner, New Letters, The Idaho Review*, and *The Southern Review*, among other places. He teaches in the Writing Program at George Mason University and the Squaw Valley Community of Writers.

Find out more about Mr. Cheuse at www.alancheuse.com.